CW01418422

ISBN 978-1491074954

Cover art by Mark Watts

To Mark Watts

My friend

Ben Blake is on Facebook, at
https://www.facebook.com/benblakeauthor

Follow Ben's blog at http://benblake.blogspot.co.uk

Or email him at ben.blake@hotmail.co.uk

Also by Ben Blake

The Risen King
Blood and Gold (Songs of Sorrow volume 1)

The Gate of Angels

Songs of Sorrow Volume Two

Book Three

Brothers to Dragons

I am a brother to dragons, and a companion to owls.

Job 30: 29

One

Once Before the End

The day when Calesh Saissan came back with his five hundred men of the Hand was the day when events began to rush down on Sarténe all at once, bursting like firecrackers in a winter night's sky. Or so Ando Gliss remembered it, after, when the hot embers of that summer had long since grown cool. Others recalled it differently, or wrote it so, when they penned the long histories that took their places in the archives of the Basilica. They peppered the pages with quotes and first-hand accounts, but they didn't understand, and it wasn't the same. Stories told when the coals have dimmed are pale, listless things. Echoes of the truth.

Ando had been there. Close to the heart of things, both before Calesh returned from Tura d'Madai and after, when events started to happen so fast they almost tumbled over one another's heels. Poets and historians wrote of the lonely, ethereal beauty of Ilenia, left alone by her husband in favour of a singer, but there was a wealth of expression they knew nothing of, a profusion of brief glances and pale cheeks, and lips that smiled below eyes that did not. Ando had seen it all, as he'd seen how people oriented themselves to Calesh when he was in the room, a movement as subtle and inexorable as stars across the sky. Those writers had not: and they lied, anyway. They wrote what their masters wanted them to write, and the truth died between their pages.

He had been there. And it began, the febrile time when Sarténe as it had been came to an end, on the day Calesh rode back to the city, and a killer came to Mayence from the south.

*

Ando was in the shadow of the city walls when Calesh returned, playing music to a gaggle of labourers as they worked clearing shacks and accumulated earth away. The slope was steep between the river Kair and the walls, but the lost and bereft had made such homes as they could there

6

despite that, scavenging boards and cheap cloth from fields or dank alleys. A few had even begun to grow tomatoes or carrots in little patches of earth, some only a foot across. It all had to go, now. Anything that might help the approaching All-Church army to get over the wall was carted away and burned. The earth was piled into handcarts and trundled away. Ando didn't know where it went.

Three crews worked in the bed of the Kair itself, behind wooden barriers that forced the river into half its usual channel. Even so, more than half each team bailed water with buckets, and still it came up to their knees. The rest hacked at the riverbed with pickaxes, then shovelled the debris into great drums that were attached to pulleys and hauled clear by pairs of horses. They worked steadily, taking rests in groups of three or four. Ando would have been exhausted in half an hour, and fit for nothing but an afternoon lying down with a damp cloth over his eyes.

In truth, there wasn't a great deal he *was* good for. He was no labourer: his hands would come out in blisters almost as soon as they laid hold of a pickaxe. He couldn't work the pulleys or supervise a work crew, and he'd never wielded a sword in anger in his life. Besides, he knew perfectly well that labourers and soldiers alike would mutter behind their hands if he tried to join them, whispering names they thought he couldn't hear. Or perhaps that they intended him to hear. *Pervert. Pederast. Invert, degenerate, sodomite.* All old names, things he'd heard many times before. Needles in his flesh.

So he did what he could, which was play music, and sing. That much, they let him do.

"Play us a ballad," one of the men called from the riverbed. "Play us a ballad of the high country, singer."

They let him do it, though he was still obliged to play the old, simple, tooth-achingly clichéd sagas of one or another of the old mountain lords, sitting on their distant crags and thinking themselves mighty when all they ruled was one valley. All those men ever seemed to care about was their pride, and perhaps their daughters. Inasmuch as their daughters were bound into their pride. Ando would not have cared if he woke one day to find he'd forgotten every mountain ballad he'd ever known. He certainly wouldn't learn them again. But this was what his gifts allowed him to do, so Ando made himself smile, and when he was ready he strummed the opening notes of *The Song of Vaunce's Daughter*. The men grinned and slapped each other on the back, and Ando began to play.

He had been very small, when he first realised he could sing. His mother taught him cradle songs, as any mother did her child, and one day in the garden little Ando began to sing back the tune she had lulled him with the night before. She was with his father by the tree, and as little Ando toddled towards them his parents turned to him with identical expressions of surprise, and then of disbelief. He hadn't understood why. All he wanted was to be picked up and dandled on his mother's knee, or failing that his father's, but neither of them moved, even when he raised his arms as a hint.

"Good God," his father said at length. "Did you ever hear him do a thing like that before?"

His mother shook her head, blonde tresses rustling. She didn't speak, and Ando grabbed her knee. "Pick up, p'ease!"

He didn't know how young he'd been that day. Very young, if he couldn't talk properly, but he could still recite back a cradle song he'd heard only once. He didn't remember anything else from the same age, but that day had lodged in his mind. Perhaps because it set his path, though nobody knew it at the time. From then on Ando had always been set for life as a troubadour.

He sang with half his attention, so sure of the refrain and the tune that he performed them without thought, his mind elsewhere. Why that memory had come to him today he didn't know, but it occurred to him now that he hadn't seen his parents for several years. They didn't even know he played for the Margrave now... or that he did other things for Riyand, too. He wondered what they would say if they knew.

He'd reached the point in the song where Vaunce's daughter had met her swain, in secret because her father would kill the suitor if he knew. The doom ordained for them was taking shape.

I'll dread no dark with you, love
Nor fear your father's rage
So tell me where to meet and I'll be there.
In the lavender we'll lie, love
And we'll shiver when we touch
As I watch the sunset glimmer in your hair.

It really was the most godforsaken piece of trite in the world, when you broke it down line by line. But still, when you added the thrumming music there was a certain power to the song, a sense of onrushing disaster that nothing the lovers did might turn aside. Ando wished he hadn't thought of that, with the All-Church army closing in on them. Even so, his own songs were more layered, more cultured, despite what that heathen Calesh Saissan had said in the tavern back at the waterfront. *The idiot who wrote those lyrics,* indeed. Nobles all across Gallene were honoured when Ando Gliss agreed to stay with them for a time, and lend the glamour of his art to their name.

He reached the last verse, when Vaunce had killed the young man who dared to court his daughter, and left his ghost pining in the hills of the Aiguille:

So I walk the dark alone, love
Over crag and trail, and grove
But love, I'd never change that distant day.
I will see you ere the end, love
When both sun and moon are gone
So love, oh love, remember me, I pray.

He drew his hand across the strings, sending out a rippling chord that deepened and then died. When he looked up it was to see that most of the men had stopped working. They were listening in rapt silence, from which his movement seemed to release them. As one they broke into applause, and Ando stood and bowed to them, acknowledging the approval with a troubadour's customary diffident air. It was as he straightened that he saw riders coming up the high road from Parrien, several hundred dusty men in the Hand of the Lord's reversed black and white, and he realised Calesh Saissan was back.

That would very likely be enough to send Riyand into a sour mood for the rest of the day, and on the spot Ando abandoned his plans to find other groups of workers to play for. As the labourers' applause faded he saluted them with a raised hand and turned away, to scramble hurriedly back along the sloping strip of land between the river and the walls.

He'd heard enough today, catching scraps of talk from a worker here or a soldier there, to know how popular Saissan had become. The man had hardly got good Sarténi soil on his boots and already the people of Mayence were swapping tales about him, each one more improbable than the last. If you believed the stories Calesh had killed nine Madai chieftains in single combat down the years, one of them because the man had insulted his wife. Every woman in the city went doe-eyed at that one. People claimed Calesh never slept, but his strange Madai wife made him a potion from secret herbs, one draught of which left him refreshed and ready for another day. And they said he went out each dawn to sharpen his sword on the rays of the rising sun, and whatever that blade struck it sliced through, like a curved knife through jellied fruit.

He noticed, though, that they didn't say he would lead the army of Sarténe to victory. After a while Ando began to listen for it, to seek out that one whisper among the many, but he never heard it. The people of Mayence might love Calesh Saissan, and trust him, but for all the wondrous tales they told they knew a miracle when they needed one.

The column of riders was coming fast, the banner at the front snapping in a breeze Ando couldn't feel in the shelter of the wall. He cursed and tried to move faster, skidding as he did on the newly-scraped rocks that had, of course, been designed precisely to make men lose their footing. When he glanced back up it was to see groups of labourers stopping work to lift their hands to Saissan as he rode by; some managed a ragged cheer, laced with shouted good wishes Ando couldn't quite make out. Calesh acknowledged them with nods and a raised hand, but he didn't slow down. Ando cursed again.

Then the column *did* slow, forced to swerve around a series of trenches that were being dug across the road. When they were deep enough sharp stakes would be placed at the bottom and the cuts covered with woven mats, and dirt spread over the top to hide them. Other similar traps were being prepared all over the plain, though the farmers had raised perfect hell about that. Hand soldiers and Guardsmen had listened to them complain, and then gone ahead anyway. There wasn't much the farmers could do about it except grumble, and they had enough of that to do with all their livestock and stores being taken away and sequestered inside Mayence. All the farmers were given in return was a token promising payment at a later date, and about *that,* they had raised pure murder.

Ando had heard that one smallholder was so enraged that he attacked the Hand soldiers on his land with a wood axe. They had killed him, of course. That sort of thing couldn't be allowed to spread.

At any rate, the delay to negotiate the trenches gave Ando the time he needed to reach the Gate of Angels just as Saissan and the cavalry rode up. It was men of Riyand's Guard who manned the gate in their blood and gold livery, but it might as well have been Hand soldiers for all the difference it made these days. They stepped aside and saluted smartly. Ando scrambled over a final treacherous slope, boots sliding under him.

"Commander!" he called.

Calesh looked over and saw him, and a moment later he spoke swiftly to the cadaverous man beside him and reined his horse to the side of the road. Four other soldiers stopped with him, and also a small man Ando knew, wearing the green robe of an Elite. Everyone knew Luthien; he was the only man in Mayence to wear glasses, and instantly recognisable. Today he looked a little drawn. The column rode on past behind him, into the city.

"What news?" Ando asked.

Calesh looked down at him without dismounting. Dust lay on his armour and skin in thick swirls, and his horse stood with its ears down and breath whuffing through its nostrils.

Obviously the group had ridden hard. "Yes. You can save me a trip if you take the news to Riyand."

"What news?" he asked again.

"The north road is blocked," Calesh said flatly. Those people close enough to hear made a strange sound, half gasp and half moan, like some unknown and chimeric creature in distress. "We found a forward camp of Justified and hit it, hit it hard; I think we killed about two hundred men. But there was another encampment behind it, a larger one, and two regiments of spearmen began to move towards us. We had to withdraw. You know what this means."

"I'm not sure I do," Ando said.

Calesh stared at him expressionlessly, then said, "We have rather less time than we thought."

"But you said it was hard to move an army through hilly terrain," Ando protested. "And Parrien only fell a week ago. How can the All-Church have advanced so fast?"

"Their commander is good," Calesh answered. "Very good. I wish I knew who he was: it's easier to anticipate a man if you know him." He ran a hand through grimy, sweat-damp hair. "Tell your Margrave that, Master Gliss. The noose is tightening. You tell him."

With that Calesh flicked his reins and was gone, leaving Ando to stand in the gateway and blink after him while a worried murmur began to rise from all around. A distant part of Ando's mind wondered what new tales of Calesh Saissan they would make from this little scene: certainly the commander hadn't seemed very much the hero, with grime crusted on his skin and exhaustion etched into every line of him. But it was a distant part indeed. All he seemed able to do was stand there and stare as the last of the riders clattered by and were gone, until a hand touched his arm and he almost jumped out of his skin.

"I believe I might accompany you to the Manse," Luthien Bourrel said. He had swung down from his saddle and now held reins in one casual hand. He looked almost indecently fresh. "Riyand might like to hear from someone who was there, and there might be some need for words of comfort."

Words of comfort. Ando very nearly laughed at that, but one did not laugh at Elite, and especially not Luthien. There was something about the neat man which precluded even such minor ill manners as that. Ando nodded – he still seemed to be having trouble speaking – and turned towards the gate.

He was forced to stop when a pair of horsemen pushed in front of him, reining their horses in when the gate officer stepped into their path and raised a hand. He had nine liveried men behind him, but suddenly Ando had the impression that they were sheep confronted by wolves, and the predators were hungry. There were only two horsemen, but one of them sat his saddle with the cocksure arrogance that only came from experience in combat. He was a muscular man, not especially tall but stocky, and he looked powerful.

"Your business here?" the officer asked. His tone ought to have been commanding, but instead it was edged with a note that was almost obsequious. *He senses it too,* Ando thought, and looked back at the lead rider again. He was aware that Luthien had gone very still beside him.

"We have come to fight against the All-Church," the muscular man said. "I heard their army was coming here."

The officer frowned. "That was quick. The army only crossed the river two weeks ago."

"We were already coming north. We've been fighting in Alinaur for five years. It's time to see home again, before we go back."

"Maybe you should go home anyway," the officer said. "This isn't your war, and the odds aren't good."

The muscular man gave a sudden, toothy smile. "We *like* fighting. And I've faced poor odds before."

He kept switching between *we* and *I,* Ando noticed, as though he was prone to forgetting there was anyone else with him. Or that the other man didn't matter. And that smile made the skin crawl on the back of Ando's head: it was wide and friendly, but it never touched those cold, unfeeling eyes. Perhaps the officer felt the same. He stepped aside without further questions, allowing the pair of riders to enter the city. When they had gone it was as though the sun had re-emerged from clouds, lifting a shadow from the day.

"Odd," Luthien said. He was gazing after the riders. "If they have been fighting in Alinaur, then they're either mercenaries or in one of the Orders. And they're not in the Hand of the Lord."

Ando frowned at him. "So?"

"So where is their home," Luthien asked, "and why do they want to forego it to fight for the Dualism? Anyone from the other Orders ought to be hurrying to join the Crusade army, not us. I will say one thing," he added, his voice dropping. "The one who spoke is a proper fighting man. I don't like this very much. That man could do with keeping an eye on."

"I don't understand any of that," Ando said.

Luthien shook himself and pushed his glasses up his nose. "Perhaps it's just as well. Men like Calesh fight so that men like you don't have to understand such things. Once you know, you've lost a little of your innocence, and you can never win it back again."

"You fought," Ando said, struggling to think, "and you understand, but you took the Consolation. Did you regain any innocence?"

Something flickered at the back of Luthien's eyes at that, a shadow that peered out through the gap between expressions. A moment later Luthien was all mock solemnity, tapping his teeth with one fingernail. "A difficult question, that. The Basilica teaches that Adjai the God-Son died to redeem the sins of mankind, which rather implies that purity of heart can be regained, does it not? And of course the casting away of worldly possessions and concerns has a cleansing effect on the soul. Everybody knows that."

"I don't –"

"Then again," Luthien mused, "a skill once learned can hardly be *unlearned,* I think. As an Elite I abstain from wine and meat, but I remember how they taste. Does that mean I have regained an untainted state, or merely that I am strong enough to resist temptation?"

"I can see why they call you the wise man," Ando said.

"Yes," Luthien said. "I'm clever; no point denying that. Sometimes I think the thing I detest most about the All-

Church is its hatred of learning. They would like to take all the books in the world and hold a great burning, a single pyre on which all knowledge is turned to ash, and men thereafter would know only what the Church decided they were fit to know." He pushed his glasses up his nose again. "Come on. We ought to hurry, or word will reach Riyand before we do."

*

He hadn't meant to spout off. Poor Ando: the man was a competent troubadour, if a little heavy of touch with the lyrics at times, but he was no great thinker. Luthien had long believed that was why Riyand liked him. The Margrave was hardly a man of intellect himself. At any rate, Ando hadn't deserved to be the recipient of an outburst like that. Earnest as he was, the singer would probably wrestle with the concept of dubious redemption as Luthien had outlined it, and then giving up would blot out his thoughts in a puddle of wine.

Here in the reception hall of the Manse Ando kept glancing across at Luthien, a small frown on his face. Evidently the wrestling had begun already. Further away the doors had been thrown open to allow spring air inside, and liquid sunlight splashed across Ilenia's brown hair where she sat nearby and brought out latent flames of red. She looked over at Luthien from time to time as well. He wished she wouldn't.

"So much for Commander Saissan's great plans," Riyand said. He was standing in the shafts of sunshine, hands behind his back and his feet spread apart. Luthien thought uncharitably that he knew exactly how he looked, a lonely silhouette limned against the light. Riyand had always been stronger in image than in actuality. "We may have been unwise to trust him."

"I think not," Cavel said calmly.

Ando gave a twitch of surprise. Luthien could understand why. The bony old seneschal was as loyal as a beaten dog, though never submissive, and he never, *never* went against the Margrave. He might guide him subtly to a desired decision, or persist doggedly with persuasion when he had to, but he didn't disagree so bluntly. Certainly not in

15

public. Ilenia turned from gazing out through the doors and fixed Cavel with a considering look, but she did so only after her husband had moved to face the seneschal, so his back was to her and he couldn't see.

"You think not?" Riyand said. "Have you turned against me now as well, seneschal?"

"Turned against you?" Cavel shook his head. "Hardly. I serve you the best I can, and as faithfully as I served your father before you. And that means I will give you my best advice, as I once did to him." He paused. "My advice is this: place your trust in Calesh Saissan. You will find no better captain. Such hope as we have of escaping the vice of events lies with him."

It did, of course. Calesh had been battle-hard when Luthien was still in Tura d'Madai: all of them had been, in truth. In that bitter land a man either hardened his heart or broke it. Now he was more than merely hard. It was as though those long dry years in the desert had been meant to hone Calesh, to sharpen him the way an armourer will sharpen the edge of a blade, and what they had honed him for was this. It was ironic, really. Calesh was the only one of them who had never wanted to come home.

"We all want to make a future for ourselves," Luthien had said to him once, trying to explain. "You never have, Calesh. All you want is to forget the past."

Now here Calesh was, back in the land he had abandoned long ago, and fighting to save it from the fire. *God makes fools of all men in the end*, Luthien thought wryly. *He certainly does of me.*

Ilenia's eyes rested on him again, just for a second before they flicked away, and his heart gave a small skip.

"Perhaps that's true," Riyand admitted finally. He scrubbed a sleeve across his eyes. "Forgive me, Cavel. You have never given me reason to doubt your loyalty. I'm just edgy these days." A smile ghosted around the corners of his mouth. "I can't imagine why."

"Quite understandable," Cavel said.

"Even with Saissan to lead us," Ando said in a low voice, "our chances aren't good. I can't help thinking it will all come down to one last, desperate charge, in the end."

If it did, then it would mean either Calesh had made mistakes or luck had been against him at every turn. His job was to make sure there were other options. Ando didn't understand that, though. The man who'd written *The Lay of Gidren Field* saw battle in terms of honour and glory, not sweat and blood and spilled, stinking guts. If God was through making men into fools, Luthien thought, he would at least spare them the spectre of Ando Gliss making battle decisions.

"We will need every man who can hold a sword, if it does," Cavel said. He cocked an eyebrow at Luthien. "And you, master Elite? Will you not fight even then, at the last need?"

"I will not fight," Luthien said. He was tired of repeating the same thing, but not tired enough to change it. He was aware of Ilenia's gaze on him again. "Not at any need." He stood and offered Riyand a slight bow. "With your permission, my lord, I will withdraw. I need a bath quite badly. And the people need to see Elite in the streets, to offer such consolation as we can."

Riyand let him go with a languid flap of one hand. Most of his movements were like that, carefully judged and studied, the same way as his light-limned pose by the doors had been. He knew how to play the great lord, but the trouble was that when the playing had to stop there was nothing behind the games. It was as though the greasepaint was wiped away to reveal no actor beneath, no mouth to speak the words. That was a faintly unsettling thought. Luthien closed the door behind himself and shook it away, starting down the corridor.

He had enough to worry him. That muscular fellow by the gates, for instance. A fighting man, Luthien had called him, but that hardly did justice to him. There was a poise about him, an air of coiled readiness that Luthien had seen only rarely. Cammar ah Amalik had possessed it; even striding across the valley at Gidren Field he had looked lethal, a cobra that had simply not yet decided to strike. Calesh had a little of it too. Come to that, Luthien supposed he had it himself, or had done once, when he still carried a sword.

He had it no longer, but he could still recognise the signs. That man was dangerous, and if he'd come to Mayence to fight for the Dualism as he claimed then Luthien was a pig's auntie. All his old senses were twitching to warn him of danger. He would have to find out where the muscular man and his friends were staying, and keep an eye on them until –

He heard his name called in a voice soft as satin, and his thoughts scattered like a reflection in water when the surface is disturbed. He turned, halfway down the corridor to the main hall, and with no surprise at all he saw Ilenia walking towards him, her yellow skirts kissing the floor with every step. His heart gave that quick skip once more.

"I thought I'd better leave the hall before Riyand loses his temper," she said as she reached him. "He usually does when he's nervous, and he will be anxious now as he's never been."

He nodded. All that was true.

"Your friend the Marshal is rather impressive," Ilenia went on. She was talking just to fill a silence, of course. "Even Cavel has begun to listen to him. I didn't think he did that for anyone in Sarténe."

Luthien drew a breath. "How may I help you, my lady?"

"By putting aside that stiff formality," she said, suddenly harsh, "for a start. Why so rigid, Luthien?"

"You know why," he snapped back, and then immediately reached for the calm place he knew was within him. "Because I'm afraid of what I might say, if my tongue runs loose."

"How unfortunate for me," she murmured, "that when I fell in love, it had to be with the one man in Mayence who values honour far above any desires he may have for himself."

"There are many such men in Mayence," he said. "And in the All-Church army, I dare say."

"There are none such as you," she told him.

He said nothing to that: really, there was nothing he *could* say. Every loving wife thought the same of her husband; every loving husband thought the same of his wife. He and Ilenia were neither. What they felt meant nothing. She was married to another man, and he had his oath.

He had spoken before in sermons of purity, and the desire in the heart of every man and woman to achieve it. Luthien had striven for purity, and when it wasn't granted to

18

him he'd prayed for strength, which he knew he had. He needed it, because the heart has other desires, always. Sometimes his appetites raged within him, lust and love, impatience and fury, but they all broke on the wall of his will. He was Elite. He would eat no meat and drink no wine, do no violence, and he would not touch a woman in love.

"I wonder sometimes," Ilenia said softly when he didn't speak, "what it would be like, Luthien. Don't you?"

"I'm not made of stone," he retorted, and regretted his tone at once. "I'm sorry. I didn't mean that."

She might not have heard him. "It's ending in Sarténe, isn't it? The Dualism. The Hand of the Lord. It will all be lost, and priests of the All-Church will stand on the ashes and sing their hard, bitter songs."

"I have not given up hope," he answered. "Not yet. Not while Calesh is here, and Raigal, and Baruch. We are taught that the greatest of God's gifts is hope. Don't let it go lightly, Ilenia."

"I still hope," she said, her voice a caress. She reached out and touched his cheek with her fingertips. "I hope that you will come to me, and love me once, just once before the end."

She turned and set off back towards the reception hall without giving him a chance to reply. In truth she had no need: Luthien could not have spoken if his soul depended on it. He stood there alone for a long time, head down as he struggled to control his breathing, before he felt able to move. He went then to his rooms and his bath, and to pray once more for strength. His will was iron, he knew that, but he wished God need not place so many temptations before him, as though testing his faith every day and with every person he met.

Two

Signs

"Did you hear?" Elizur asked, once they were past the guards. "Did you hear what he said about the raid?"

Galien nodded grimly. *We found a forward camp of Justified and hit it, hit it hard; I think we killed about two hundred men,* Calesh had said by the Gate of Angels. It was the second time already that the Servants of the Justification had been attacked by this misbegotten dog of a man, after the treacherous slaughter at the bridge outside Parrien. Good soldiers of the All-Church, true men of the Faithful, were being slaughtered in this war. It was worse even than the desert. At least there the enemies of the Faith wore their heresy openly, their loyalties plain to see.

Not here. The men of Sarténe had fought beside the other Orders, struggling against the Madai in the east and the Jaidi in the south. They had bled and died in the name of a God they had never believed in, hiding behind deception and trickery like cowards. God only knew what atrocities they'd practised in the privacy of their own camps, shielded by walls of stone or canvas as they worshipped their false idols. It made Elizur burn inside with hate. Not that he needed another reason to despise Calesh Saissan.

I was five steps away from him, Elizur thought as he rode into Mayence. *Five steps away with a sword at my side, and yet Saissan still lives.* He could feel his cheek twitching, a reaction to stress he'd never been able to stop.

But there was more to this than killing the dog of Tura d'Madai, much as Elizur hated to admit it. There had to be at least a chance of his escape; that was drilled into Highbinders from the start, and he supposed he agreed with it. Not because he owed the Servants of the Justification anything, of course, but there were other things he wanted to do before God took him home, other ambitions to fulfil. Although he couldn't think of one that made his blood fizz the way the thought of killing did.

Especially killing Saissan. The man wasn't just a dog, he was a cheat as well, a fake who had lucked into a reputation he'd never deserved. He was a chancer who got lucky, that was all. But here in Sarténe the apostates thought he was the image of salvation, and they painted him onto walls and sang songs in his honour. Elizur had heard one of them on the ride north, sung by an indifferent bard in a grubby roadside inn. It was a poor tune, as far as Elizur was any judge: he didn't care about such things. But the ragged farm folk had demanded the bard sing it three times before the night was done, until Elizur had to fight down the urge to pull his sword and lay about himself. It was only the prospect of settling a score with Saissan that had stopped him.

He'd killed the bard though, late the next morning as the man made his way north. A knife in the belly, the way a kill should be made. Nobody could survive after their innards spilled out of them.

"I will kill *him* that way," he said to Galien, though quietly. They were in the city now, on the broad avenue called Waggoner's Way, and it wouldn't do to be overheard. Galien nodded as though he understood and made no reply.

Elizur rather approved. There weren't many men he liked, and fewer still that he trusted. He liked to say that the only men worth trusting were the dead, who couldn't betray you. But he thought the lean, almost silent man who'd ridden with him might be deserving of a little faith. If Galien played his part in this endeavour he might prove it.

On the other hand, the man *was* from Sarténe. Only the eastern side of it, close to the river Rielle; but still, he was Sarténi, and this was where the heresy had grown like suspicion in the dark. Perhaps it would be best to dispose of him, once Saissan was dead. Elizur would have to think about it.

Saissan. His thoughts circled around again, coming back to that moment in front of the Gate of Angels when the Hand of the Lord had ridden by with Calesh at their head. *I was five steps away from him, and yet he lives.*

Elizur wouldn't have been able to reach him though. That was the truth of it; five steps was a long way when there were armed men all around, each of them watchful despite their weariness. There wasn't a swordsman on the planet who could stand with Elizur Mandein, but five hundred of them would kill him quite easily. Ten would manage it, in all honesty, tired or no. The Hand of the Lord trained its soldiers well, for all that they were a bunch of heathens who deserved to be scoured from the earth. It was unpalatable, but Elizur prided himself on facing the truth even when it was distasteful to him, and he had to admit that he would not have been able to kill Saissan there at the gate.

Well then, he would wait. The senior men of the Hand would sleep at the Preceptory, naturally enough, and there would be no chance of reaching Saissan there. But he would have to come out to do his job. He'd have to tour the walls, confer with the boy-loving monster who was Margrave, scrutinize the defences being flung up outside the city… a dozen things, any of which might present an opportunity to a watchful man. And Elizur was very good at being watchful.

Not very good at being patient, but he could be for this, oh yes. He'd waited eight years. He could wait a few days longer.

"Barricade," Galien said.

The crowd had already forced Elizur to rein in, something he'd done unconsciously while thinking of other things. He hadn't noticed the rampart though. It was only half built, a head-high wall of stones that blocked both sides of the avenue and left only a narrower gap in the middle, just wide enough for one wagon to pass through at a time. Several waited in a long line, all of them heading out of Mayence; Elizur assumed anything coming in now had to take a different route. People were thronged on both side of the wall though, waiting until they could pass through. Twenty or so soldiers in red and yellow kept order, some of them speaking to the wagon driver to confirm something or other. Elizur felt his lips tighten.

The Sarténi were getting ready for a siege. He'd known that already of course, from seeing the extensive earthworks and trenches being dug outside Mayence, across the plain where farms had been. That might be a problem when the army came, Elizur knew. The river especially would pose some difficulty for men trying to reach the city beyond it, especially given that the Sarténi were dredging the riverbed and strewing rocks across the far bank, nearest the walls. And the fields had been cleared of crops and livestock, just as around Parrien, everything swept up and carried away to deny the All-Church any forage from the land. It would be hard to bring supplies all the way from beyond the Rielle to here, over a hundred miles of increasingly hilly roads.

But it was one thing to see the land being cleared, and quite another to see defences being prepared inside the city as well. That spoke of both organisation and strong command. Elizur knew exactly who would have been responsible; Baruch Caraman for the first, and Calesh Saissan for the other. The muscle jumped in his cheek. *Damn* whoever had sent that message to warn Calesh of the coming assault. If not for that Calesh would still be counting scorpions in Tura d'Madai, and Sarténe would be afire from river to sea before he even learned something was wrong.

On the other hand, if that if that had happened Calesh would still be in the desert, and beyond the reach of Elizur's vengeance. Perhaps he should be grateful. And besides, having the Hand of the Lord here meant all the heretics could be obliterated at a single stroke, which might not be easier as such but was certainly more elegant.

He made himself wait calmly, or at least with the outward appearance of calm, as the Guardsmen dealt with the crowd and wagons. Finally he and Galien reached the front, and two liveried men came over and looked them up and down.

"Mercenaries?" one of them asked.

"From the south," Galien agreed. As he was Sarténi it made sense for him to do the talking when possible, since he had the right accent. He'd also been fighting in Alinaur until Elizur's message reached him, so he knew recent events in that war-torn country. "Come to help, if the pay's right."

"Pay's standard rates unless you've a special reason to deserve more," the Guardsman said. He didn't seem to think there was much chance of that. "Go back to the last turning on your right. There's a barrack house down there that can take you, or else direct you to one with spare beds. They'll find work for you until the fighting starts."

"Thanks," Galien said, as sparing with words as ever. He and Elizur turned their horses and made their way back out of the crowd, down the road they'd just passed up.

So, in addition to everything else, the Sarténi were also being careful about who was allowed into the central part of the city, beyond the barricade. Elizur was sure there would be other roadblocks as well as this one, encircling the heart of Mayence, and all the important places and people would be inside that cordon. The Hall of Voices, the Hand's Preceptory, the Margrave's Palace: all sheltered inside this ring of ramparts. And Saissan, of course. Although he would have to come out.

"They'll put us to work," Galien said, when they were away from the press of citizens and unlikely to be overheard. "Digging ditches or the like."

"I expect they will," Elizur agreed. Warmth was spreading through him now, joy that he was close to settling the score with Saissan at last. It would take a good deal to upset him now. "That's all right. It gives me a chance to gauge the situation."

Galien nodded and said no more. He really was a good companion, dependable and very nearly silent. It would almost be a shame if Elizur had to kill him after this was done.

But he needn't worry about that for now. He was inside Mayence, and by the end of the day would be a hired mercenary working on the city's defences. Not quite trusted, perhaps, but close enough. He'd be able to spy out holes in the defences, and most of all he could study where Saissan went and what he did, and pick the best time to kill him.

It wouldn't hurt to spend a few days planning. For this, above all, Elizur could be very good at patience indeed.

*

"In Sarténe our brothers in the Order fight to save our people," Rissaun said. "It's natural for those of us here to want to join them. We were fighting men once, and it aches our hearts to sit behind the walls of Adour while other men risk their lives for our cause."

The days when these men fought in the deserts of Tura d'Madai, or the mountains of Alinaur to the south, were long gone. Rissaun was somewhere in his mid-fifties, and those years had thickened him around the waist while his hair turned grey and blew away in the breeze. The others were no better. Seran was past fifty too, his face lined and his nose a battered blob of veined red flesh. At least two of the garrison of the castle were the wrong side of sixty, and more in Haun's case, though he stubbornly insisted he was two years younger than Seran. Perhaps three. But his skin was wrinkled parchment and blue eyes were faded pale, like cloth from which all the colour had washed out, and beyond ten or fifteen feet away they could see nothing but a blur.

They had all spent their lives in the Hand of the Lord, and while age had now overtaken them they had nowhere else to go. And they could be useful, in their way. Farajalla thought they would sink into quiet despair if they were taken from this lonely outpost and set down amid the bustle of Mayence, to waste their days drinking thin ale in run down taverns and telling long, disjointed tales of the things they used to do.

"But we have a duty of our own," Rissaun went on. He looked around the tiny chapel, into which all the occupants of Adour castle had crammed themselves for this sermon. Twenty soldiers and five guests, Farajalla among them. Beside her sat Kendra with little Segarn in her arms, peering around as myopically as Haun and sometimes waving his arms in the air. Across the room Gaudin sat beside the small figure of Ailiss, the Lady of the Hidden House. The soldiers still called her that, though the house itself was no more. Ailiss had ordered it burned when they left. *So those murdering beasts cannot walk through these rooms of ours,* she had said, *and make stories of what we did there.*

"Our duty is to provide a haven for the Lady," Rissaun said. He kept turning as he spoke, to face in turn the people ranged in the seats that formed circles around him. "Perhaps we won't win glory by it, but I don't think any duty I ever had in the past gave me as much pleasure, as much pride, as this one. And I believe God will forgive me the pride, when in my time I leave this world and pass through the Gate of Angels into Heaven."

There was a quiet murmur of agreement. Nobody spoke up, much less clapped his hands. Not for these men the impetuousness of youth. As silence descended once more Segarn gurgled happily. Rissaun went on without seeming to notice. *One of God's chatterers,* Seran had called him the day Farajalla came here, and that was exactly right. He was a good speaker though. When it came their turn to give the sermon most of these ageing men could do no more than mumble a few halting words, but Rissaun could really talk.

"The All-Church has come to burn us, and everything we are," Rissaun said. "The Lady tells us that all gods are the same god, dressed in different cloaks made of ritual words and prayers. It's too pure a thought for me, but I defer to her wisdom, of course." He gave her a little bow, which brought a smile to the old woman's lips. "But the All-Church has forgotten that, if it ever knew. Their priests have become defiled by their own greed. They have fallen into error and a manifold dogma, thinking their authority comes pure to them and only to them, from God himself. They are dumb dogs, and dry canals. Whatever communion with the divine they may once have had has long been lost in ritual, and an ambition for power. They don't believe they need to ask for forgiveness for their sins, because they claim they do God's work, and so cannot sin at all."

"Listen to me, letting my mouth ramble on." Rissaun waited for the soft chuckle that brought to die down before he continued. "It's said that the greatest of God's gifts is hope. Well, let us hope that he grants understanding to the leaders in the Basilica, and they see the pointlessness of this war they have launched." He raised his hands, palms upwards. "You have suffered me to speak, and this shall be your consolation. Go in love."

"He'd make a good Elite," Kendra said as the men began to rise. "Rissaun is the best speaker of anyone here."

"He has the most practice," Farajalla answered. "It's getting him to shut up that's the trick."

She heard the absent tone in her own voice, one she'd heard often these past four weeks in the castle. Her thoughts had gone elsewhere again, to the Lady's belief that all gods were one, if you stripped away the incense and rituals and endless, wearying formality. Farajalla had a better understanding of it now. She had read the *Opening of the Ways* until her eyes ached and words blurred on the pages, and she knew that the origins of religion lay, as did so many things, with the ancient people known as the Gondoliers.

Ailiss had said that they showed mankind what he could be, if he freed the spirit inside him. Perhaps that was why men always imagined their god as looking like themselves: who else should he look like, if he came from within? All-Church priests had portrayed their deity in different ways as time passed: bearded when there was a fashion for beards, hard-eyed and towering in years of war, then gentle and forgiving in more peaceful days. A reflection of themselves, always, or of how they imagined themselves to be. Other peoples did the same. In the desert the Magani had pictured their supreme god as being the sun, the factor that so dominated their lives. The Madai, her mother's people, followed Anu, who they said lived behind the sun so his radiance would not leave mortals blind. Both gods, behind the glow and the gleam, wore bodies indistinguishable from those of mortals. The Long Barrow Men had worshipped a seasonal god, one who died each midwinter but rose again in the spring, just as they emerged from their longhouses and flowers pricked their way through the melting snow. An image of themselves, written large across the sky and all the world.

Farajalla wondered if it mattered. All gods might be one god, but if so it was a truth that had eluded the All-Church. And if one representation of that god became too twisted, too much warped from what it had once been, then in effect it became a new deity after all.

"I feel I am being unfair to you," Ailiss said. She seated herself on the bench at Farajalla's side, resting her hands on the handle of the cane she used now to lean on. That was a new thing, one she hadn't needed when they arrived at Adour. She had aged in the month spent here, wrinkles deepening in a face that was a fraction paler than it had been before. Farajalla wondered if it was the journey that had wearied her, or the loss of her home. Or something else, a failure of hope perhaps, as the All-Church advanced and Parrien burned by the sea.

"Unfair to me?" she asked. Kendra was gone, she realised. Farajalla had been too wrapped in her thoughts to notice.

"You ought to have had time to study the lore," Ailiss said. Gaudin hovered not far away, watching her with anxious eyes. "The wisdom of the Gondoliers isn't easily learned. A student ought to have months, or better yet years, to even begin to master it."

Farajalla could believe as much. She didn't even understand the instructions for some of the more complex conjurings in the *Opening of the Ways*. There were words she didn't recognise – inevitable when the text had been translated through several languages – but more, the concepts themselves were often baffling. She didn't understand what the authors were trying to tell her to *do*. Ailiss had tried to explain, but even that didn't always help very much.

"The time I have is limited by the world," Farajalla answered. "Not by you. There's no reason for you to reproach yourself."

"I do, even so. I studied for more than a year before I began to understand more than the simplest glamours, but I thought I could shorten that time for you. I believed I was a good teacher. Evidently I flattered myself."

She had to smile. "It could as easily be that I'm a poor student."

"Hardly." Ailiss waved that away. "Yours was the face I saw. I told you that, back at the Hidden House. And you can open yourself to visions already, much earlier than I was able to."

That was true, but thus far Farajalla was able to do no more than achieve the odd blend of calmness and concentration that enabled a capable mind to receive what Ailiss called visions. *Absorbed serenity* was the phrase used in the book. But Farajalla's grasp was imperfect at best, giving her glimpses of insight so brief that the scene flickered across the inside of her eyelids and was gone before she could recognise it. She might be able to recognise a wagon on a road, or the face of a man on a street corner, but what good was that on its own?

Yesterday she'd had a fleeting sight of Calesh, eating from a metal tin with men in the black and white of the Hand of the Lord all around him. Farajalla had time to see that much and no more, even whether he was wounded. He might have been riding out on what he called a dragonnade, the battle assault of the Hand, or he could have been riding back from one. She didn't know, and unless she could gain better control of what she did, she wouldn't learn.

"Believe in yourself," Ailiss said, as though aware of Farajalla's thoughts. She probably was, in fact. The Lady was an intelligent woman, and besides that she had the tricks and glamours of the Gondoliers to call upon. "The fact that I saw your face leaves no room for doubt. It's you who will carry the lore on."

"If it's to go on at all," Farajalla said.

"There is that." Ailiss stood up, leaning on the back of the bench for support. Gaudin moved swiftly to take her arm. "If you feel unfairly dealt with, by me or by events, I apologise for it. This has been thrust upon you, I know. Still…" She folded bony hands on the head of her cane. Farajalla almost thought she could hear the old woman's skin crackle. "Learn quickly, if you can. Time is pressing. It may be that nothing you do can be made to matter, but my instincts tell me otherwise. The story is not over yet."

Gaudin helped her into the aisle, though Ailiss grumbled that she could manage perfectly well on her own, thank you. He didn't take the slightest notice of her. He did turn his head to look at Farajalla, very briefly, as though assessing whether she was a worthy successor to the Lady he served, or too frail a vessel in which to place such trust. Then the two of them were gone, save for the falling murmur of Ailiss's words as Gaudin guided her down the crazily uneven steps to the fortress below.

Farajalla stood up, kneading her back to loosen a knot of muscle, but she didn't follow them at first. She walked slowly into the middle of the little temple, where Rissaun had stood while he spoke. The Dualists claimed there was no such thing as hallowed ground, no place on earth that was sacred to God, because all matter had been made by the Adversary and was tainted with his evil. Still, there was a sense of peace here.

Farajalla had felt the same in the temples of Anu, back in Harenc, among the women of her father's household. The one time she'd entered an All-Church tabernacle she'd had a similar sense of sanctity, if she was honest, though the ceremonies there had struck her as rigid and dry. The bishops of the Basilica seemed to believe God was best found through repetitive responses, formal and precise, spoken from a hundred mouths in unison. Perhaps they were right. Perhaps only one faith held the true keys to Heaven, and it was the All-Church's. How was the average woman supposed to tell?

The book might hold the answer. The *Opening of the Ways,* a tome that held what Ailiss assured her was the collected teachings of the Gondoliers, those long-ago people who had taught all other men how to build, and how to be. They were nearly gods themselves, Farajalla thought wryly, or at least God's trusted servants, like angels clothed in flesh. The idea would be abhorrent to the Dualists, of course, but they were not immune from error. The great books in which Ailiss set such store might be the keys to Heaven, or they might not.

"If my husband is lost in the name of a lie," she told the empty temple, "I will find every house of Dualism and tear it down, and spit on the rubble before I walk away. This I swear."

She turned then, and walking quickly she left the temple and went down the crooked stairs, trying to put that last terrible thought from her mind. It clung stubbornly to the edge of her awareness though, and was still there an hour later when the foresight came upon her all at once, unbidden, and for the first time she saw the future as it might become.

*

She was sitting on the edge of the tank, the little pool of water where a spring bubbled up from the rock beneath, with the remnants of her breakfast on a plate beside her. Prayers always came before food, among the men of Adour. It was a practice taught on the estates where young recruits to the Hand trained and became men, and a habit that had stuck with them. Calesh always rose early as well, though not always to go to prayers. He had never been criticised for it. If someone wanted the comfort of cast-iron ritual he could find it in the All-Church.

She wondered just how different the two religions really were. Oh, there were doctrinal distinctions, most notably the Dualist belief that Adjai had been merely a man, and not the divine son of God clothed in mortal flesh. There was a chasm between the two methods of worship too, one using set rituals in ornate churches and the other with few set prayers or sermons, often spoken in the open air. But in the end the God was the same, just as Ailiss said: he simply wore different clothes. Heaven was the same too, a place achieved by good deeds and pure hearts, and where a soul could live forever in bliss. To Farajalla the similarities outweighed the differences, many times over.

But this war wasn't about God, not really. It was about power. The All-Church had declared that mortals could only approach God through its priests, and they were prepared to commit horrors to protect that claim. The holocaust at Parrien was proof of that. Twenty thousand citizens had been butchered in a day, including hordes of villagers who had fled to the town for safety as the crusading army advanced. Farmers and labourers, peasants and craftsmen, all slaughtered without compunction and regardless of which religion they followed. Sarténe knew now what it could expect when the All-Church army came. Any possibility of negotiation, much less surrender, had burned away in the flames of Parrien. Perhaps that was what the All-Church had wanted all along.

And her husband stood in its way. Fighting for what might be a lie. Farajalla seemed to have spent her whole life in the midst of religious wars, first in Tura d'Madai and now here, and still she didn't know which religion was true and which ones were false. God ought to have left signs, if he truly cared for humans, clues to help them choose between the bewildering profusion of churches and creeds, so that nobody had to die fighting for the wrong cause, or be slaughtered for believing the wrong thing.

But she was chasing the same thought around her mind, repeating herself over and again. She wished Calesh were here, or she with him, so they could steady each other.

Nothing had been the same since he dismounted in the courtyard in Harenc and she saw him for the first time.

She decided to clear her mind. Closing her eyes, she imagined a shell of darkness around herself, a shroud which shut out all sounds and scents, all awareness of the world. It took a moment to form: Ailiss could achieve this at a whim, but it came harder for Farajalla as yet. Once it was done she extended it further out, deepening her isolation until she could feel nothing but the slow beat of her heart, and that faintly. Then she opened her eyes.

In the darkness she saw a man with a bloodied sword, standing over a second man fallen to the floor. The blood was his: he had been wounded several times. There was a robed figure in the background, a woman perhaps, but Farajalla couldn't tell and didn't try. The figure on the floor was her husband.

The vision broke apart as she shot to her feet. Sounds and colour intruded on her and she threw up a hand to shield her eyes, stumbling backwards until her legs struck the stone coping of the pool. "That wasn't battle. Someone is going to try to kill him."

"Who?" Othaer asked.

Farajalla turned her head, surprised to find the young man there beside her. He was standing with her used plate in his good hand, the one not withered by childhood polio, and staring at her with wide eyes. He was the odd man out at Adour, a young man never able to fight surrounded by oldsters whose fighting days were long past. Rissaun and the others were proud to help the Lady but not in awe of her, or at least not much, but for Othaer there was hardly room for anything *except* awe. She could see it in his gaze now.

"My husband," she said. "Leave the plate, Othaer. I need a horse and I need it at once. Hurry!"

He gave a jerky nod and dashed away across the courtyard, towards the broad doors cut into the fortress walls behind which the horses were kept. Farajalla turned towards her room, on the other side of the castle, but after one step she stopped in surprise.

"What did you see?" Ailiss asked. She was standing in the middle of the yard, with Gaudin beside her as usual. Both of them had travelling bags in their arms. Gaudin had Farajalla's as well as his own. She found herself beginning to frown.

"What did you see?" Ailiss repeated.

"Calesh is going to be assassinated," Farajalla replied. "A short man, stocky, with dark hair." She nodded towards the bags. "How did you know?"

"I didn't," the Lady said. "I knew you'd see *something*, but I had no idea what. I had to wait for that."

"But you've packed."

"Ah, well," Ailiss said. She leaned on her cane, a small woman bowed by years and responsibility. "I thought it almost certain that whatever you saw, you'd want to go rushing off and help. I didn't need any raptures or glamours to understand *that*."

"So you're not going to try to stop me?"

"Stop you? Why would I want to stop you?" Ailiss limped closer. The journey through the Aiguille had been hard on her, and she wasn't fully recovered yet, but her eyes were as bright as ever. "Calesh is the key to all our hopes. I've told you that. You can't want to save him more than I do."

"Yes I can," Farajalla said. Surprisingly Gaudin smiled a little at that, only a curl at the corners of his lips but still more emotion that he was prone to display, except for Ailiss herself. For her he fussed and fretted like the worst of old grandmothers. Farajalla thought that was more to do with Ailiss herself than the office she held.

Othaer was bringing her horse out of the stable. Not only hers, Farajalla realised; there were three mounts on his leading reins, and another man brought three more behind them. A trio of soldiers was standing by the main gate, making the last-minute checks of armour and the hang of their swords that she'd seen Calesh make so many times. She looked at Ailiss.

"As I told you," the old woman said mildly, "I knew you'd see something. Shall we go?"

Three

Consolations

The blade whipped over Ando's head as he ducked, so close that it riffled his fair hair. He caught the reverse stroke with his own sword, winning just enough time to back up. A third attack was aimed at his head. The musician deflected it with a wooden clack and retreated again, across the floor of the hall.

Luthien was sure Ando could have slipped under that third stroke, and delivered a killing blow to Riyand's stomach. The singer was no swordsman, but still, the move would have been no more than moderately difficult for him. If this was a real battlefield the Margrave would be dead already. But Ando was being kind, trying to build up Riyand's confidence in himself to the point where he might just about be able to survive a battle. Battle was certainly coming, and when it arrived, Riyand would have to fight beside his men.

Luthien would have taught the Margrave differently, as he knew old Rissaun would, training raw recruits eleven years ago and more. Riyand would be black with bruises by now, and each error he made would be punished with another to add to the welter. Every recruit to the Hand of the Lord spent his first few months wincing with the pain of the knocks he'd taken and there was never any respite, never any excuse. Enemies in battle make no allowance for your hurts. One lad had sprained his ankle and still been made to complete a five mile fitness run across the Aiguille. He'd struggled home hours after the others, bathed in sweat and hobbling like an old, old man, but he had learned the lesson. There is never time to stop and bind a wound when the melee is screaming all around you.

The Margrave needed to learn that too. Ando could be as kind as he wished: battle, in Sartene or Tura d'Madai or anywhere else, was not. Mistakes were rarely forgiven.

"Better!" Ando cried. He had dodged away from another blow and was still retreating up the hall, his worn old boots sliding on the tiled floor. Riyand stalked after him, his face flushed with a combination of effort and exultation. "But can you finish it off?"

Riyand attacked again, grinning as he launched stroke after stroke. At least half of them were wild, lashing blows that left him unbalanced and open to a riposte. Some of those times Ando struck back, but always too slow or too short, allowing Riyand to brush the counters aside and come on. Wooden blades clattered together as Ando defended.

Luthien was careful not to let his lip curl. Battle training meant next to nothing if one of the combatants was able to grin. He should be dreading the impact of a heavy practice blade into his ribs, or cracking into the angle between neck and shoulder. Both men wore leather padding, of course, but the blow would still hurt: it was meant to, after all. Yet Riyand was almost laughing, treating the exercise as a game, something to play at while men built up the city walls or dug cavalry traps in the fields.

Luthien made himself take several deep, calming breaths. The intricacies of warfare meant nothing to him now, or should not. He was Consoled, his spirit given to God. Such ugly earthly things as warfare were not his concern any more. Even with wooden practice blades.

There was a sudden rattle of wood on tiles, and he opened his eyes to see Riyand leaning on his practice sword with his chest heaving. Ando's blade lay on the floor some distance away. The musician himself was holding his right wrist in the other hand, but he was smiling.

"Bravo!" he said. "Bravo indeed. I'd applaud, but my hand seems to be sore. Well done, Riyand."

The Margrave grinned at him. "I'm improving, aren't I? I might even be a match for my poor brother, I think."

"I think so too," Ando said.

Bohend had been a decent swordsman, before the plague took him and left his younger brother to inherit the High Seat. He could have cut Riyand into slivers without working up a sweat. Ando must be aware of that. He was doing his lover no favours with this sycophancy.

Bohend had been clever, too. He wouldn't have ordered the All-Church priest killed by the river, as Luthien was almost positive Riyand had done, and brought the disaster of war down upon them.

A door on the far side of the hall opened. A page entered, clad in the blood and lime livery of Mayence, and right behind him the people he had come to announce. Reis was first, the tall commander of the Margrave's Guard, his worn face unreadable as always. Behind him came Calesh, taller yet but less bulky across the chest, and not so weather beaten. *Give it time,* Luthien thought. Calesh wasn't thirty yet, two decades younger than Reis, and if he spent those years in saddles and on trails he'd likely take on the battered-oak visage of the general. He looked weary almost to death, which would bring that worn look on more quickly if he kept it up, but he glanced at Luthien and smiled. He was limping a little on his injured right leg, the way he did when he was tired, but still, he could still smile at a friend. Luthien felt his heart lift.

Behind Calesh came a much smaller figure, brown hair tied back and held in a net. Ilenia, the Margrave's wife, whom rumour said was still a virgin after nine years of marriage. This time Luthien's heart skipped. She saw him and smiled a tiny smile, as though she knew a secret.

Behind them all, on the wall facing Luthien, was a towering scene of battle in the desert. In the centre stood Calesh Saissan, one foot planted on the fallen form of a swarthy Madai, while beside him a smaller figure threw a broken green banner to the ground. The image didn't much resemble Calesh, in fact, any more than the second man was a good portrait of Luthien. But it was odd enough to stand in a room with a depiction of yourself looking down on you, as you had been in another life. It was outright disorientating to see Calesh as he really was, beneath a stylised image of how a painter thought he ought to be.

"My lord," Reis said, not waiting for the page. He bowed as he spoke, but Calesh merely saluted, right fist to left shoulder as the Hand of the Lord did. Riyand didn't seem to notice. Perhaps he was used to it by now.

"Commander," Riyand said. He lifted his wooden sword. "Ando and I have been practising. I'm becoming quite good."

"I'm sure you are," Reis said.

Calesh's eyes shifted to Luthien, who shook his head very slightly in reply. That made the corners of Calesh's lips twitch. There were no words and very little in the way of expressions, but Luthien knew they understood each other perfectly. Riyand would be a liability in a fight. He might manage to kill one enemy soldier, even two if he was lucky, but then he'd be cut down and even his own side would breathe a sigh of relief. Nobody wanted to have a wild-swinging incompetent beside them in the ranks.

Riyand laid his sword down on a table. "Well then, commanders. What brings you here today? Is the All-Church about to descend upon us at last?"

It was almost a month since the fall of Parrien. Everyone in the town had been butchered, as far as reports and rumours could tell. Twenty thousand people lay dead in the streets when the town was set ablaze. For two nights the flames of that burning had licked at the eastern sky. People gathered on the walls of Mayence to watch, red-limned silhouettes murmuring softly to one another. The next morning hundreds of extra citizens volunteered to join the work details repairing the walls, or clearing livestock and spring crops from the fields. Everyone worked at a feverish pace, with one eye always looking east, to the roads and trails along which the All-Church Crusade must come.

Except it hadn't done so. Days became a week, then two, and the All-Church army remained camped north of the ash and black stone that had once been Parrien. Even so, Mayence did not relax. The enemy might be delayed, for whatever incomprehensible reason, but he was coming.

Luthien knew why the All-Church had stopped, of course. So did others.

"They're staging," Calesh had said, as soon as scouts reported that the army had pitched its tents on the plain. "The All-Church can't have expected us to strip the farms as thoroughly as we did, so they're probably short of food and need to bring some up from east of the river Rielle. And they'll want to scout, now the Hand is back from the desert and standing in their way."

Luthien thought that last was the more significant factor. The All-Church army would have had supplies of its own, gathered and stored for the long voyage east to Tura d'Madai. It wouldn't make much difference that they were being used now in a land war to the west, rather than a sea journey to the east. A soldier needed to eat and drink no matter where he was.

"We're in no immediate danger," Reis said now, in answer to Riyand's wry question. "But the All-Church has brought up forces forward to cover the main approaches to Mayence. You know they closed the north roads three days ago. We've heard now that there is a force of Crusaders in the passes south of the Raima Mountains, blocking the routes to Alinaur."

Luthien winced inwardly. Those southern forces made it impossible for the Hand to recall its men from Alinaur, as Calesh had hoped to do. It was only a few hundred men, but every sword was going to matter in this war. And if they lost it, and had to retreat, there was now nowhere to go. The All-Church had placed the noose already.

"Additional troops?" the Margrave repeated. "How many?"

Reis spread his hands. "It's hard to say with certainty. Something over five thousand, I would say. At any rate, if they cut the roads they'll stop our supplies. We'll starve, sooner or later.

"They've begun to close the noose," Calesh said, echoing Luthien's earlier thought. They were the first words he'd spoken, and typically they were blunt to the point of rudeness, going straight to the point. "We have to cut it before they draw it tight."

Riyand looked at him. "We were outnumbered at least four to one before this. Now it's worse. How can we affect anything they do?"

"They're spread out," Calesh answered. "Not thinly: their general is too clever for that. But there are places where terrain forces a group to separate from the ones on each side of it. I can take advantage of that."

"My lord," Reis said, his tone surprisingly diffident, "I think you should go with him."

Luthien stared at the commander in surprise, and he wasn't alone. Ilenia, silent and still at the back of the group, looked as though she'd been slapped. Ando blinked and then went white: he *did* know how bad a swordsman Riyand was, then. Some instinct turned Luthien's attention back to Calesh, to find his friend's gaze already on him and a wry look on his face. Luthien barely had time to see that before the expression was gone, before anyone else might notice, but it was enough. No words were needed. Calesh didn't want Riyand anywhere near his soldiers, and certainly not on a raid.

"Me?" Riyand said. He sounded stunned.

"It makes sense," Reis told him. "The people need to know you're beside them, and sharing the same dangers. You can't do that here, and I'm not prepared to send the Guard out on the kind of risky foray the Hand of the Lord is capable of. My soldiers aren't as well trained, or as experienced. I need time to improve them, to assimilate new recruits into the ranks, so they have to stay behind the wall until the last moment. The only other way is for you to go with the Hand."

"But I need more training too," Riyand protested. "I'm not ready yet. Unless you think differently, Commander?"

It was Calesh who answered. "Nobody's ever ready. The best trained man in the world might freeze the first time he goes into battle, and be chopped into sausage while he's still crying for his mother. You can practice the steps all you like, but you won't be a dancer until you dance."

"You have an eloquent turn of phrase, Marshal," Riyand said dryly. "But I think I can be sure that you don't really want me with your men."

"Of course I don't," he said, even more arid-voiced. "But Reis is right. An example has to be set."

"Are you really going to help dig ditches while others put their lives in danger?" Ilenia asked from the door.

Her voice was very quiet, but it cut through the conversation and stopped it cold. Reis looked down at his boots, while Ando took a step forward and then halted as though unsure what to say. As for Riyand, he looked at the wife most people believed he'd never touched in love, and a brief spasm of anger passed across his face. It often did, when Ilenia spoke. She never gave a sign that she noticed it, and never let it stop her speaking.

Forget Bohend, Luthien thought, watching her as she met her husband's stare.

This is the woman who ought to have been heir to Sarténe, and not the craven excuse for a man to whom she's married.

"I suppose not," Riyand said at length. "When do we leave, Marshal?"

"The day after tomorrow," Calesh answered crisply. "Noon. I'll send a detachment to pick you up, Margrave. Bring your best two horses. We'll move fast, and won't stop for a man whose mount goes lame."

"You'll stop for him," Reis said.

"Of course I will. But as far as possible he follows the same rules as my men." Calesh turned back to Riyand. It was odd, but beneath that towering likeness of himself on the wall, it was still the real Calesh who dominated the room. "One thing must be clear from the start, my lord. Once we leave the city command is mine. I won't abuse that trust, but if I give you an order you obey it, the same as any raw-handed recruit with straw in his hair and a tremble in his hands. You obey it *immediately*, and if you don't I'll knock you down just like I would anyone else. Is that clear?"

"Perfectly," Riyand said.

Calesh nodded. "Until tomorrow, then. Luthien, will you walk with me for a moment?"

"Of course," he said. He bowed to Riyand and walked across the hall, following Calesh through the small door by which the commanders had entered. The corridor beyond was wide and lavishly decorated, mostly with expensive tapestries from the Jaidi kingdoms of Alinaur, what they used to call the *Taifa* before the All-Church had sent soldiers to reconquer them. They were very good. Luthien was quite certain that had they been appalling, Calesh would still like them more than the mural in the hall.

"God damned foolish thing to do," Calesh muttered as soon as the door was closed. "What's Ando been doing? Feeding the Margrave honey and smiles until Riyand starts to think he's a fighter?"

Luthien blinked, then smiled. "I keep forgetting how astute you are. Yes, that's more or less what he's been doing. If you think it's foolish to take him, why are you doing it?"

"Because it needs to be done," Calesh growled. "Reis is right about that. The people need to see Riyand out there battling for them. Only trouble is, he's so useless he's likely to stab himself before the enemy even sees him."

"You stabbed yourself once," Luthien reminded him.

"I know. My heart and eyes, I know, Luthien." He sighed, looking more tired than Luthien could remember seeing him before. "I'll find a way to cope. Maybe I'll give Baruch ten men and tell him to worry about nothing but keeping Riyand alive until we get back."

It was time to lighten the mood, Luthien decided. "What did you think of the mural in the reception hall?"

"What mural?" Calesh frowned.

Putting a hand on the other man's arm, Luthien came to a halt in the middle of the corridor. "Calesh, if you didn't even notice a ten-foot likeness of yourself on a wall, then you must be exhausted. Go back to the Preceptory and go to bed. If you're in this state when you ride out tomorrow then you'll be putting yourself in more danger than you need to, and your men as well."

"I have to –"

"You have to rest," Luthien said gently. He knew how his old friend hated to sit idly when there was work to be done. "Amand and Baruch can handle things for one evening. They're both good organisers and you know it. Let them do their jobs."

Calesh hesitated, but Luthien tightened his grip on his arm and at last his friend nodded. "I suppose you're right. My heart and eyes, I miss Farajalla. I can't seem to sleep right on my own."

"Then bring her back from Adour," Luthien said. He held up a hand when Calesh opened his mouth. "Yes, I know it's a risk, but what isn't these days? Anyway, that's a thought for another time. Go and get some sleep, Calesh. The city will still be here in the morning."

"What are you, my physician?" Calesh asked. He didn't even smile at his own wry joke. He clasped Luthien's hand and went away down the corridor, still limping slightly on his right leg. It was new, that limp, something Luthien hadn't seen in him when they were in Tura d'Madai together: the injury had happened later, when a Justified Highbinder had tried to murder Calesh in the courtyard at Harenc. One of the soldiers had told Luthien it was Farajalla who saved his life, and killed the assassin besides. Luthien would have dearly enjoyed watching the expression on the killer's face when that happened.

He loathed the Justified. Always had; it was a constant in his life, like enjoying sunshine on his face or laughter with friends. An Elite should be able to let go of his hatreds, really. Luthien knew it, but still, he loathed the Justified, with their sneers and swagger, and bravery which evaporated the moment a struggle began to turn against them. They were typical zealots, ruthless in terrorizing the weak but slow to face the strong, and too quick to wilt and withdraw even when they did. In Tura d'Madai it had been one of the few things the Hand could laugh about with the Glorified, or even the Shavelings: they skulked in shadows, everyone said, like slugs afraid to come into the light.

Justified thought they could excuse any act – justify it, in fact – with the words *in the name of God*. They thought it was acceptable that their assassins wore gloves backed with human bones. Luthien did not, and though an Elite should be able to let go of hatred, there were some things that deserved anyone's hate. He was glad Farajalla had killed that highbinder in the courtyard at Harenc, leaving one fewer black crow to darken the light of God's sun. If that meant his own soul was tarnished he'd make recompense as best he could, and hope the deeds of his life stood him in good stead when he passed through the true Gate of Angels into Heaven, but if not he would accept it.

The tapestries really were good. The Jaidi wove on cotton, eschewing the wool preferred by most others, and it gave the colours a texture Luthien found smoother. Some weavers in Mayence had picked up on the habit years ago. The tapestry nearest him showed hundreds of men kneeling before a priest in a valley, while behind them a town burned against the dark evening shadow of the mountains. You had to look closely to see that the priest was actually a green-robed Elite. Longer examination might betray the fact that the two halves of the picture were almost identical, if folded over a vertical line running down the middle, except for the colours – dark mountains on the right, flame-lit mountains facing them, and the priest in the centre. The praying Hand soldiers were on the side of light, while across from them men with crimson crosses on their shields knelt in the dark, picked out only by the gleam of firelight on metal. Justified, of course. But it was done so subtly that an observer would only see two groups of men in prayer, both facing the same priest, and not understand the subtext.

It was still hard to see if you were a Dualist, and knew. There was beauty in that and wit too, the cleverness to show your beliefs openly and yet hide them at the same time. It was the sort of subtlety Luthien had once hoped he might achieve himself, in his writings on history and philosophy. He might not have been able to manage it, but he would have liked to try. He didn't know when he might be able to, now, if ever. The Academy had been burned and its books were on their way to Samanta, if they'd managed to get through the passes before the All-Church Crusaders blocked them. If not there would be a bonfire one night soon, when the soldiers found the texts. Anything not written by the All-Church was regarded as morally suspect. You couldn't hope that Crusaders, of all people, would be immune to that.

He needed to pray. Too much was happening now, more than he was used to. Life since he'd returned from the desert had been slow, thoughtful, a pace only dampened further when he joined the Academy. He turned and then stopped, watching as three women came down the passage towards him.

Ilenia led them, of course. The other two were ladies in waiting, women who seemed interchangeable to Luthien, floating in and out of any room that had Ilenia in it without ever leaving an impression. They hadn't been with her in the hall, so they must have been outside; probably Luthien and Calesh had walked right past without seeing them. He didn't really see them now. All his eyes took in was Ilenia, graceful as a dove and almost shining, her eyes aglow when she glanced at him.

"Elite Luthien," she said, with a nod of her head that was perfectly formal, perfectly correct.

And then she was gone, walking away, leaving only a tightness in Luthien's chest as a mark of her passing. No, not only that. His blood was racing too. Ilenia could do that to him so easily, every time he saw her really. Most of the time it was his oath to abstain from meat that gave Luthien the most difficulty, or from wine, both of which he'd enjoyed in considerable amounts prior to taking the Consolation. But when he was near Ilenia the vow of celibacy seemed impossible to keep, an urge against which he could only stand for a short time while the throb of his desires beat against him, and beat, until he crumbled under its weight.

"I am beset on all sides," he murmured to himself, and his lips curved in a wry smile that was almost invisible. The All-Church assault had forced him from Parrien and into Mayence, close to Ilenia and temptation, and at the same time it forced him to watch his friends risk their lives while he could do nothing to help. Temptation was everywhere, it seemed. He shook his head and pushed his glasses up his nose, trying to shake the mood.

He *really* needed to pray, and he couldn't use the palace chapel because Ilenia might meet him there. Even if she didn't the thought would always be with him, distracting his mind. As for the chapels of Mayence, they lacked the solitude Luthien preferred; the city was too big, and the people at the moment so afraid that they packed the benches for every service. But in the villages people still prayed outdoors when the weather allowed, and that would do well enough for Luthien too. There were parks, and if those were now full of labour crews and crosshatched with ditches, he could walk outside the walls. If he could find a patch of farmland not also scarred by fortifications.

He turned and made for the main entrance, and the guards let him pass without a word.

Four

Preparations

"These are good people," the priest said. About thirty civilians were grouped behind him, most of them clutching bags or sacks in their arms. "Your neighbours. It's barbaric to turn them out of their homes."

"It's barbaric of your church to come here to kill us all," the Guard captain told him. He hadn't bothered to dismount. "We're not going to let the Faithful of the All-Church wait in the city until they have a chance to open the gates and let the army inside."

"They wouldn't –"

"Some of them would," the captain cut in. "In this group, or another. Now get gone."

"Give them until sundown," Calesh said.

The officer looked around, surprise already being replaced by anger that someone had contradicted him. Both expressions vanished when he saw who had spoken. "Uh, is that wise, sir?"

"The army isn't here yet. There's no danger today," Calesh said. "And look at them. They didn't believe we would expel them from the city. Half of them haven't packed. Let them."

The priest was glaring at him as though he'd ordered the citizens slaughtered, not given them time to salvage what they could. Well, that was to be expected, probably: Calesh was the All-Church's great enemy in this war, the figure they encouraged their soldiers and clerics to hate most of all. He knew it and accepted it, for the most part. It was just hard to feel determined when desperate women were standing in the street with pleading eyes, and children clung to their skirts or hid behind their fathers' legs.

In truth, Calesh wasn't sure anyone would let the All-Church army into Mayence. They knew what had happened in Parrien, where the church's Faithful had been slaughtered alongside Dualist Believers, without even an attempt to distinguish between them. But *not sure* was a long way from *certain,* and the risk couldn't be taken. Besides, every mouth removed from the city was one that no longer needed to be fed, which improved the chances of withstanding a siege. Calesh had given the order yesterday, before going to the palace with Reis, and then spent the rest of the day with the taste of horse dung in his mouth.

The Guard captain nodded, and Calesh turned away. Twenty Hand soldiers moved with him, forming a circle inside which Calesh, Baruch and Amand walked side by side. The precaution probably wasn't necessary, but again, probably was a long way from certainly.

"You did that because of the children," Baruch said, once they were away. He kept his voice low; the street wasn't very busy, but there were always ears to hear, wherever you were. "Didn't you?"

"I suppose I did," Calesh agreed. "Poor little devils. None of this is their fault, after all."

"None of this is ours," Amand put in.

"True enough. So should we punish children because strangers want to punish us?" Calesh snorted. "I'm not going to do that. Giving them a day to pack doesn't hurt us and it will help them. War is always cruel, but that's no reason to make it crueller than it needs to be."

"Remember Raigal, and the girl in Elorium?" Baruch asked.

Of course he remembered. Raigal Tai had flung himself across a street to pull a little girl almost from under the wheels of a rattling, laden wagon, rolling over one vast shoulder with the child held safely in his arms. The girl had been Madai, one of the enemy, supposedly. She'd fled straight to her mother and then the mother had vanished too, scuttling away rather than speak to the filthy outlander even if he had saved her daughter's life. But he would do it again, and Calesh would too. War was ugly enough without finding new horrors to add to it.

"Let's get on with this," he said, a little brusquely. He'd slept like a dead man last night but he was still tired, a long sea journey and the pressure since catching up with him. "I need to finish the dispositions for the defence before I take Riyand out on a raid this afternoon, and there's a lot to do."

"Not least with Riyand," Baruch said, sotto voce.

Calesh glanced at him and didn't reply. Riyand was worse than a buffoon, a fool who was hardly capable of running his lands during peacetime, even with the help of capable men like Reis and Cavel, the seneschal. In war he endangered Sarténe just by being Margrave. Ideally Calesh would like to kick him out of the city along with the few All-Church adherents who remained, and replace him with a son or nephew who could at least wield a sword and was willing to work to defend the country. But there wasn't anyone; the family had been sparse for generations, and the plague fifteen years ago had killed off the last alternatives. Including Riyand's elder brother Bohend, who should have been Margrave while his younger sibling frittered the years away in bar rooms and poetry readings.

There was nothing to do about it now. Calesh tried to dismiss it from his mind, but he'd tried before, and it kept creeping back. "Never mind Riyand. What are we looking at first?"

"The east road," Amand said.

Calesh nodded. "Then let's look."

It wasn't that easy. Once on the main streets their progress slowed, because it seemed everyone in the city wanted to crowd close to Calesh Saissan, shout his name, shake his hand if at all possible. The twenty escorts tightened their protective ring until their bodies made a solid circle, but faces still appeared over their shoulders and hands reached over, and Calesh shook them when he could while trying not to slow too much. There was work to do, yes, but part of that work was in raising morale, helping people to believe they *could* stand off the All-Church, however grim the odds might be.

So he shook hands and smiled encouragement, and in response to shouted questions he said that yes, he was very confident, he knew the people of Mayence were tough and could stand anything thrown at them. That got a cheer no matter how often he said it: he heard it being murmured back through the crowd each time, a ripple of expanding confidence that showed in turned heads and sudden grins. Baruch stole a glance at him once, probably pondering whether to say something wry about Calesh's ability to inspire, but he held his peace. Amand just stalked along of course, watching the throng and saying nothing.

They reached the end of Waggoner's Way, where the small plaza just inside the gate had suffered changes. The two narrow streets that ran off parallel to the wall had been blocked with stone walls seven feet high, behind which archers could stand on plinths and shoot into the square. Windows had been bricked over too, and breastworks built of unmortared stone formed curves on rooftops all around. Any soldiers who forced the Gate of Angels would find themselves in a killing jar, bottled up and under fire from all sides.

The Guardsmen on duty saluted as they walked through. When Calesh had led the Hand into the city a month ago they'd tried to bar his way. That was unthinkable now.

Outside, the walls of the bridge had been broken down, the blocks presumably taken inside to form the new defences there. The deck itself looked bare without them, like a winter tree shorn of its leaves. Men were working beyond it, in what had been fields until recently, digging pits and driving sharpened wooden stakes into the ground in lines facing outward. Others, resting between shifts, turned to look at the party on the bridge; several raised their hands in greeting.

The stakes were *chevaux de frise,* hated by cavalry everywhere because the points were at just the height to disembowel a horse. The approaching army would be able to clear them, of course, but only under fire from the walls, and it would take time. They would have to be careful of the pits too, covered with thin mats of branches and a coat of earth, enough to deceive the eye but not enough to support a man's weight. Anyone who fell in would impale himself on more spikes. Foot soldiers hated the pits almost as much as horsemen hated the stakes.

It would all count. Every day the All-Church was delayed brought autumn, so distant now, a day closer. And with autumn would come the rains, the winds that brought winter riding on their tails, the cold nights and mist-wreathed mornings that would make Raigal Tai feel right at home.

"It's like this all around the city," Baruch said. "I'll check the north gate later, because the bridge there should have been destroyed by now. We don't need it: nothing but the army can come down that road now."

Calesh nodded. "The Kair doesn't run along the wall on the north, though. It's further away, and I remember a bridge half a mile out that could do with breaking, when the army gets close enough."

"Already done," Baruch said complacently. "Mostly we're making do with small boats, but anything large can come down the east bank to here, and enter the city this way."

"Make sure the boats —"

"Are tied up on our bank," Baruch interrupted, "or else burned. I know, Calesh. It's in hand."

Amand leaned forward to look across Calesh at the other man. "He does that to me too. Reminds me of things I've already done."

"Has he ever reminded you of something you *hadn't* done?"

Amand managed a very small smile. "Once or twice."

"Which is why I do it," Calesh said, and the two men answered in unison, "We know that."

He couldn't help chuckling. Even after a good night's sleep he was still tired half to death, and the thought of the advancing All-Church army appalled him when he let himself think about it too closely. He tried to avoid it by concentrating on the details, dealing with a hundred little things instead of the one big problem, and it worked in a way. He was still functioning, at any rate.

"Look under the bridge," Baruch said.

Calesh got down on his belly and hung partly over the side, so the Kair frothed along above his head. Near the far end of the span he could see two small barrels hooked into brackets under the stonework, each with a thick cord protruding from one end. "Fire oil?"

"In case we have to break the bridge quickly," Baruch explained. "I don't want to be caught by surprise. Besides, we're talking about Justified and Shavelings here, and either might be stupid enough to fall for the same trick we pulled out by Parrien last month."

They had blown a bridge then too, hurling dozens of Justified cavalry to their deaths, men and horses alike. Fifty riders had been trapped on the Hand's side of the ravine, easy meat for the larger force, but Calesh had ordered them spared. He'd still hoped that the war could be an honourable one then, with both sides prepared to observe the rules of chivalry and offer terms of surrender when they could. What had happened in Parrien after that day had put an end to such optimism. Now he knew it was to be a war of annihilation, one side or the other crushed so utterly that the mud itself turned red.

"What else do I need to know?" he asked. "Make it brief, if you can. I have to look over the assignments for wall duty before I take Riyand out on our little jaunt this afternoon."

"Arrows," Baruch said crisply, lifting a hand with one finger held out. "We don't have enough, and we're not going to have unless we can find more glue. Feathers we have, but we need glue. That means butchering horses. And we need to do it soon, or we're likely to run out of shafts."

"Speak to Reis while I'm gone," Calesh said. "Tell him my advice is to slaughter as many horses as necessary. Our cavalry will be no use behind a wall in any case. What else?"

A second finger shot out. "Children. I want permission to requisition the All-Church Cathedral for use as a sanctuary when the fighting starts, to keep the young ones out of the way. And out of danger," he added, almost as an afterthought. A good military planner thought of necessity first and compassion second.

"Agreed," Calesh said.

"I also want to use the Hall of Voices," Baruch went on, "and the Margrave's Manse as well."

Amand barked laughter, and Calesh grinned. "Also agreed. But wait until Riyand and I have ridden out, and then ask Cavel. Or Ilenia, for that matter. I don't think they'll protest."

"Splendid," Baruch said, and a third finger popped up. "Next, Amand and I want to start rationing food as of now. That means gathering all food into central storage and putting guards on every chicken coop and pigsty in the city. If we wait until the All-Church arrives we might find we made a mistake, and it will be too late then. This is going to be close as it is,

Calesh. Very close. A day's worth of food might make all the difference."

"Do it," Calesh said. "However you and Amand see fit. You don't need to check something like that with me, Baruch."

"Given that you're effectively the ruler of the city right now, I think we do," Baruch replied. He poked out a fourth finger. "Lastly, we want to send some of the locals out of the city into the Aiguille, before the siege begins. The half-trained men, for the most part, with a smattering of old campaigners for seasoning. They can live off the land and try to break up All-Church supply lines, and meantime it leaves us fewer mouths to feed."

Calesh frowned. "I can't see many men volunteering for that."

"You misjudge them," Amand said. "I asked around a little, unofficially, and we could send out five hundred if we wanted to. I don't recommend we do – half that number will be enough, and more would strip the walls too much – but we'll have the men."

"It was Amand's idea," Baruch put in, a little wryly. "Here I've been in Mayence all these years, and it took a desert rat fresh back from the sand to show me something so simple."

"That's what we desert rats do," Calesh said. "We trust you soft home folk to know the streets and the city, and make the plans we can't. Which you've done admirably, Baruch. I agree to all your ideas, and Amand's too. He's coming on the dragonnade with me, so you're the one who'll have to put them into effect. Reis will help you."

"I'm glad someone will," Baruch grumbled.

Calesh put a supportive hand on his friend's shoulder, but he didn't bother to reply. Baruch had always been the same, complaining about his workload even while trusting nobody else to do it for him. Come to that Amand was the same as well, though the gaunt man managed to make it look easy, somehow. He'd had time to iron neat creases into his uniform again today. After five years of working with him Calesh was still half-persuaded that the man never slept.

He felt uncomfortable though, and not because of preparations or the problems they would cause. *You're effectively the ruler of the city right now,* Baruch had said. Calesh supposed it was true – in fact, being honest, he knew it was true. It was just strange. He was the son of a pig farmer, a yokel who'd left Sarténe more than a decade ago with no intention of ever coming back. And yet here he was, back on home soil, with the Margrave's Guard under his assimilated command and the lord himself acquiescing with his demands. Reluctantly, to be sure, but Riyand did jump when Calesh said goose. Witness this expedition planned for the afternoon, when Calesh would take the effete Margrave on a raid and try his best to bring him back alive.

He had work to do before then. Calesh turned, his two friends and the twenty man escort turning with him, and set off back into the city.

*

Half an hour later he was sitting at a large table in one of the visitors' rooms in the Manse, with piles of paperwork in front of him and not enough time to do it.

Paperwork is more Amand's thing, he thought, but it wasn't really. Both the cadaverous man and Baruch were gifted organisers, able to think of all the myriad tasks which needed to be done and to see they *were* done, but they didn't have Calesh's strategic ability. He knew that; he wasn't being arrogant, or claiming a talent he didn't have. The other two could look at a summary of the food reserves and understand what it implied for the future, and Calesh could do the same for troop dispositions and co-ordinations. This was what he was good at. He sighed and picked up the first report.

> *Gate of Angels – two towers with linked parapet.*
> *Two squads of Hand of the Lord,*
> *two of Guard, four of militia. Arranged in*
> *rotating shifts of twelve hours.*

> *Wall section, Gate of Angels to Southpoint Tower.*

One squad of Hand, one of Guard.
Arranged in rotating shifts of twelve hours.

Southpoint Tower – single tower over river.
One squad of Hand, one of Guard,
one of militia. Arranged in rotating shifts of
twelve hours.

The three positions covered the section from the Gate of Angels to where the city wall bent back east, along the edge of the low rise on which Mayence was built. Calesh was never going to be able to remember all the details for each position all the way around the city. He needed a map, and a pen to make notations. He pushed back his chair and stood as the door behind him opened.

"I brought you some maps," Luthien announced as he walked sideways into the room. He had to crab his way in because of the rolls of paper under one arm; in the other hand he held a plate piled with fruit and sliced meat. "I had one of the scribes start copying them out a week ago, so they're mine. Feel free to scribble all over them if you want."

"I'm well served by my friends," Calesh said, smiling. "But I'm sure there should be guards on that door."

"There are," Luthien agreed. "One of them was going to search me, but the other one just laughed."

"Good for him," Calesh said. He realised he was famished: after going to bed so early last night he'd been up before dawn, and breakfast seemed a long time ago. He took the plate from Luthien and popped a large piece of cheese into his mouth. "Thank you."

Luthien winced a little. "Please. Chew or talk, but don't try to do both unless I'm ten yards away."

Calesh swallowed. "And this from the man who used to use strips of bacon fat as a bookmarks."

"Don't remind me," Luthien shuddered. He fumbled in his robe and produced a bottle and one glass. "I brought this too."

"Wine?" Calesh asked, surprised. "From you?"

"I've sworn myself to abstinence," Luthien said. He pushed his glasses up his nose. "Nothing stops me from serving the need in others. And I think you could use a drink."

He nodded. "I could, but I'd best lay some food in my stomach before I touch that, or I'll wobble where I stand." He rolled a slice of beef in bread and took a bite, careful to make sure it was smaller than before. "Does one of your maps happen to show the city walls?"

Two minutes later they had it unrolled on the table, weighed down on two corners by paperweights and on the others by the wine bottle and Calesh's plate. They started with Calesh calling out troop positions and Luthien marking them, but Calesh was still trying to eat and that caused a lot of indistinct mumbling and a spray of crumbs, so they swapped around. Luthien moved the stool to the far end of the table, closer to the window where the light was better.

After a while Calesh went back to the plate and was surprised to find only an orange left. He began peeling it with one thumb as he went back to the map. "All right, what's next?"

"We're done," Luthien told him. "That's the whole circuit. What changes do you want?"

"Let me think a bit," he answered.

Luthien sighed. "You might not have heard it, but the late morning bells rang a little while ago. Quarter of an hour, perhaps. That leaves you thirty minutes before you have to go to the Preceptory to lead the men on your raid."

He hadn't heard the bells, and hadn't realised time was so short either. Calesh was about to protest that he needed time to think anyway, and then saw Luthien's slight smile and the perception in those green eyes and gave it up. They knew each other too well for deception. "Fair enough. Will you need to write down my suggestions?"

"Call them orders, since that's what they are," Luthien said mildly, "and no, I can remember well enough."

Too well for deception, indeed. Orders were exactly what Calesh wanted. Luthien wouldn't let him hide behind loose phrasing or weasel words, any more than he'd allowed it ten years ago in the desert. Some things changed, like marriage or the swearing of a sacred oath; other things never changed at all.

"All right then," he said. "First of all, we don't have enough men, but Amand and Baruch know that already. Reis too," he added as an afterthought. He was still used to thinking only of the Hand of the Lord when he gave commands. "There's nothing to be done but train more men, and put them on the wall as soon as they can avoid stabbing each other by accident. They know that too, I'm sure, but it bears repeating. It matters."

Luthien nodded, hands folded in his lap.

"One thing we *can* change is the shift rotation," Calesh said. "Baruch has got everyone on twelve-hour watches, changing at the same time every day and all along the wall. The general of the All-Church army will spot that on the first day and plan around it. If he's thinking straight – and this man does think straight, whoever he is – he'll launch probing attacks an hour before the guard changes, when the men on watch are tired and their replacements are still in bed."

"So what do you want done?"

"We need to change things around, have different shifts for each section of the wall, so people change over at staggered times. Even then we'll need to alter things every few days once the siege begins." He rubbed his jaw. "Every week, say. That way the enemy can't adapt to any patterns."

"I seem to remember," Luthien said, "that the Madai used that tactic, when the first Crusade invaded Tura d'Madai."

"They did," Calesh agreed. "One of a number of things they taught us. Now, I want to –"

He broke off as the door opened, turning towards it. As he did so he was aware that Luthien had gone very still on his chair, staring past Calesh towards the door. A decade of honed instincts had Calesh's hand straying towards the hilt of his sword even before he could see for himself.

"Look out!" a woman screamed from the corridor. Calesh was still turning, the moment seeming to stretch like dripping honey, but he realised with stupefaction that the voice was Farajalla's, she was *here,* and warning him. Then he was facing the door, and could see the body of one of the guards face-down on the floor, twitching as blood ran from his throat in a thick stream. The other was tumbling backwards into the room, arms splayed as his heels clattered and slid away, and he fell on his back as his hands went to the great slice in his own throat, identical to that of his colleague. Two Hand soldiers, killed like sheep in the Manse itself.

A smallish, muscular man stepped into the room and turned to close the door. Farajalla screamed *"Calesh!"* and he had a fleeting glimpse of her, throwing herself at the oak just as the little man slammed it shut and shot the bolt, all in one motion. The door rattled as Fara hit it but was never going to break; these doors were made to stand up to assault with an axe. Inside it the man turned, smiling broadly. He held a bloodied dagger in one hand.

"Calesh Saissan," he said. He was dressed like a mercenary, a boiled leather jerkin covered with a fairly poor mailshirt, and leather vambraces on his forearms. "At last. At long last."

"Do I know you?" Calesh asked. Blood was humming in him. He had no idea what was happening but two men were dead, and it was going to be his turn next. That had to be why the muscular man was here. His weariness was gone, banished by the familiar surge of energy that came before a fight.

"The whole world will know me after today," the man said. He flashed a quick, toothy smile that made Calesh feel suddenly cold: there was madness in that sudden grin, or he'd never seen it before. "The man who killed Calesh Saissan, and broke the spirit of the heretics. And it's been coming. Ever since you stole my glory at Gidren Field, it's been coming."

Calesh drew his sword, exactly as the stranger did. The other man was advancing slowly across the room, taking his time, savouring the moment. Calesh still didn't know who he was, but he held his sword like a man who knew his work, and his eyes flickered around the room as he memorised the positions of furniture and any loose or uneven floor tiles. And he wore black gloves on his hands. Black gloves backed with bones.

"You're a highbinder," he said. His stomach clenched. "One of the Justified's assassins."

A muscle jumped in the muscular man's cheek, but he made a mocking bow. "Elizur Mandein. A name to take with you to the grave."

He frowned, trying to remember where he'd heard the name. When the memory came the tightness in his belly grew worse. "You won the sword tournament at Caileve."

"I did," Mandein said.

He was shockingly composed, certain of himself even for a professional assassin, and with good reason. Anyone who won a single match at Caileve had to be more than merely good: anyone who won the entire competition must be stunningly gifted. Calesh wasn't. He had killed Amalik all those years ago, but that had been competence in battle, not brilliance in single combat. He was almost certainly going to die here now, and with the thought the tension in him vanished and he felt calm, as composed as Mandein himself.

If he had one chance it was to unsettle the killer, so Calesh looked him up and down and said, "I thought you would be taller."

The muscle jumped in Mandein's cheek again, and he snarled like an angry cat and attacked.

Five

A Spin of the Blade

Saissan wasn't armoured, had been caught entirely by surprise. There were no guards after the two at the door, only one of the heretical priests of this Dualist cult, the Elite. He was framed in light streaming through the window, still as a statue: probably in shock, Elizur thought. He could be dealt with later.

But now there was Saissan, at *last* there was Saissan, and Elizur went to meet him with the small, pattering steps of a dancer.

The blades met, then slid over each other with a squeal. Elizur pivoted on one heel and brought his sword around on the reverse, only to be met with another wrist-grinding clash as Saissan anticipated the move. But that was all right: Elizur was holding back, gauging what Saissan could do and how fast he was, and the answer so far was that he didn't have enough. Not nearly enough. It paid to be careful though, so Elizur engaged him once more with a series of forehand blows, driving Saissan along the edge of the table but not really trying to strike him. The other man fell back easily enough, making his own stroke-by-stroke assessment of his foe. Saissan was a good swordsman in fact, and an experienced soldier beside, so he knew the game and how to play. Much good it would do him.

There was shouting from outside the door now, the words unclear but the tone at once urgent and angry. Probably they were calling for axes to be brought. It was time to be done with this, to kill Saissan and the false priest and be gone through the window, along the wall Elizur had carefully scouted out last night. He stepped back and gave Saissan a wide smile.

"I only ever failed in one task for the Servants of the Justification," he said. "That was in killing Cammar a Amalik. I was at Gidren Field, you know. If not for your rashness I'd have had his head that day."

Saissan was watching him warily, making no move to attack. In the brief clash of arms he'd taken Elizur's measure then, and knew exactly how much trouble he was in. "You're angry with me for that?"

"I *despise* you for that," Elizur said, still smiling. "I've despised you for eight years. And now I'll take the price for what you did that day."

"If you can," Saissan said.

Elizur actually laughed. "You know I can."

"Not yet I don't," Saissan retorted. He waggled his blade, openly taunting. "And they say the greatest of God's gifts is hope."

Hearing this man, this apostate, talk of the gifts of God brought fury rushing into Elizur with such force that he was half sure his boots lifted from the floor. He lifted his blade and stepped into the attack.

This time there was no hesitancy, no cautious testing of Saissan's speed or reflexes. Elizur knew them well enough already. He'd noticed that the other man was a fraction slow in pushing off his right leg, the one he'd been shot in long ago. He wasn't quick enough cutting back on the forearm either, perhaps as the result of another wound, one Elizur didn't know about. In truth he wasn't quick enough anywhere, but those were the obvious places, the ones Elizur had identified in the first short clashes.

Now they engaged for real, and in the first exchange Elizur laid a gash across Saissan's thigh when he turned too slowly on his right leg. It was a surprise, actually: Elizur had thought the cut would kill, but Saissan saw it just in time and managed to twist away. Blood leaked through the slice in his trous though, a fair stream of it. On the second pass Elizur wounded him again, this time pushing Saissan onto his forehand and then slashing up and across before the other man could adjust. Again he thought it was a killing blow, and again Saissan avoided it, arching his body backwards so the tip of the blade only raked a furrow across his chest, leaving the black shirt to flap around the cut. Saissan backed up a step, hunching slightly now as he gained room.

Elizur went after him without pause, without thought.

Saissan was slow, but his peripheral vision must be astonishing, for him to have read those two moves of Elizur's in time to dodge the cuts. Very well then; if cuts didn't work Elizur would kill him another way. Behind him the door jumped in its hinges as an axe was buried in the wood on the far side. He registered it distantly, focused on the fight at hand.

He spun his sword into a blur. Saissan parried once, twice. He was backing up desperately now, trying to turn to make room as he fended off another blow, this one a raking forehand.

It never arrived.

Elizur moved his feet, pushed against his own slash and turned it into a straight-ahead thrust. It took Saissan in the lower left side of his chest, slipped between two ribs and went into his lung. Black blood bubbled around the wound even before Elizur pulled his blade out. Incredibly Saissan was still on his feet, still standing with a sucking chest wound gushing blood over his stomach, staring at Elizur from a whitening face. Then his knees buckled and he fell. His sword rattled away across the tiles.

Elizur stepped forward, and reversing his sword he stabbed downward to end the hated man's life. Tried to stab downward.

His blade was met with a crash that ran up his arm and rattled his shoulder in its socket. Only the reflexes of an assassin saved him then; he sprang back, utterly unaware of what had happened or who had thwarted him, and the green-robed Elite's backswing passed harmlessly an inch in front of him.

"Pick on someone your own size," said Luthien Bourrel.

It was him. Of course it was him; had he not been standing by the window when Elizur came in, outlined by the light, Elizur would have known him at once. It was the glasses which gave him away. Nobody else in Gallene wore spectacles, certainly not another Elite. Back in Tura d'Madai people had spoken of Bourrel as the finest swordsman in the Crusade army.

Mind you, nobody had known what Elizur was, in those days. He had seemed just another soldier among the Servants, one appointed to rank directly by the commanders, but a soldier nonetheless. And Bourrel hadn't lifted a weapon since he took that fool oath, however long ago that had been; and he was wearing an ankle-length robe besides. Such things mattered among fighting men. On the floor Saissan gasped and more blood bubbled over his chest.

Elizur spun his blade and went forward.

He was met and matched from the first blow, Bourrel's sword flashing to counter every pass Elizur made. Each time the shock was enough to jar Elizur's bones. The other man hit *hard,* and he didn't seem to move his feet, or need to. After half a minute Elizur realised why; it was because Bourrel's feet were already where they needed to be before the blow began, so he never had to adjust to counter it. He was anticipating. It was the kind of thing Elizur was so good at noticing, a chink in the other man's ability. What was a strength became a flaw, against him. He could take advantage of that.

In the midst of the next exchange he swung his weight around a bent leg, changing the angle of his strike. It was a difficult move, one beyond most fighting men, and he accomplished it neatly and at speed. His blade lashed back across and cut only air.

Something stung his shoulder and Elizur fell back with a gasp. He looked down to see blood welling through his shirt. Bourrel was standing a yard to the side of where Elizur had thought he was, his sword held casually downwards, looking at Elizur with eyes that burned with rage.

"God damn you," Bourrel said. His voice was thick, slurred with fury. "God damn you, and anyone of your blood. My oath. You foul, shit-smeared, stinking piece of offal, you made me break my oath."

Elizur didn't understand. He lifted a hand to touch the blood soaking into his shirt, amazed to see scarlet on the tips of his fingers.

Bourrel sprang forward. Elizur had never seen anyone move so fast, hadn't thought it was possible. He deflected a blow but another came, another, streaks of flashing silver that struck like hammers, shaking his bones. He fell back but it wasn't enough, he wasn't *quick* enough, and he took wounds to both arms and one hip, then from a blindingly deceptive backhand that sliced his right cheek open from nose to jaw and left a flap of flesh hanging from his chin.

He was still trying desperately to fend that off, just realising he'd been hit, when something white-hot went through his middle. It barely hurt and for an instant Elizur thought he was just short of breath, and the little stab of pain was a sudden stitch. Then he felt the blood, his *own* blood, and he had just enough time to look down and see Bourrel's blade pulled free before everything ended and he fell.

*

Luthien waited for the axe to hit the door before he slid the bolt back, so the people outside didn't cleave his head when he tried to let them in. The handle turned at once and he moved aside as three people all but fell into the room: Raigal Tai with a huge lumberjack's axe in his hand, an aged and portly Hand armsman Luthien didn't know, and Farajalla. She pushed him aside with a cry and threw herself towards her husband.

"Blood of the God," Raigal whispered. He was staring at Calesh's fallen body. "Is he dead?"

"He will be," Luthien said. His hands were shaking. "I wasn't fast enough, Raigal. If I'd acted straight away –"

"You broke your oath," the big man said, understanding flooding his face. "You killed the assassin."

Luthien swallowed. "Yes. I killed the assassin."

"I'm sorry you had to do that," the portly man said.

Luthien looked at him, wondering for a moment who this stout old fellow was, but then he recognised him. Or remembered him: both of them had changed in eleven years. Just now it didn't seem much of a shock to find him here. "Rissaun. Good to see you."

He could be polite it seemed, the habit so deeply ingrained that it held even now. More people were coming in into the room, two of them physicians Luthien had seen in the Manse before. More of Riyand's pet court favourites, like

Ando Gliss. Behind them came Ailiss herself, the Lady of the Hidden House here in Mayence, which Luthien couldn't remember happening before. He realised he was still holding a bloody sword, and dropped it with a clang.

"Lady," he said. He had to swallow again. "I'm so sorry. I –"

"He wants you," Farajalla said from behind him, and Luthien turned. Her voice was very calm. "He wants to speak with you."

Luthien went over to his friend. Black blood still pulsed from the wound every time Calesh breathed, but there was less than before. His eyes were open and there was a terrible pain in them, but they shifted as Luthien knelt on the tiles. "I'm here, Calesh."

"Broke your oath," Calesh whispered.

Speech was beyond him, so he just nodded.

"Didn't have to," Calesh managed. His voice was hardly more than breath, but he forced a faint smile. "My brother to dragons."

Brother to dragons. The men of the Hand called each other that: they were the men who stood as one and rode together in the charge, what they called the dragonnade. Luthien had once been proud to be such a man, then later he'd been proud to have left it behind for God. Now it seemed he was a warrior again. He didn't know what to say to that.

Farajalla folded one of Calesh's hands in hers. She was weeping, Luthien saw, though her expression was perfectly serene beneath the tears. "Oh, my love. Wait a little longer with me."

Calesh was still looking at her, but he didn't react. His eyes had begun to glaze over. Farajalla moved his hand to her belly, and Luthien was suddenly sure she was pregnant. He thought then he could feel his heart breaking, that it was cracking like glass and everyone would be able to hear it. Across the room Raigal Tai stood with Baruch, who had appeared from somewhere, both of them crying. The doorway was crammed with soldiers in the black and white of the Hand, all of them motionless, and all of them silent.

It was then, as Calesh's eyes slipped closed, that the Lady said, "There is no need for him to die."

It drew every eye to her, a small woman crinkled with age, leaning heavily on a cane. That was new, a concession to age and infirmity, but she stood straight enough now. "Lift him onto the table. Right side first, if you will. Keep him as straight as you can."

Farajalla looked up sharply. "He'll die if we move him."

"He will die if we don't," Ailiss corrected her gently. "Girl, have you learned nothing? You've spent the last month reading the sacred books. You of all people should know something of the arts I possess, and which will be yours one day. But since that day isn't now, trust me." She met Farajalla's stare. "Lift him to the table. Right side first."

"Lift him," Farajalla said, and it was her order that was obeyed. Luthien would remember that, later when there was time to think, and sorrow had been driven back awhile. It was he, Baruch and Raigal who slid their hands under Calesh's body and raised him, of course, taking care to keep him flat. When they laid him down Luthien thought that if a butterfly had been resting on his shirt it would not have been in the least disturbed.

"Now leave, all of you," Ailiss said. There was still enough command in her thin voice that everyone began to move towards the door without thinking. "Not you," she pointed to one of the physicians, "and not you, Fara. You ought to see this done."

Farajalla was very pale, but she nodded. Luthien followed the others to the door, stealing glances over his shoulder as he went, but the three who'd stayed were bent over Calesh's unmoving form and he couldn't make anything out. Then he was in the corridor and he pulled the door shut behind him. He felt sick and dizzy, overwhelmed. Too much had gone wrong today.

I broke my oath. There was something that followed from that, a thought he'd had before, but he couldn't think what it was.

"Can she really save him?" Baruch asked.

Luthien's own question, but one he had no answer to. "I don't know."

"Course she can," Raigal said stoutly. "If she says so, then she can." But his eyes strayed to the door, and a child could have read the worry there, and the fear.

"What happened?" Baruch asked. "Tell me. I don't know anything of what led to this."

"An assassin," Luthien said tiredly. There was blood on his hands and he wiped them on his robe. They were shaking, he noticed. "Justified, a highbinder. Called himself Elizur Mandein."

"Mandein?" Raigal repeated in astonishment. "He's famous. He won the Caileve tournament three, four years ago."

"He won't win any more," Luthien said.

Baruch looked at him, then at his hands, and finally back at Luthien again. "You killed him?"

"I broke my oath," Luthien said tonelessly. "I couldn't stand by and watch while Calesh was killed. But I was too slow. I don't know," he added, "which shames me more."

"Shames you?" Raigal echoed. It seemed to be his day for repeating Luthien's words. "You put aside your vow, your own soul, for the sake of a friend. If God damns you for that then I'll stand before his throne and spit in his eye, and come right down to Hell with you."

"So will I," Baruch added.

Luthien looked at them, fighting tears. He couldn't have said then if he wanted to weep for Calesh, or for his lost and shattered oath, or for the love of two such men as these that held them by his side even now. Or for Sarténe, in such peril now. His head felt ready to burst. He said, for no reason he was aware of, "He called me his brother to dragons."

"We're all that," Baruch said. He reached out and gripped Luthien's shoulder. "If you take the Consolation again and never raise a hand in violence from this day to your death, you'll still be our brother to dragons."

"I can't take the Consolation again," Luthien said. His throat was thick. "Oaths aren't made to be broken and then sworn anew. Especially not that oath. One time pays for all, and I failed."

But he knew, suddenly, what it was he'd been forgetting.

It's ending in Sarténe, Ilenia had said yesterday, in the corridor outside the Manse's reception hall. *It will all be lost, and priests of the All-Church will stand on the ashes and sing their hard, bitter songs.*

It seemed hard to argue with that now. Luthien stood by the door with blood on his hands and robe, and the best friend he had ever made dying in the room he'd just left. More than a friend, in fact; Calesh was Sarténe's best hope, their one real chance of fending the All-Church army off until winter came or circumstances changed, and some sort of peace could be made. Without him Mayence was in more danger than ever. Elizur Mandein was dead but he'd wreaked his share of damage before he fell.

Luthien was almost sure that Sarténe was doomed, now. That might be only misery talking, the voice of grief at his forsaken vow, but he didn't think so. And it brought another thought into his mind, one which followed from the other thing Ilenia had said in that passageway; *I still hope that you will come to me, and love me once, just once before the end.*

"I must," he started to say, and then broke off. Baruch and Raigal were looking strangely at him but there was nothing he could say, no way he could explain. Not now. He made a brief, abortive gesture and turned away, walking up the corridor past the ranks of silent armsmen.

Once before the end.

He'd thought holding to his oaths would be easy. No violence; he'd left that behind in Tura d'Madai. It was another man's life, that time of riding with a sword at his hip under the burning desert sun, no more important to a Luthien returned home than the toys he'd played with as an infant. No alcohol; that was easy, since Luthien had almost stopped drinking when he came home, and no longer had fresh barbarities to wash away with wine. Doing without meat was more difficult because he loved a bit of pork, or a chicken cooked until its skin was golden and crisp, but he knew he could manage well enough.

No love.

He reached the main corridor and turned left, away from the entrance atrium and the main halls, all the places where soldiers and leaders would be talking and laying out their plans. As he walked he kept his hands in his pockets, hiding the streaks of blood. Servants might see the dark smear on his green robe but they'd think it was wine from another man's glass, or meat from another's plate, because Luthien would not break his oath. He'd spent enough time in the Manse for such things to be known.

No love.

He had been a fool, to think he could ignore love because he'd never known it, except for the quick hot passion that is so much like lust, overpowering for a time and then wilting once the urge is gone. Except for God, as well, to whom Luthien had given his soul and, he'd thought, his heart as well. And then Ilenia had come and proved him wrong, had taken his heart from him and proved it wasn't God's after all, but had still been his to give away. Since then it had been hard, so very hard to keep to his vows. He'd taken to spending as much time at the Academy as he could, immersing himself in books and histories, using erudition to smother what he felt under layers of paper and ink.

The Academy was gone now, its halls and gardens burned by All-Church soldiers even though they were empty by then. Luthien's oath was gone, his best friend was gone or would be soon, and not long afterward Sarténe itself would be lost. The things he loved were being taken from him one by one, stripped away to leave his soul naked and cold. He was being driven like a boar in the hunt, forced towards the one thing he never wanted to do again, which was to wield a sword in battle. To kill men. He'd sworn it would never happen, and more than that, it was the wish of his life that it would not. But he was being left nothing else.

He emerged into a wide, plain anteroom, at the foot of the servants' stairs. Several of the staff offered him nods or warm smiles as he passed, but he hardly saw them, and the smiles slid away into perplexity as he passed. He ignored the many doors and went straight up the wooden steps, trying not to hurry but his heart beating madly now. He could feel sweat on his brow and resisted the urge to wipe it off, and leave a bloody trail on his forehead.

If he was left nothing else but war, then war it would be. Luthien had believed his place in the world was as God's servant, robed in green and offering solace to those who asked for it. Perhaps he could be God's servant still, but clothed in steel instead of a simple robe, and with a blade in his hands instead of words of comfort on his tongue. Perhaps. It was a fool who believed he knew the intentions of the Lord, but Luthien had; he had, for so very long. He would not deny himself any longer in the name of a life he could not live.

No longer.

He came to a richly decorated passageway, studded with occasional doors. This was where the nobles lived and slept, not the Margrave himself but his visitors when they came to Mayence, and his children as they grew. Not that Riyand had any children, nor was likely to have either. These days only one person lived in this wing, preferring the solitude she found there to her husband's indifference or his moments of petty vindictiveness. Luthien had stopped visiting her here some time ago, when it became too hard to conceal his feelings. But he knew her door, and lifting the handle he opened it and went inside.

She was sitting by the window, on a divan angled to catch the afternoon sun where it slanted across the room. She was alone, blessedly. As he closed the door she looked up from the book in her hand and her expression changed from mild surprise to concern in a moment, and she stood.

"What is it?" Ilenia asked.

Luthien took a step forward. He couldn't speak at all, suddenly. His mouth worked but no sound emerged.

"Why – is that *blood?*" she gasped. The hand he'd used to open the door was still at his side, not hidden, and she'd seen it. She had always been quick. With the thought something in him opened and he could speak again, and he took another step across the room.

"I broke my oath today," he said.

Ilenia's hands went to her mouth. Over them her eyes were huge, wounded. He couldn't look away.

"An assassin came to kill Calesh," he went on. Another pace. "I killed him, instead. I'm not Consoled anymore."

"Luthien," she said, aghast.

"You said you wanted me," he said. He was very close to her now. "Do you still?"

Her hands came down and she smiled. That was all, but it was enough, and a moment later they were kissing and she was pulling at the belt of his robe, even more eager than he. His breath came in short, desperate gasps. Their legs hit the divan and they fell onto it, and as Ilenia grabbed hold of his face and pulled his lips to hers again Luthien closed his eyes.

Six

A Revelation

She was there when he woke, of course. The first thing he saw when he opened his eyes.

For a long time Calesh only looked at her, letting his cloudy thoughts drift. She was sitting in a chair by the bed, asleep, so lovely it made him ache. Farajalla's beauty had stopped him cold in the courtyard of Harenc, when he turned and saw her for the first time. It stopped him cold still, sometimes, when he came on her unexpectedly or caught her framed by shafts of sunlight, or sleeping with her hair a curtain over half her face. He didn't know what she saw in him, to be honest. He was just a fighting man, all calluses and bruises, and picking up more scars every year. With that thought he tried to move, and pain blossomed immediately from his neck to his hips, filling him so completely he couldn't even cry out before his mind gave up and he submerged once more.

When he woke for the second time Farajalla was sitting on the side of his bed, patting at his face with a damp cloth.

"Hello, you," she said.

He smiled at her; there wasn't enough breath in him for words. Now she was closer he could see the strain in her, lines of weariness etched deep around her eyes and mouth, and across her brow. He thought she'd look a little like this when she was old, in fact, and if so he was a lucky man. Luckier even than he was to be alive, in fact. He tried to speak and only managed a gasp.

"Ailiss saved you," Farajalla said. She shook her head slowly. "All the reading I did, all the struggles to decipher a word or glyph, and I didn't understand until the Lady showed me what her glamours can do. You're going to live, Calesh, and be as strong and fit as you ever were. But not," her eyes flashed their familiar fire, "if you try to do too much too soon. Ailiss says the charms she worked take a great strain on the body, so you're going to lie there and be still."

He didn't think he had a choice about that, actually. Earlier he'd only tried to move his arms, but the pain had been so great and sudden that he'd blacked out again. Obviously walking was going to be beyond him for a little while yet. Speaking was beyond him for the moment, in fact. He tried anyway, mouthing silent words as Farajalla frowned down at him.

"A week," she said finally, and with some reluctance. "You have to stay in that bed for a week. And don't even *think* of arguing," she added fiercely. "I almost lost you once. I will *not* come that close again, especially not because you're a fool who can't stand to do nothing."

He shook his head. Mimed words again.

"Oh," she said. "I see. Well, you've been here for two days. Really," she said when he raised his eyebrows. Even that hurt; whatever the Lady had done, he must be black and blue from neck to knees, and from his skin right down to the bone. "I won't lie to you."

Calesh started to say he knew that, but the darkness stole over him again like a thief before his lips even moved.

He woke for the third time to find Fara asleep in her chair again and Luthien standing by the window. The small man turned as Calesh opened his eyes, either from intuition or chance, and took a step closer to the bed. There was fog in Calesh's mind again and he knew something was different about his friend but couldn't decide what it was; something in the stance, perhaps, or a new sorrow written in the eyes. It took him a long moment to realise it was both those things, and more.

Luthien was wearing armour.

"I'm sorry," Calesh whispered.

"You have nothing to be sorry for," Luthien answered. "I made my choice that day in the map room. I decided I would better nourish my soul through saving a friend than by devoting myself to God. And if I'm wrong the decision was still *mine,* mine alone, and I refuse to let you diminish me by treating me like a child and taking the responsibility for it yourself."

He managed to smile. "Clever with words."

"Yes I am," Luthien said. "But not so clever as I am with a sword. It seems to me now that this is my vocation, the thing I was born to do. The thing God wants me to do. I have spent a lot of years denying that to myself, though my friends tried to tell me. I regret that."

"You have nothing," he had to pause for breath, "to be sorry for."

Luthien chuckled. "Clever with words."

"I used to be jealous of your three friends," Farajalla said. Calesh couldn't move his head across to look at her, and had to wait until she came around the bed to stand beside Luthien. "Even in Tura d'Madai, when they were half a thousand miles away, I envied them. Isn't that silly?" She shook her head and her braids rattled softly. "But I'm jealous of them no more. I think I understand the bond you share now. Anything Luthien wants, ever, or that Baruch and Raigal want, is theirs if I can give it, for as long as I live."

"There's no need for that," Luthien said.

She glanced at him. "The decision is *mine,* and I refuse to let you diminish me by treating me like a child."

"I think I'm going to stop speaking to you two," Luthien said wryly. "You're both so infernally quick."

Calesh wanted to laugh, which he was sure would have hurt amazingly, but he didn't have the energy. He was slipping away again, pain and tiredness conspiring to pull him back into oblivion. Farajalla seemed to realise that. "Enough talk, now. You need to rest."

"You do," Luthien agreed. "Don't worry, my friend. The city is locked down tight and the supplies are all in place. Nothing larger than a tick can get in without the sentries spotting it. You can sleep safe."

He knew he was safe, it was being inactive that bothered him, when other men would be risking their lives. Luthien knew that, of course. Farajalla knew it as well, he was sure. But it seemed too much trouble to say it, so Calesh let his eyes slip shut and sank away once more.

*

"He's going to live," Luthien said, and there were sighs of relief all along the table. "But he won't be organising anything for a while. The defence of Mayence will fall to us for the next few days."

The assassin had succeeded at least in part, then. He hadn't killed Calesh but he had managed to deny his skills to the defenders, and deal a heavy blow to morale at the same time. Ando wondered how the men were feeling now, standing on the walls and building the last extra defences. The All-Church army was only a day away and Sarténe's great hope was absent.

At the head of the table Riyand looked very pale. That might be for any number of reasons; shock at Calesh's injury, tension over the approaching army, or just the leftover of the morning's terror, when the Margrave had thought he was about to ride on a dragonnade for the first time. Ando suspected it was the latter. Riyand had vomited twice during the night before the aborted raid, sheer stress keeping him awake almost until dawn. It might have been battle he was afraid of, but Ando suspected it was at least partly Calesh himself.

Cavel sat on Riyand's right, opposite Ando. The seneschal looked tired and overwrought, but then everyone did these days. If it wasn't fear keeping a man awake then it was the hammering of workers building yet another wall across yet another street, or fletchers churning out more barrels of arrows and smiths melting down railings to make spear points. Ilenia was next to him, her colour high for some reason, with Elisande beside her. Next to the Elite Ilenia was usually a pale bird indeed, but today there was a light in her which turned that around.

Reis sat at the foot of the table, with Luthien off to one side towards the window.

Luthien in armour looked strange, like a farmer in silks or a cavalryman astride a goat. Even stranger, the new appearance suited him in a way that Elite green never had. If asked, Ando would have said Luthien made a fine Elite, as suited to his robe and sandals as any man or woman in Sarténe, but the contrast now was impossible to miss. Armour became Luthien. In it his priestly grace had become deadly, his once-comforting poise a flagrant threat.

Listening at that door in *Kissing the Moon,* the day Calesh came home and brought all the eastern Hand of the Lord with him, Ando had heard Farajalla say something he remembered. *They said men feared Raigal Tai for his size, and for the axe spinning in his hand like a split twig. They trembled when Baruch Caraman strode forward, and shook when Calesh Saissan sounded the charge. But it was Luthien Bourrel they fled from, crying out to their gods for protection and succour as they went.*

He understood that now. This small man was even more deadly than Calesh, if a less forceful personality, and if the assassin had taken the one and given them the other, he might not have done them a disservice after all.

"What's left to do?" Riyand asked.

It was Reis who answered. "Not much. The storehouses are full and the defences are as good as we can make them, given the time. All we can do now is wait for the All-Church."

"And the raid?"

"Pointless," Reis said. "The Hand could ride without their captain, but to what end? The force to our north is too big to dislodge without stripping the walls. Same for the Crusaders to our south, across the mountains, and they're too far away besides. So we do nothing, and wait."

"Calesh wanted the men to know I fight," Riyand said.

"Calesh realises that needs change with events," Luthien put in. "What was possible three days ago isn't necessarily possible now. Calm yourself, Margrave. You'll have the chance to risk your neck, but rushing off to attack a superior foe now would be utter foolishness."

A less forceful personality, Ando thought wryly to himself. On the basis of this meeting Luthien seemed to be imitating Calesh's bluntness more with every sentence. Others seemed to have noticed that too. Ilenia turned slightly in her chair to study him, anyway. She really did seem to glow today. He wondered briefly if she'd taken a lover and discarded the idea: not her, and not now. Ilenia was too prim and cautious to risk an affair with the Manse so busy.

74

"Very well," Riyand said finally. He sounded reluctant, of all things. All night he'd been shivering with fear, and now he almost seemed to *want* to hurl himself into the teeth of the enemy. "We have to last a siege until winter, in that case. Are we able to?"

Cavel nodded. "I believe so. We have access to fresh water, and much of the earth dug out of the fields has been brought inside the walls and made into make-do planting beds, wherever there was room. The park has been ploughed up too, and your father would have been distraught to see what has happened to his two hundred year-old lawn."

"My father cared more for that lawn than he did for me," Riyand snapped. "Pigs can shit on it all summer for all I care."

Ando blinked, taken by surprise by his lover's ferocity. He'd been studying Luthien again, trying to decide why a faint smile kept appearing on the man's face and then fading again, only to re-emerge moments later. It seemed odd, for him to be so distractedly happy just when he'd been forced to abandon his oath. Perhaps it had freed him somehow, released his spirit in some way Ando couldn't begin to guess at. Neither could Elisande, to judge by the way she was frowning at him, but that was as likely to be disapproval as anything else. She wouldn't like it that Luthien had abandoned his vow, for any reason.

"Well, quite," Cavel said after a moment. "And I believe pigs will indeed 'shit on it all summer', as you so eloquently put it. In short, even without the remarkable mister Saissan, we are well prepared."

Ando had noticed before that Cavel held Calesh in high regard, and here was more evidence to show it. *He is what every noble ought to fear,* the seneschal had said once, *a base-born man brought by events to a position of power, and with the talents to use it.* There had been something admiring in his tone then, hinting at a shift in his thinking if not in the balance of power.

Noble blood doesn't stop a blade or get someone a single step closer to Heaven. The times when common people remember that are the times when kings fall. That was the rest of what Cavel had said, that day on the lawn that was now a field for farmers and their livestock. Ando wondered where the old man's loyalties now lay, and to whom he would bow when the siege was over and Sarténe safe again. If it could be saved at all.

"Of course we may face unforeseen problems," Cavel was saying now, "such as disease, or hungry citizens stealing food from our gardens or warehouses as the siege wears on. Not," he added thoughtfully, "that they *would* be unforeseen, since I just foresaw them."

Ando let out a brief chortle. It wasn't really appropriate, but then neither was Cavel's odd digression into pettifogging. But it seemed to ease the mood, and for the first time smiles were exchanged. Well, the first time except for Luthien, of course. What *was* that about?

Well, he could ask about it later. For now what mattered was that it seemed Mayence could hold the All-Church off through the summer, and Ando looked forward to seeing how the besieging army coped here in the Aiguille when the season changed. The most common winter winds came from the south and west, the first freighted with snow from the Raima Mountains, the second bearing icy spray from the ocean which froze in the air and fell as sleet or hail. Farmers and townsfolk alike made sure their homes were sealed tight long before then, because those winds slipped through the tiniest cracks and sucked away warmth in moments. The All-Church soldiers, prepared for the heat of Tura d'Madai and not for the cold of the Aiguille, would be shivering inside thin tents as the wind shrieked. Ando didn't envy them.

But then, he couldn't honestly claim that he cared very much how they suffered, either.

Secrets all around, he thought as the meeting broke up around him. Cavel was hiding divided loyalties, and not hiding them very well. Ilenia had her lover, or whatever it was which had put that high colour in her cheeks, and Luthien had the smile that had flickered on and off his face like the glow of a guttering candle. Riyand hid the truth of his love for Ando, though that was such an open secret that *hid* wasn't really the right word. Refused to acknowledge, perhaps. No doubt Reis had secrets as well, the dispositions of his men kept from everyone except officers, to reduce the chances of information findings its surreptitious way to the enemy outside the gates. It was possible that Elisande was the only person in the room who didn't have an enigma to conceal.

Then again, perhaps she did. Not all the Elite could be as comfortable with their lives of purity as they seemed, and claimed to be. There must be times when they were tempted, days when they longed for meat or wine and nights when their beds were cold and they yearned for a warm body to lie against, or to move against as desire took them. Ando didn't suppose there was an oath in the world that could guard against the weaknesses of the heart.

"Ruminating?" Riyand asked.

They were alone in the hall. Ando hadn't even noticed until now, but he managed a smile. "More or less. Although I doubt a song will emerge from this particular moment of introspection."

"You haven't written anything for some time."

He shrugged. "I can't seem to find the peace I need to compose."

"There will be peace again after this is over," Riyand said. He seemed to consider the words for a moment, then sighed and pushed a black ringlet out of his eyes. "Or perhaps not. Come up to the terrace with me, Ando. I want to feel the sun on my face."

There had been days, in summer and when the air was still and clear, when it had been possible to see Parrien from the terrace. It was the highest vantage in Mayence, and mountain air made the tumble of hills to the east so clear that Ando could pick out individual farmers six miles or more away. Even so, distance turned Parrien into a mere gleam of sunlight from windows, like a rogue sparkle reflected from the surface of moving water. On one occasion, an early summer's day like this one, Ando had sworn he could pick out the forest of masts in the harbour. He wasn't so certain now. Eyes could play tricks, especially in the early-morning glare of the sun.

He couldn't see Parrien now, of course. There was nothing to see. The All-Church army had slaughtered every person found inside the walls and then set torches to the buildings, sending up a column of black smoke that was visible from Mayence's streets, a hundred feet below the terrace. It had burned for five days, so when the sun rose it glowered through a curtain of smog and ash, like a brutal red blaze. Calesh said it was a mistake, probably done over the objections of the clever general who commanded the All-Church forces, at least in theory. Probably a Church envoy had demanded the townsfolk be butchered. Whether that was true or not, the burning of Parrien had told Mayence what it could expect if it surrendered, and so the city never would.

Ando thought Calesh was right; he was sure of it, in fact. But for himself he couldn't see things in so cold a way. When he thought of Parrien it was the people he saw, cut down in swathes or roasting in the great pyre, their flesh melting and peeling as they shrieked. On the terrace now he resolutely looked anywhere but east, towards those charred remains, because if he did so he might convince himself he could see the ashes and the bones.

Or he might see the All-Church army, emerging from the hills like dark spirits of the dead.

"I wish you *would* write," Riyand said, apparently apropos of nothing. He'd settled himself on a lounge chair, hands folded in his lap. It took Ando a moment to remember what they'd been talking about, in the meeting room two floors below. "You never seem wholly happy unless you're composing something. And I can't remember when you last went so long without a quill in your hand."

"I can't write with all this hanging over us." Ando waved a hand to indicate the world in general. "I once told you that if the All-Church wins they'll leave no songs here in Sarténe except songs of sorrow. Do you remember?"

"We were here on this terrace," Riyand said, "the day Cavel and Reis brought the letter from the Basilica that declared Crusade upon us. The first day of war. Of course I remember."

"Songs of sorrow," Ando said, "aren't something I can write. I can do love songs, or battle paeans." He thought of Calesh's contempt for *The Lay of Gidren Field,* claiming the lyrics could be improved with an axe, and pushed the recollection away. He didn't need more angst, not now. "But I can't write mourning, or laments for the lost. I'm too… optimistic."

Usually Riyand smiled at such comments, but this time he only looked at Ando without smiling. "If we lose this siege, you may have to change that belief. Or it may be changed for you."

He shook his head. "If we lose this siege, I won't have to believe anything ever again."

"Then we must not lose," Riyand said thoughtfully. "I think I can help ensure we don't, you know."

Ando hesitated. His lover had been out of sorts all afternoon, first seeming eager to ride into battle and then erupting with fury at Cavel over nothing. Riyand had a temper, of course, but it rarely burst out of him with so little warning, or against such a surprising target. He hardly seemed himself. Ando was aware that he wasn't himself either, and that might be affecting the way he saw others, but he knew Riyand well and he didn't think that was it.

"How?" he asked finally.

Riyand kept his hands folded, but the fingers writhed over one another like eels in a fisherman's creel. "By leading the men on a raid."

"What?"

"You heard me," the Margrave said. "Calesh said the men need to see me fight, to know I share the same dangers they do, and he was right. I need to go into battle, even if only briefly."

"Baruch will never allow it," Ando said bluntly. He realised his hands were shaking. "Not with Calesh wounded. And the Hand of the Lord would never follow you."

"Not the Hand," Riyand said, smiling. It looked like a grimace. "But the Guard obeys my orders."

Only because Reis promised your father he'd do his best to support you, Ando thought. He bit the words back before they more than trembled on his tongue. If he said that aloud he'd only aggravate Riyand's temper, this time predictably, and the Margrave would *demand* the right to lead soldiers then. But he didn't know how to respond. He could only stare at Riyand, feeling his face whiten as he realised what his lover meant to do.

"You want to hit them when they arrive," he said.

Riyand nodded. "There will be chaos while they try to deploy. Calesh said so, and Reis does too. The All-Church will have regiments criss-crossing all over the plain as they try to find their positions, so half of them will be tangled up with each other and the rest will be isolated. If we're careful, and quick, we can hit them and be back inside the wall before they can react."

"This isn't a good idea," Ando said.

"Why not?" Riyand asked, pleasantly enough. "You said yourself I was good with a sword now."

Yes, he'd said that, but only in an effort to boost Riyand's confidence. Ando had thought his friend would be riding out in the midst of the Hand of the Lord, the best fighting men in the world. They would be able to shepherd him safely through a minor engagement with All-Church outriders or a forward company, then see him back to Mayence with nothing more than weariness and a few bruises to show for it. But the Hand would be vital, they were *needed,* because the truth was that Riyand was an appalling swordsman, worse even than Ando. A musician needed at least a little hand-eye co-ordination, if not much strength; even so, Ando could have landed his wooden practice blade on Riyand half a dozen times if he'd wanted to. Now he wished he had. If he'd known it might prevent this ridiculous overconfidence, he would have done.

And if he said as much? Riyand's confidence would vanish in a blink, just as he prepared himself for the siege. There were traps whatever Ando said, but one thing he could do was think quickly, and he was able to answer with hardly a beat of hesitation.

"You're reasonable," he said, and couldn't stop himself from adding, "If you're careful."

"There you are then," Riyand said. His voice was perfectly calm, but still his fingers twisted, the knuckles white. "One quick strike, that's all. We'll hit a regiment as it tries to set up and be back inside the gate before anyone can respond. You'll see. It will be easy."

Ando's heart quailed at those words, but Riyand gave him no time to reply. Still in that eerily calm voice, the

Margrave asked, "You do believe I can do this, don't you, Ando?"

Trapped. There was only one thing he could say, and so he said it, speaking through numb lips. "Of course I do."

"Thank God for that." The fingers stopped writhing at last. "There are times when I feel everyone in this city despises me, you know. I don't mean the commoners; they can whisper about you and me all they like, and it doesn't matter. But Reis, and Cavel. Ilenia." He paused. "I think they'd be gone from me in a second if Calesh asked them to."

"That isn't true."

"I think it is," Riyand said. "I need you to believe in me, Ando. I'd walk away from it all without that."

"I need you to believe in me too," he said. He hadn't actually known he was going to say that. His lips were still numb, his hands still shaking. "I have to tell you something."

Riyand sat up. "What is it?"

Secrets, Ando thought. Cavel hid his trust of Calesh, Ilenia her lover, if that's what had her glowing within. Luthien smiled at a private pleasure; Ando wondered briefly if he was Ilenia's lover, then dismissed the idea. Luthien had broken one part of his oath, he wouldn't hurry to break another. Riyand concealed his love for Ando and Elisande any doubts she had, any inner fears. They were all closemouthed, all hiding something. But what Ando hid was the biggest thing of all, and he had kept it too long alone.

"It was me," he said, "who killed the priest. By the river."

Riyand stared at him, and then a full second after Ando had stopped speaking his eyes went wide in shock. "You? Why, in God's name?"

"Because of what he said," Ando replied. "What he called you, in your own hall. He said you –"

"He said I was an abomination in the sight of God," Riyand broke in. "He called me unclean, and a desecration. But why does that matter to me, Ando? His God means nothing, you know that. His whole religion is a mishmash of half-truths and outright lies. I never cared what he said."

"It was too public," Ando said. "Too flagrant. If he could say those things and walk away, then what was to stop another man repeating them? A noble, or a musician, or an Elite. You and I have been able to stay together because we've never acknowledged... what we are."

"Oh, Ando." Riyand rubbed at his eyes. "We've stayed together because we didn't care what people said about what we are. My dear, you didn't need to do this. Not for me."

"I know," Ando said. He couldn't meet his lover's gaze. "I realised it on the way home from the river."

There was a silence. Ando turned to look east for the first time, towards the ruins of Parrien and the advancing All-Church army, filling the valleys that led into the Aiguille and to the plain outside Mayence. All those people had died because of his mistake, in the end. He could rage against All-Church cruelty, despise the barbarism of men who ordered innocents killed, women and children among them, and still know it was his act that had started the slaughter. His match which had begun the burning.

"My father used to tell me never to waste time regretting the things that are already done," Riyand said at last. "In the days when he still had some love left over for me, he did. He used to tell Bohend the same thing, come to that. Done is done, Ando. Let it go."

He said, choking on the words, "I need to – I want –"

"Then I forgive you," Riyand said. He'd come up behind Ando and now slipped his hands around the musician's waist, linking them in front of him. "And I need you to forgive me."

He closed his eyes and leaned his head back, resting it on Riyand's shoulder. "For what?"

"For needing to lead my men into battle at least once," the Margrave said. "For needing that much of their respect."

Words that left him no choice. There didn't seem to have been a choice for any of them since that day by the river, when Ando had killed the priest with a staff thrust into his throat, crushing the windpipe. The only man Ando had ever killed, or tried to. Every day since he'd wished he could take the act back, undo it, but in this bitter world of mortals that wasn't possible. Perhaps it would be in the next, in Heaven, if Ando was allowed there. He might not be. The Dualist God was no fonder of murderers than the All-Church one.

"I forgive you," he said.

He felt his lover's hands tighten around him and took it at first for affection. But then he heard Riyand's intake of breath, felt the sudden tension in him, and Ando lifted his head and looked across the plain and there at the line of hills he saw the gleam of sunlight on iron.

Seven

The Last Thing

Baruch had reserved a table outside, in the welcome sunshine of early summer. When Luthien arrived he found the *Languorous Nymph* almost full, somewhat to his surprise. He'd expected the rationing of food to have reduced custom to a trickle, and that dissatisfied, but if Baruch hadn't booked ahead the three of them would have had to eat on the street.

"There are always ways to find what you want," Baruch observed, when he noticed the same thing. "I should know; as quartermaster I've spent time dealing with the black market, both here and in Tura d'Madai. But you're right. I'll have to put a stop to this."

"After lunch," Baruch rumbled.

"I can't be seen to –"

Luthien put a hand on his friend's arm. "*After* lunch."

The carved panels had been taken down from the windows, letting air into the tavern. It was a sign that summer had arrived, and it was warm enough to eat in the open instead of huddling inside and wishing there was a bit more wood on the brazier. Luthien was cheered by that, in the normal course of things. Now he wished it was autumn, the panels closed for the first time in months because the chill mountain winds had begun to blow. The All-Church soldiers would fall like plucked feathers then, if Mayence could hold long enough. Luthien thought it could, but he wasn't sure, and a whisper in his mind nagged that he was allowing hope to cloud his judgement.

They drew several appraising glances as they sat down. A dozen of the tavern's customers wore armour, even if mostly it was made of boiled leather, or once of slices of wood drilled with holes and knotted onto a shirt. That was new, something not seen in Mayence since the early days of the reconquest of Alinaur a hundred years ago. But even so, the three friends attracted some attention. People knew who they were, now. Most had always known, in Baruch's case, but the situation was different today.

The menu turned out to be a single choice; beef slices and eggs, or nothing. Baruch was actually mollified.

"They're not sneaking food from the black market after all," he said. "We had to butcher a lot of cows because there isn't enough grass for them inside the city, so beef we have, for a few days. And as long as we have chickens we'll have eggs."

Luthien heard him without really listening. He was thinking about Ilenia again, something he seemed powerless to stop himself doing. She'd intruded on his thoughts before, had been doing so for years in fact, but not very often and not with much intensity. She was something else he couldn't have, because of his oath, and he suffered pangs of longing for her exactly as he sometimes did for meat, or wine. He'd told himself that was all it was, the yearning for something forbidden, and both natural and forgivable.

She used to be that, anyway. Now she was something more. They'd made love three times since he'd gone to her in her chambers, always cautiously, making sure nobody knew or could gossip. That was hard to do in the Manse today, crowded as it was with officers and guards, servants and workers throwing up hasty defences or bricking in windows. So they snatched an hour where they could, and then tried to go about their lives as normally as they could until time and opportunity gave them another chance, on another day.

And here in the streets the sunshine seemed brighter, the world warmer. He was lapsing into cliché, reverting to tired old phrases because his mind was too befuddled to think as clearly as it usually did. The thought brought a small chuckle. If this was what love did, he welcomed it.

"Incidentally," Baruch said, "you need to be careful."

Luthien turned back to him. "Why?"

"Because of the grin that keeps appearing on your face," his friend told him. "Especially when Ilenia's in the room. Keep simpering like a fool and people will know you're doing her, you know."

It never occurred to him to deny it, but Luthien shook his head. "Such a delicate turn of phrase you have, Baruch."

"You make cow eyes at her too," Raigal put in helpfully.

"I do not," he started to protest, and then saw their smiles. "Well, all right. Maybe a little bit."

Baruch shook his head. "When you break your oath you really go all out, don't you?"

"I do everything with my whole heart," he answered, remembering something Calesh had once said. It was true: the things Calesh said usually were. If Luthien was the scholarly one then it was Calesh who had the insights, the instinctive understanding of what it was that made a man do the things he did. Both things could be called cleverness. So could Baruch's ability to organise, and Raigal's gift for lifting morale with a joke at just the right time. All of them knew what to say, or what to do, and when. Sometimes it seemed they always had.

The food came, not as much of it as Luthien would have liked, which was only to be expected. They salted their eggs and dug in. The beef was fatty, poor quality cuts, but to Luthien it tasted wonderful.

"Will you be all right with that?" Baruch asked at one point, around a mouthful of beef and bread. "The meat, I mean."

"Him?" Raigal said. When he laughed the whole shop seemed to tremble. "Old iron guts? Blood of the God, in Tura d'Madai he could eat pork still dripping with blood and it never bothered him a bit."

"This is not Tura d'Madai," Baruch noted.

"No," Luthien agreed. "And we were younger then. But a few slices of beef won't hurt me, Baruch, just because I've lived on nuts and fruit for three years. Worry about our large friend here, if worry you must. How he'll manage on short rations I dread to think."

Raigal chuckled. "I can afford to drop a little weight." He forked eggs into his mouth and swallowed almost at once.

"You can afford to drop five stone," Baruch said.

He had missed this. Oh, how he'd missed it, in those years wearing Elite green, when he'd immersed himself in study and worship. The priestly life had suited him, he knew, it had made his heart ache with joy sometimes; but still, he'd missed the easy camaraderie of friends. Of *these* friends, these fighting men with weapons at their belts and one other man, the captain who changed them from three individuals into a group, into cohorts. Luthien had a sword on his hip again now, something which still hurt when he let himself dwell on it, but that had meant he could be a part of the foursome again instead of standing just beside it.

That had never been the same. He'd told himself it was good enough, and perhaps it was, but since when did *good enough* fill a man with joy? He had managed though, and he thought he would have continued to manage, except that Calesh came home from the desert and everything changed. Luthien suspected it would have changed even without the All-Church's war. The simple fact of Calesh's presence altered what the other three of them were, how they behaved towards one another. Without him they had drifted apart; once he returned they were drawn back together again.

The Dualism needed them to be. Luthien knew without arrogance that he was the best swordsman in Sarténe, and probably better than anyone in the approaching army as well. Elizur Mandein had been one of the best fighting men in the world and Luthien had cut him apart, even wearing a restricting robe and without having held a sword for years. The Dualism had other Elite, other priests, but it had only one Luthien Bourrel. His place was with his friends, bloodying his blade beside them until either Sarténe was safe of they were dead.

Perhaps afterwards – if there was an afterwards – he would be able to lay his weapons down once more, and retreat to a clerical order somewhere. If he couldn't be Consoled again, at least he could spend his days in contemplation, as a sort of apology for having sworn an oath to God and then broken it for the sake of a friend. It would be nice to think so. It would be even nicer if he could believe his apology might be accepted.

"I'm surprised by how quiet it is," he said.

"It's always calmest just before the attack," Raigal answered. They'd all finished eating by now. "It was the same in every town in Tura d'Madai, do you remember?"

"I remember. But those were towns that had been fought over for decades, taken first by one side and then by the other. Everyone was used to sieges and assaults. The people here aren't."

"But they used to be," Baruch said. "And not long ago, either. Two hundred years back Mayence wasn't much more than a mountain fort that was a bit larger than most."

Luthien smiled. "Are you saying the citizens remember what happened two centuries ago?"

"I'm saying their blood does," Baruch countered. "Everyone's grown up with the tales of the bandit chieftains in their castles in the mountains, or here in the Aiguille. They used to go to sleep dreaming of armies camped outside thick walls, and the brave men who defied them."

"They might think that means they know what siege means," Luthien said, "but it doesn't. Not really."

Baruch made an exasperated sound. "I realise that. But it does at least mean they're not going to panic. People here are tough, Luthien. Tougher than the All-Church understands."

"I hope so," he said.

He hadn't meant to needle his old friend. Maybe he hadn't: they were all tense, and Baruch was as likely to have over-reacted as Luthien was to have prodded him a little too hard. He looked away, down the length of Old Palm Street with its crowded shops selling almost everything imaginable: food and drink, clothing and fabric, pots, pans, cutlery and crockery, shoes and knives of a hundred kinds. Just from where he sat he could see two Madai onion domes, a Jaidi minaret further down the street, and several examples of the fluted pillars typical of the All-Church, some standing at the front of simple shops. The pointed tips of two Alinauri spires poked above the rooftops to his right. Cultures met here, peoples from strange lands who mingled in peace and sometimes built, leaving a lasting mark on the city they'd walked through.

He could see the linked circles of the Dualism, the arc of each passing through the centre of the other. It symbolised the endless struggle between good and evil, God and the Adversary, Belial. The All-Church knew that now. For decades their priests had walked past the circles unaware, blind to the growing strength of a new belief. Or an old one: the book he and his friends had brought back from Tura d'Madai was proof of just how old. But here in Sarténe it had found new life, a new form perhaps, and had begun to grow strong.

Past most of the other shops he could see the window of a bookstore, crowded with tomes. Luthien knew without checking that the All-Church would disapprove of most of them. Theology from Boromil, where clerics had formed heterodox beliefs concerning the indivisibility of God. Philosophy from Caileve in the distant east, as far as Tura d'Madai, where learned men pored over the ancient writings of the Empire and drew new conclusions from them. Mathematics from Temujin, a near-mythical city on the steppe as far east of the desert as Sarténe was to the west. Once Luthien had dreamed of going to Temujin one day, to sit at the feet of the teachers there and listen to them teach.

Once, he thought with an inward snort. He'd still been dreaming of it a week ago, even after the fall of Parrien and the slow closing of the noose around Mayence. There was no point now. He had picked up a sword again, and he had wanted to go to the steppe city as a scholar, not a fighting man.

But Mayence could have become something great, given time. All of Sarténe could. With the proliferation of culture and learning here it would have been hard not to. Nobles had been sending their sons to be educated at the Academy in Parrien for years already, prizing the tin badge of a graduate as much as skill with a sword or a horse. That university could have been the heart of a new enlightenment in a hundred years; less, in fifty. Now it was ashes. The books might have been saved, sent south to Samanta in a caravan of wagons, but there was no Academy for them to be brought back to.

"What might have been," he murmured, hardly aware that he'd spoken aloud.

"Pardon?" Raigal Tai said, and didn't bother to wait for a reply. "I'm still hungry."

"I have a few coins," Luthien said. He stood up and went next door to the pie shop; they might be served again in the *Languorous Nymph,* but it would set a terrible example if the leaders of the city indulged themselves that way. Buying pies wasn't much better, but it helped a little. His two friends were waiting when he came back out, a beef and onion pie in each hand and a third balanced precariously on top of them. Raigal took that one with a hasty word of thanks and bit into it.

"I'm amazed your stomach can stand this," Baruch told Luthien. "Sliced beef and now a pie? Raigal's right, you must have guts of iron."

"He'll be slurping wine next," Raigal grinned.

"I will not," Luthien protested, and then as they opened their mouths he added, "Well, perhaps I will, at that."

They both laughed, each lifting a hand in identical movements to cover their mouths full of half-chewed food. Luthien would remember that, later. The last thing before the end began was laughter shared with his friends, in the moment before a sudden stillness in the street made them turn.

Hardly anyone was moving. A pair of ragged-trousered boys wove their darting way between adults, all of whom stood motionless as they stared down Old Palm Street towards the east wall. The ground fell away slightly as it receded, but not enough for someone standing here to see outside the city. The citizens stared anyway, as though trying to pierce the stones of the wall by force of will, or sheer numbers. Baruch and Raigal followed suit, pies forgotten in their hands.

Luthien did not. Stepping forward, he caught a burly man by the shoulder. "What is it?"

"Get your – oh. Sorry, Elite Luthien." The man could see he was in armour, not his usual green, but he used the honorific anyway. "The army has come. That's what I hear."

It's always calmest just before the attack. Baruch's words, just a moment ago, and proved true once more now. Luthien let go of the hefty man and looked back at his friends. "Baruch."

"I'm already gone." Baruch crammed the last of his pie into his mouth and swallowed immediately, something he normally left to Raigal Tai. "I'll see you this evening. Be safe, my friend."

"And you," Luthien answered. Baruch trotted up the street, away from the wall but towards the Preceptory, and

Luthien turned to Raigal. "If you've nothing to do, could you come to the wall with me?"

"Well," Raigal said. He tipped his head back and let the uneaten half of his pie slip off its paper tray and into his mouth, so it slithered down his throat like fish being gulped by a dolphin. "I should be with the Hand, really. But Baruch will have them turned out in no time. I'll come with you."

The odd stillness of the street had started to break up, as people formed hurried clumps and began to whisper in tight, tense voices. Luthien raised his voice a little. "There's no need for panic, now. It will take a day or two for the All-Church to deploy its army, so we needn't fear an attack just yet. I'd suggest you all behave as though this is just another day."

He was a soldier again now, but he knew that to the people of the city he was still Luthien the Elite, and they listened to him. Some of the worry left their faces and their tones: not much, but a little. It would do. Luthien turned and set off down Old Palm Street, taking care not to hurry. The sight of running men in armour would bring panic about more quickly than anything else.

"Do you believe that?" Raigal asked quietly, as they walked away. "There's no need to worry?"

"I said there was no need for panic," Luthien corrected his friend. "But worry? We should all do that."

A knot of Guardsmen in their blood and gold surcoats trotted past, heading towards their place on the wall. It was almost certainly not necessary yet, but it was good for the men to hasten to their posts at least once before the actual assault, because then they came to see it as more real, even normal. Once was enough. It had always astonished Luthien how quickly something new came to be usual, when it had been a cause of unease and even terror before.

The city folk were generally going about their business, if with tighter lips and quicker steps than before. Luthien thought most of them would do their most urgent chores and then head home, to be with their families, just in case. Tomorrow they'd feel safer and could go out again. Meanwhile children dashed through the streets on their way to rooftops and towers, anywhere that offered them a vantage from which they might see the enemy army arrive. Most had already been taken by the soldiers, to be used as lookout posts or shooting nests, but Luthien expected the kids would find somewhere to watch from.

"Come on," he said, dismissing the thought, and turned towards the wall.

*

"I dread to mention this," Calesh said. "But I'm hungry. Could you please allow me a shred of dignity and not feed me this time?"

Farajalla looked up from her book. "Maybe."

"Maybe?"

"If I do," she said, "will you promise not to claim it means you're strong enough to walk a little way?" She gave him no chance to interrupt. "Because I know, Calesh, that when you say 'a little way' you actually mean 'right around the walls to make sure all the dispositions are right', don't you?"

"I couldn't manage that," he said.

"Not even part of the way? I haven't heard a promise from you yet, I notice."

He couldn't help laughing, though he had to hunch over slightly to stop it hurting too much. "All right, I promise. I won't leave this room."

"Then I'll find something to eat." She stood up, her spine cracking as she stretched up and back to work out the kinks. "I've been sitting down for too long. I feel as stiff as old wood."

"You think you have problems," he said from his bed, a little sourly. "Is it making any sense?"

"Some," Farajalla allowed. "I was never very good at picking up new languages, and this book is full of them." She indicated the *Opening of the Ways,* resting on the table. "But some of the words... I can almost understand them on sight, as though I've always known what they meant and just forgot. It's strange."

"It unsettles you," he observed.

Farajalla smiled. "Clever man. Though it's more than that; it *frightens* me, to be plain. To think that this understanding has always been hidden inside me, waiting to be awakened, is disorientating."

Ailiss said the knowledge in the books of the Dualism dated back for thousands of years, to civilisations and peoples Calesh had hardly heard of. The Magani, most recently, and before them a line of ancestors who dwindled into myth until it reached the Gondoliers, the fabled ancestors of all the cultures of the world. Every child had heard of *them*, both here and in Tura d'Madai, and probably everywhere else as well. The stories said they were responsible for every invention, every art and craft; whatever more recent peoples did was mere rediscovery, not invention at all.

According to Ailiss, the stories were true. The *Opening of the Ways* gave an insight into how those wonders had been achieved, the magics the Gondoliers used to attain high civilisation in the first place. It was more grimoire than anything else, a book of spells, which made it utterly different to the *Unfurling of Spirit* and the *Book of Breathing.* Those tomes spoke of Adjai and Muret, his acolyte, and of the teachings and parables that had passed through many mouths and countries to become the twisted words and lies of the All-Church. But the teachings themselves were old, millennia older than Adjai, who had simply taken them and given them new life, in a new land. It had happened a dozen times, Farajalla said, the seed of the idea surviving wreck and fire to put down roots again, a thousand years later when the last burning had been forgotten.

Calesh didn't like to think of that. It made Sarténe seem meaningless, just another patch of fertile ground in which the ancient ways had flowered once more, but of no value in itself. All the people here could die, all the temples burn and the fields be sown with salt, and the idea would go on uncaring and whole. Well, the Gondoliers who had written these things might not care, but Calesh did. This was *his* fertile ground, and that made all the difference. He'd spent his adult life in a foreign place, never intending to set eyes on Sarténe again after the pain he had suffered here as a boy: his mother and brother dead, both of plague, and then his father's slow dwindling into grief before he too passed on.

But when the letter had come from the Basilica, delivered to the house he and Farajalla had shared in Elorium, there had been no choice anymore. Calesh had issued orders for the Hand of the Lord to return at once, and once he was back in Sarténe a peculiar thing had happened. He would have sworn that the desert had become his home, the ancient cities and time-worn hills of Tura d'Madai the hearthstone of his heart. But back in the west he'd discovered it was Sarténe he loved after all. He remembered standing at the bow of the *Promise of Plenty,* with the land a smudge on the horizon ahead, and telling Farajalla this was a wonderful place for them to raise a child.

It was. There was beauty, and poetry, and a dozen cultures mixing in the markets and the cities. There were great palaces and churches, temples and spires. Or there were wide spaces where hardly anyone went, the hills of the Aiguille and the woods to the north of them, wildernesses in which a man could lose himself and never be found unless he wished it. It was the perfect place for a family. Or would be, once the war was won. If it could be.

When Farajalla was gone, Calesh used his arms to lever himself more upright in the bed, something she nagged constantly at him not to do. If he'd tried with her in the room she'd have crossed the room in a flash to help, even plumping his pillows for him as though he was an invalid. Well, he supposed he was an invalid, in fact, but not a helpless one. A man had to be allowed to do *some* things for himself or he'd wither away into rags.

He couldn't do much without pain though. Bandages still gripped him tight around the chest, and when he moved his torso at all it felt as if knives were lacerating him from the inside. It was hard to breathe too deeply as well; that caused a burning in his lungs that left him gasping like a fish. But he was sure he would be able to walk, if ever Farajalla left him alone for long enough to dress. Since she wouldn't, he was forced to spend his days lying in bed, with nothing to do but read whatever books Luthien brought by. Today he had a choice between *The Genealogy of the Margraves of Mayence* and a thick tome titled *Epicureanism and Positivism; the Struggle for the Mind of the Empire,* which Luthien said was the best book on philosophy he knew.

Calesh had been trying, but he didn't understand half of what he read. He wished he had just a taste of his wife's newfound ability to comprehend sentences based on almost no evidence.

Someone was shouting outside. Several someones in fact, to judge by the noise, all yelling in the street. He heard a distant clatter that he recognised immediately as hoofs on paving slabs and frowned to himself. The horses were moving too fast for them to be a routine patrol.

So. A hubbub among the populace and soldiers moving in a hurry. He looked at the door and sighed, knowing Farajalla was going to be furious with him about this.

It took him a couple of minutes just to throw back the covers and sit up, pushing himself upright with both arms. Then he needed to rest before he swung his legs around and put his feet on the floor; he was hunching by then, trying to soothe the fire in his chest. When he felt able to he stood, still scrooched over at the shoulders, and wrapping a blanket around himself he shuffled to the window and looked out.

Because the Manse stood on a slight rise, it overlooked the rest of Mayence and Calesh was able to see into some of the streets. He turned west, knowing that was where the All-Church would come from, and saw citizens standing in clumps and pointing, or talking urgently among themselves. More distant figures scuttled along the city walls. As he watched a squadron of cavalry came flying around a corner, and scattering pedestrians galloped out of sight again. It might have been the same riders Calesh had heard before, or different ones, but he thought it didn't matter. The reason for their hurry did.

The army was here.

He was already exhausted and he turned to go back to bed, but he was only halfway there when the door opened and Fara came in with a tray in her hands. She saw him standing – well, nearly – and her eyes darkened at once.

"I said I wouldn't leave the room," he said, forestalling her, "and I haven't. The All-Church is here, isn't it?"

She put the tray down beside the *Opening of the Ways,* careful not to spill soup on the pages. The tantalising smell of onions had begun to fill the room. "Whether it is or not, you can't fight them, Calesh."

"I know that." He reached the bed and sat, trying not to show how much effort it cost him. To judge by Farajalla's scowl he didn't succeed. "But I can still be told what's happening."

"I suppose you can. Very well, the All-Church is here." She came over and rearranged the linen, pulling it into place more firmly than was necessary. "Now get back into bed. The more you flout instructions, the worse you make it for yourself, and the longer it will be before you're well enough to walk again."

"I can already walk," he answered. "Just... not very far. And I don't have to for a while."

Her eyes narrowed. "That sounds ominously as though you're planning something."

"I need to be seen, Fara."

"You need to rest! If you –"

"Fara," he said gently, "please don't trot out that line about making it worse for myself, not again. I know the dangers. I also know what the men need to see before the fighting starts."

"You mean that they need to see their commander hale and well," she said mulishly. "But what you need is rest. You know that, too, or you do unless you're a complete fool."

"Not a complete one, I hope." He caught her hand. "Men are about to fight in the places I've ordered them to be, Fara. Some of them will die. I can't ask that of them while I lie abed, unwilling even to take a little stroll because my wife says it's too much for me."

"They won't die today," Farajalla retorted, "and you know it, Calesh. It will take until at least tomorrow before the All-Church tries an attack. Stop trying to shame me into backing down. We'll see in the morning if you're strong enough to take this little stroll of yours."

"Tomorrow you'll say the same thing," he pointed out.

"I will if you're not strong enough," she said, not abashed in the least. "Now get back into bed."

He was saved the need to reply when the door opened. Farajalla was in the way so he couldn't see who entered at first, but he heard the tap of her cane and knew it must be Ailiss. The small woman came over to sit beside him on the bed, settling with a sigh of relief.

"You should rest," Calesh began, and Farajalla gave a snort and broke in, "Look who's talking!"

"We can none of us rest now," the Lady of the Hidden House said.

Only that, but Calesh felt unease worm into his belly at the words. By the look on Farajalla's face she felt it too; her expression was suddenly all tension, and her fingers curled into loose fists. She opened her mouth and then closed it again. That wasn't like her at all, and Calesh thought he might have to ask Ailiss how she'd been able to induce such respect in his wife. She'd never shown any before, to anyone. It made him nervous.

"I have seen the city burning," Ailiss said. "We have time to leave, but only if we hurry."

Calesh stared at her. "The city is secure. Isn't it?" he added, turning to Fara. "Have you been hiding things from me?"

"She has hidden nothing," the Lady told him. Her voice was very quiet, but flooded with finality. "Mayence is as secure as you and your captains could make it, but there is a flaw. I saw it just now, not quarter of an hour ago."

She meant she'd had a vision, of course. Ailiss had set him on a course once before as a result of a vision, when she'd seen the location of the *Book of Breathing* in Elorium, and then the faces of the four young soldiers who would fetch it for her. It seemed history was about to repeat itself, something Luthien said happened all the time. He managed to keep his voice level. "What flaw?"

"Riyand," Ailiss said. "He's leading a force of Guard cavalry on a raid through the Gate of Angels."

"He's *what?*" Farajalla said, but Calesh only closed his eyes.

Reis had asked him to show a modicum of respect to the Margrave. It had been against Calesh's instincts, but he'd agreed, judging the price of antagonising Reis to be too high to pay. He should have paid it with a smile. He should have shut Riyand up in the Manse and refused to let him out, no matter how shrill the young man's cries became. He should have *killed* him, cut his damn throat and tossed him in the river, the first day Calesh had been back in the city. That he hadn't might be why Mayence would fall. He didn't know if he could live with that.

"Visions can be wrong," he said.

"Yes," Ailiss agreed. "Rarely. But yes."

"I have to get to the Gate," Calesh said. He opened his eyes and stood up, taking care not to move too fast. "Fara, where's my armour?"

"Armour? Are you insane?" she snapped. "Have you lost your mind entirely? You're barely strong enough to walk and you want to put twenty pounds of copper on your shoulders? You'd make it halfway down the corridor before you collapsed. And then I'd kick you where you lay –"

"Fara," he said, and she stopped. He could see in her eyes that she knew, she understood that he was going to work now, and he went to her and smoothed braids back from her brow. "I have to. You heard the Lady; Mayence will burn if I don't, and we'll have to flee."

"Mayence will burn if you do," Ailiss contradicted him. "Visions can be wrong, but not this one, today. Yet you wouldn't be the man you are if you didn't try. Give him his gear, Farajalla."

She stared at him, rebellion in her lovely dark eyes now, and then said, "I'm going to have a baby."

He stopped. Stopped breathing, he thought. Just looked at her with his hands still in her hair.

"Ailiss's doing," the woman he loved so dearly said. "One of her arts. I may be able to do it myself, one day. But I will need you there, husband, and I will *not* let you be such a fool that you never see your child. I want your promise not to fight, or I'll stop you leaving."

"I can't make that promise."

"Make it!" she said fiercely. "I'll push you down on the floor and sit on you if I must, so make it!"

"I promise not to fight unless I'm attacked," Calesh said softly. "I can't do more, Fara. And I *will* be back." He moved a hand to the flat of her stomach; there was no sign of a baby yet, at least. But he believed her. She wouldn't lie about this, knowing what a child meant to him. He could trust her, and Ailiss too, as much as he trusted his three friends.

She shut her eyes for a moment, breathing hard, and finally said, "I will fetch your armour."

She turned and left the room, almost running. As the door closed Calesh sat beside Ailiss again, more tired than he wanted to admit just after standing for a little while. Farajalla was right: wearing armour was going to be torment. But if it had to be done then complaining wouldn't help.

"I want you and Fara to find Amand," he said. "He'll be at the Preceptory; or if not, someone there will know where he is. Tell him I said to escort you to the south gate and wait for me there."

There was a smile on Ailiss' cracked lips. "I sent Gaudin to Amand before I came here. He should be on his way already with Rissaun, and a squad of men from the Hand. They'll take your wife and myself to the temple by the south gate. Do you know it?"

"I can find it," he said. He'd been away too long to remember every building in Mayence. Not that he'd known them all even before he left for the desert, country-raised as he was. "If it looks as though the All-Church is going to close the road to Adour then you leave without me. Amand will know how long to wait."

"A good man, Amand," Ailiss said.

He was. There were a lot of good men in Mayence, in the Hand of the Lord, and if Calesh couldn't reach the Gate of Angels in time to stop Riyand's foolish escapade then most of them would die. He glanced at the door, willing Farajalla to hurry.

"Some things are fated," Ailiss said. He turned back to find her eyes on his, still as piercingly blue as the first time he'd seen them, all those years ago. "It may be that the fate of the Dualism is to end in blood and fire. The flowers of the Lore have been destroyed many times before, Calesh, and yet the Lore itself always goes on, always find new soil in which to grow. Tragedy need not mean an end."

"But I like this soil," he said, without thinking.

She smiled. "Of course you do. I chose right when I called the four of you. Giant, soldier, wise man, king: the icons of so many legends. Whatever comes next, I don't regret it." She broke off, probably hearing what Calesh heard: his wife's footsteps in the hall. "Go and save your soil, if you can. But don't sell your life for a fight that can't be won."

"Not if I can help it," he said. Then Farajalla was back in the room, laden with his armour. His *pregnant* wife, and it was no time to be talking of death anymore.

Eight

The Only Songs Left

They came through the gate in perfect order, already halfway to a gallop as they fanned out into a chevron aimed directly at the leading elements of the All-Church army.

Reis would have forbidden the Guard to be part of this raid, Riyand knew. The stocky soldier only obeyed out of respect for Riyand's father. Well, the old man was more than five years dead, and his son had inherited at least a few of the family skills, and a few tricks besides. He'd once seen his father avoid a confrontation with Reis by simply not telling the general what he was going to do. Riyand had followed that example this afternoon. It was too late to stop the strike now, and Reis was going to be *so* embarrassed.

Cries were going up from the wall now, men pointing in surprise. One fellow bellowed for the riders to stop, his voice an enraged lion's roar, and Riyand turned his head to see who it was. Vision from his helmet was limited, except straight ahead, but he could hardly miss the enormous figure looming on the wall and waving for him to stop. That had to be Calesh's northern friend, the one who'd owned the inn in Parrien. Raigal Tai, that was it. Well, let him watch. Reis wasn't the only one who'd have to revise his opinion of the Margrave after this.

"Form up!" he shouted.

They called him a weakling, he knew. Said he was soft and effete, like any lover of boys. Feeble and gentle, and not a little stupid besides, a shadow of what his brother would have been if the plague hadn't taken him. Always there had been that, the shadow Bohend case over his younger brother, even in death. *Bohend was twice the man this one is. Ten times.* Words heard in a doorway once, spoken by the head of the kitchens, and never forgotten. When you heard those things said time and again, all the years of your life, they gained a weight of their own where they lay close and cold against the heart.

Ahead the All-Church soldiers were scrambling, trying to prepare to receive cavalry in the time they had. It was impossible, really, even without all the wagons and pack horses in the way, and lines of camp followers like cooks and blacksmiths trailing behind them like grubby ribbons. Riyand knew enough to be sure of that. *I have inherited a few of the family skills,* he thought again. It was a nice idea, one he must remember to mention to Ando after he got back into the city.

A driver hauled his reins to turn a supply wagon left, off the road. The front wheels had barely begun to turn when the ground beneath them collapsed and the wagon tilted, then crashed over with its right side wheels spinning. The four horses screamed, fighting to get out of the traces. One of the men who scattered away from them wasn't fast enough and a flying hoof caught him full in the eye with a crack Ando heard a hundred yards away.

"Narrow wedge!" he cried to his cavalry. Three hundred of them, the best the Guard had to offer. He knew the commands as well as they did. They formed into a wedge, a more steeply slanted version of their earlier chevron, like a sliver-thin arrowhead. That ought to keep them out of the traps Calesh had ordered dug. Riyand settled his spear into the couched position under his arm, hearing a rattle as the men around him followed suit.

He felt all right, actually. His heart was hammering fit to break his ribs, and his neck and face were slick with sweat, but his hands were dry and they held steady. Soft and effete, indeed. He howled a wordless challenge and the cavalry gathered speed, driving at the enemy line.

At the last moment the right flank *did* go down, in a sudden welter of shrieking horses and plunging men as they ran over the top of a pit. Riyand saw it from the corner of his eye but he didn't look around, couldn't spare the time; all the lessons his tilt masters had failed to drum into him were rushing back all at once, like bells ringing in his head. One of them was *keep your focus on your own work, always.* He couldn't remember who'd said that to him. It could have been any of a dozen different men, and it didn't matter. None of it had done any good at the time anyway.

He was full of a wild, skirling exhilaration, and his hands hardly trembled as the charge went home.

There was a moment, just before the cavalry rampaged into the half-formed enemy lines, when fear flashed through him like a wash of hot water, scalding him. But it was too late by then. The point of his spear went solidly into the chest of a soldier in a white tabard and lifted him from his feet, to crash back down among his fellows like a wooden ball scattering skittles. A man to one side began to lift his sword, only that, and then the horse's shoulder rammed into him and sent him flying into the mill of panicking men. Everywhere men were being thrown backwards, some pinwheeling their arms and others limp as rags, very obviously dead.

Many of the Guard still had their spears, while others had drawn their swords, but either way they kept on carving a path through the white-coated men. They were the Order of the Basilica, of course, not renowned for their sturdiness under attack at the best of times. Even Riyand knew that. He hacked downwards and missed his target completely, the blade whistling a good six inches past the man's arm, but it didn't matter because the horse was still stamping its way forward and the Shaveling was lost in the fray behind.

Then he was through, past the enemy unit and into open ground where he could turn the gelding with his knees and one hand on the reins. Other riders had broken through as well, and were now slashing at the Shavelings as their discipline failed and they began to flee. One bolted past Riyand, but he couldn't see the point of killing him now, with the brief engagement won. The man didn't even have his sword. It wouldn't be much more than murder.

He was alive. He'd come through the fight without a scratch, though there had been nobody there to guard him. Bohend could not have done better. Riyand let out a whoop, shaking his sword in the air, and as he did so he spotted a line of wagons coming up the road, stacked high with baskets and cages of chickens.

"Food supply," he said aloud, though there was no one to hear in the chaos. If his men could destroy that it would be a heavy blow against the All-Church, with the farms already stripped. He stared at it, wondering if it was worth the risk, and was so engrossed that he didn't even notice when the cavalry captain came up beside him and cut down a Shaveling with his sword already raised for the blow which would have laid Riyand dead in the mud.

"My lord," the captain said hurriedly, "we have to go. There are more men flooding into the valley. If we –"

"Food supply," Riyand interrupted, pointing with his blade. "Reform the men, officer. We're going after it."

"My lord, it's –"

"You're wasting time," he cut in. This was how Calesh behaved, a quick decision first and then make everyone fall in with it as quickly as possible. "Form them up, captain."

The man wheeled his horse around with a curse. "In ranks, at me! Lines for a strike down the road!"

Some of the riders hesitated before they obeyed. Riyand supposed that was all right: men had probably doubted Calesh too before Gidren Field, and every other commander besides until they proved themselves. He could hear All-Church horns blowing all around now, and see regiments hastening across the plain in response to them, turning to cut off the Guard's retreat. But there was time for the wagons. He was sure of it.

"My lord, please reconsider," the captain said quietly. "We don't have spears anymore and the horses have had one charge. We should get back to the Gate of Angels while we can."

"There is time." Riyand smiled, blood thundering through him. "There is time for this."

*

"Close the gate!" Raigal bellowed. "Close it, you goat-spawned sons of bitches, close the bastard thing!"

For once, Luthien didn't have a quarrel with the giant man's language, but he didn't think it was going to do any good. The men on the Gate of Angels were from the Guard, not likely to lower the portcullis and slam the great oak doors while the Margrave was still outside. He and Raigal were racing along the wall like a couple of boys, dodging sentries and leaping over holes that dropped down to ladders, but they were still some distance away.

He risked a glance to his left, over the wall. All-Church units were pouring onto the plain now, emerging from every low point in the surrounding hills. They must have sent men down every little vale and valley as they came, making it impossible for anyone to counter attack their divided force because another element would slip around behind and cut the sortie off. *Anyone but a complete fool*, he thought bitterly. If Riyand did make it back to the city Luthien was going to shake him till his teeth fell out.

"We spent two weeks digging all those traps for the All-Church to fall in," he panted, hurdling a box left on the parapet. "Not so he could go careering all over them. The idiot!"

"You knew he was that already," Raigal gasped, almost purple in the face. He swerved aside and slowed suddenly. "Go on without me. I'm too heavy for sprinting. Get that gate shut!"

Luthien nodded and sped on. Sentries had begun to point across the plain now and he slowed enough to follow their fingers, to where a cloud of dust and screaming men showed that Riyand's mad charge had found a mark. It was quite a long way out, three hundred yards perhaps. Other companies had begun to swing around, moving to cut the raiders off.

"God-damned bloody fool," he muttered. Evidently he was going to take up swearing again, along with everything else. Violence and women already; maybe he'd been slurping wine by the end of the day. Come to that he'd call it a triumph if he was, because this mess could get ugly *very* fast.

There was an awning under the wall, on the city side. Luthien hardly more than saw it before he threw himself off the side of the parapet, mailed shirt or no, to plunge down on the canvas with an impact that tore it right through. He'd landed on his back though, spread out like an upside-down cat, and he managed to catch one of the tie ropes that secured the awning as the cloth ripped. The rope hissed across his leather glove and nearly broke his wrist, and as a bonus he crashed down in the middle of a stall selling bolts of cotton in various colours, all of which were flung into the street and quickly became dusty brown. The stallholder shrieked in outrage and Luthien flung an apology over his shoulder: he was already running again, glad it was his wrist he'd hurt and not an ankle.

There was a knot of soldiers in front of him, men with battered swords and armour that needed to be hammered out, or perhaps already had been. Luthien called out to them, glad to see *someone* was taking this idiocy seriously. One of the men looked back and snapped an order.

I've seen him before, Luthien thought, still running. *Where did I see his face before today?*

A moment later another of the group, a big man who reeked to the skies of pigs and their filth, cannoned into Luthien and knocked him flying. He kept his arms around Luthien's chest and they smashed into the side of a window, shattering glass under Luthien's back. The memory came to him as he hung there, pinned by the big man's arms with jagged splinters of glass behind his back and no way to draw his sword: where he'd seen the man before. *He was with the assassin. They came through the gate together, the day Calesh came back to Mayence.*

His hands moved without thought, even while sudden terror gripped his innards in cold fingers.

There was no way he could reach his blade, not caught in the big man's bear hug, and Luthien didn't try. He hit him under the chin with the heel of his right hand, and as the man grunted and his head came up Luthien poked fingers hard into both his eyes. The man reared back, mouth opening to let out a scream that never came. Luthien pivoted on one foot, caught him by the throat, and thrust him down onto the splinters of glass still poking up from the bottom edge of the window frame. He was armoured but not helmeted. His head banged into the wood and his boots thrashed spasmodically on the street, then were still.

"Sorry," Luthien gasped to the family sitting at their dinner table, all of them frozen in shock as they stared at the pig-smelling dead man in their window. "More Raigal's sort of opponent than mine, you understand. Excuse me, I have to run."

Run he did, though he was almost sure now he would be too late. They had always known there must be some All-Church devotees in Mayence, some who still counted themselves among the Faithful and were devout or just crazy enough to try to let the besiegers in. Calesh and the others had anticipated it, planned for it. But they hadn't reckoned on a second assassin in the city because Luthien had forgotten, it had simply slipped his god-damned *mind,* while he was all caught up in the agony of his broken oath and the refuge he found in Ilenia's arms. He had indulged himself, and now the price might be higher than he could bear.

Please let me be in time, he prayed as he raced along crowded streets. *Please. I'll pay any forfeit, accept any torment, but please. Please.*

He burst into the open space inside the Gate of Angels, where Waggoner's Way ran into the city. Most of the roads had been blocked off by new barricades now, some of them closed completely, to provide an extra layer of defence. What mattered at the moment was the gate, and it was towards it that Luthien turned in time to see the last of the knot of soldiers vanishing into the gatehouse. A single Guardsman in blood and gold lay sprawled on his face on the stones, blood pooling under him. It must have only just happened now, a second ago, because nobody had raised the alarm yet, or even noticed.

Luthien flung himself at the gatehouse just as the iron-bound door shut with a clang. He struck it with his shoulder and bounced off, cursing. Someone in front of him laughed and someone behind cried out, spying the dead guard at last. They were too late. All of them, too late.

But they must not be.

"In the towers!" he yelled, backing away from the door. "Hey, you men in the towers, look down!"

A face appeared over the wall, peering down at him. Luthien gave the man no time to ask questions. "How do I get into the gatehouse?"

A frown. "The door's right in front of you."

"I *know* that!" he yelled, goaded beyond endurance. "I need another way in, quickly!"

"There isn't another way in," the Guardsman said, as though talking to an idiot. "One way makes it safe, see?"

He did see. Vital points like the wheel that controlled a gate were always heavily protected, to make it as hard as possible for attackers to gain access. But that meant that when they had, it was almost impossible for defenders to get access *back*. It almost never happened, but when it did it was nearly always disastrous. Luthien fought to control his temper and spun to face the crowd.

"I need axes and strong men," he shouted. "And right now! Go! Why are you standing around?" He turned back to the perplexed tower sentry as men began to spring out of the plaza. "Get that portcullis down! I don't care what you have to break, just get it down."

"But the Margrave –"

"Damn his heart and eyes!" Luthien nearly screamed. "Forget the Margrave, it's the city at risk now. *Close the portcullis!*"

The man glanced back, perhaps at someone behind him, and when he looked down at Luthien again his eyes were suddenly wide. "We can't! Something jamming the wheel!"

Oh, sweet Heaven, Luthien thought. "Then for the Lord's sake, man, sound your horn and summon the defence! And keep trying! Mayence itself might rest on the fate of that wheel."

If it did, things were looking dark already. Parrien had fallen in less than a day, its wall breached almost as soon as the All-Church army looked at it. Luthien hadn't believed it possible that Mayence might go the same way. It still might not. Strange things happened in battles, mistakes born of confusion and chaos. It might be that the All-Church army wouldn't realise the gate was being held open for its men to walk breezily inside.

A trumpet began to blow from atop the tower, summoning the city men to their places on the wall. Other horns followed suit from other points. Those civilians who hadn't already fled the plaza began to do so, mother gathering children close even as the youngsters tried to break free so they could see what was going on. Luthien ignored them. He'd worry about the souls of the innocent when there was time.

"What's going on?" Raigal asked. He lumbered up still red-faced, and breathing hard. His shrewd eyes took in the scene before Luthien could answer. "The gatehouse?"

"All-Church sympathisers," Luthien confirmed. "We need that door open as soon as possible."

"On it," Raigal rumbled. He unhooked his axe from the loops on his back and stepped forward.

"The iron on that door will ruin the blade," Luthien warned him.

Raigal shrugged. "Hardly the time to worry about that."

Which it wasn't, of course. A moment later the heavy blade of the axe thudded into the door, driving an inch deep into the oak. At the same time the Guardsman's head popped over the wall above once more and he yelled down, "Horsemen coming!"

"Perfect," Luthien muttered. He drew his sword and moved to stand in the middle of the open gateway. A few men had started to hurry to join him, cramming helmets on their heads and hefting spears as they came, but they would need a lot more. Six or eight men would hardly slow cavalry down.

"I'll do my work," Raigal Tai said in his deep voice. His axe slammed into the door again, ringing off the iron bands but shaking the thick oak in its hinges. "And you do yours."

*

I'm afraid that the only songs left to us after this will be songs of sorrow, my dear.

His own words, those, spoken to Riyand on the terrace overlooking the city, on the day word had come that the All-Church had ordered its army west.

They had expected the news, of course. It had grown more and more likely while spring took hold of Sarténe, and Cavel became steadily grimmer as all his attempts to negotiate were turned down. Ando had grown gloomier too, gnawed inside by the realisation that this was his fault, his responsibility. It was he who had killed the All-Church priest by the river Rielle. He who had given the Basilica the excuse they were looking for.

It had seemed so necessary, then. Rabast had thrown insults at Riyand in the Margrave's hall itself, in front of everyone. That couldn't be allowed to pass, no matter what powers stood behind the priest. Kings and princes fell when they were made to look like fools. Ando had thought Rabast had to die.

He knew now, standing on the wall with the battle swirling below him, that he'd had to live.

Cavel knew his work, had a lifetime's experience to tell him which men could be reasoned with, which cajoled. He understood when to plead and when to stand in pride, and with whom, across much of the world. Across all of it that mattered, really. If Rabast had gone untroubled to the ferry, and then home, Cavel would have gone on exchanging letters with the Basilica and various nobles, making promises when he must and vaguer undertakings when he could. He would even have kept some of them. And the army massing by the river Rielle would have been sent east, across the sea on Glorified ships, to drive the heathen Madai back into the desert and make the holy land safe under God once more.

Sarténe would have been safe. All that was changed, all ruined by one impetuous act, one moment of rashness. Ando's fault.

Every death, his fault.

He stood on the eastern wall, looking out over the wide plain on which All-Church soldiers crawled like flies on a corpse. They were still flowing in, pouring out of every valley in a torrent that went on and on. Some had already begun to work their way around to the north, vanishing from Ando's view. Not that he spared much attention for them. His gaze was riveted almost due east, along the main road, where a splash of crimson and yellow pooled around a handful of wagons. Flames licked at the carts as he watched.

Blood and gold: the colours of the Margrave's Guard. Somewhere among the riders was Riyand himself, if he hadn't fallen already. Ando's fingers curled over the stone of the wall, clutching it tight.

"Come back," he whispered. A soldier to his right threw him a sideways glance, then went on struggling into his mailshirt.

He could not bear it if Riyand died. All the deaths Ando had caused, all the grief: those he could bear, though it tore at him, if he had Riyand. If he had love. What did it matter, if your heart was given to a woman or a man? He had never understood why the priests made such a commotion over it. Love was wonderful, a bright and shining thing, and very rarely wrong. Ando loved Riyand with a fierce abiding power, something he was helpless before, like a broken ship in a storm. If you loved, helplessly, how could you be blamed for it? And why should you be?

"Please come back," he said.

All-Church regiments had begun to move to cut off Riyand's retreat. They came amid a din of shouted orders and tramping feet, moving in a curl as they peeled off from the front of the main army and swept both south and north, like pincers. Just to Ando's left a company came too close to the wall and there was a staccato rattle of bowstrings, followed seconds later by a sound like hailstones pattering on a tin roof. Eight or ten soldiers fell, some motionless and others screaming or cursing. The company made a hasty retreat, tangling as it did so with another group moving behind, so that both had to stop while they disentangled their ranks.

A few moments later the leaders of another formation sprang one of Calesh's spike traps, and this time the results were more impressive. The pit covers were designed so that when one section fell in it collapsed the rest, so twenty men or more found the earth vanishing under their feet and vanished with panicked shrieks. The next men in line scrambled backwards into their fellows, desperate not to be pushed over the edge by the regiment's momentum. Some were, anyway. Ando had no compassion to spare for them.

His lips shaped *please come back,* one more time.

The delays had bought time, but the flash of blood and gold was still close by the wagons. And now the pincers were closing, lead elements marching nearer and nearer to the main road… and then they met, turning to face east. Again bowstrings twanged, and again a handful of All-Church soldiers fell, but the regiments only moved twenty yards further from the wall and then stopped. Ando could hardly breathe. He was aware of still more companies moving towards the Gate of Angels, one of them cavalry in full plate mail, but his eyes never left the Guard.

They were moving at last, heading back towards the city. He thought there were still more than half of them, a hundred and eighty perhaps, and hope flared in his chest. The horses would be weary now, and most of the riders would have thrown away broken spears and would use swords instead; but still, that many charging horses were formidable. He looked back at the waiting infantry and saw spears come down like the bristles of a quill-pig, just as the Guard gathered speed and crashed into them.

The plain was full of shouting and movement by then, and the city wall no less so, but still Ando heard the screams of the horses as they spitted themselves on that thicket of steel points. Riders were flung forward, to crash down amongst the infantry in a tangle of limbs, where they were quickly dispatched. In a few places it was the All-Church men who suffered, their line broken and men thrown aside by the impact of several horses tight together, but it didn't happen often enough. Ando could see that. His hands gripped the wall tighter.

There was a moment, just a splinter of time, when he saw Riyand. He was sure of it, despite the chaos and confusion. His lover was standing in his stirrups to slash down at a soldier by his bridle, trying to urge his horse forward into the tightening morass of men and corpses. Ando was looking right at him when that scintilla passed and Riyand went down from his saddle, vanishing into the heaving mass, and Ando threw his head back and screamed at the clouds.

When he looked again there was nothing but All-Church soldiers, and a few riderless horses galloping hither and yon across the plain.

Men were watching him, all along the wall. Rather than meet their eyes Ando looked down, fighting the urge to throw himself over the palisade and end it, end all the pain. All the songs of sorrow. He didn't even know why he fought; he just did, instinctively, the way a bird flutters even in its cage. But looking down, he saw the cavalry force he'd noticed earlier, still trotting towards the Gate of Angels with their shields held up against the arrows that showered down on them from the wall. A double line of Crusader archers was forming up as well, to match the fire of the defenders if they could. The Gate was still not closed, for some reason. There would be a battle there soon.

Ando turned his gaze back to where Riyand had fallen, and he blew a kiss without caring that two hundred men were watching what he did. "Goodbye, my dear. Wait for me in Heaven if you can."

He turned then, and went down from the wall to find his sword. There was no need to throw himself to his death when the end was so near anyway, for all of them. It would find him soon enough. He prayed he would be given the grace to take a man or two with him before he fell.

Nine

At the Gate

Horsemen were coming, the guard in the tower had said. But they didn't appear, while men began to hurry to join Luthien in the middle of the plaza behind the gatehouse. They came in ones and twos, running from one street or other to form a rough knot a little behind him. Luthien was so absorbed in watching the gate that he didn't even notice them at first.

"Elite Luthien?" one of them asked at length, rather nervously.

"Don't call me that," he snapped. He'd lost any right to that title when he killed Elizur Mandein in the Manse, and broke his vow. Nothing to be done about that now. He turned as he spoke though, and saw the gaggle of some twenty men looking at him, waiting for orders. There were no officers among them, Luthien saw. Any orders would have to come from him.

Spearmen in the middle of the gate," he said. "Don't go too far forward; we don't want to give their archers a shot at you. Stay back, but stay in the tunnel, where it's narrowest."

"But there are only seven of -"

"Do it!" he snarled. "More will join you, and if they don't you have my permission to run like rabbits when the cavalry arrive. Everyone else, form lines in the middle of the plaza and stand ready. What are you waiting for?"

They scrambled to obey, perhaps out of a lingering respect for the man he'd been, when he wore the green robe of a Dualist priest. Or perhaps because they had needed commands to follow, and he had been the man who gave them. The seven men with spears formed a pitiful line across the near end of the tunnel, too far back really because one charge would push them out into the wider space of the plaza. But then, one charge would slice through them like a sickle cutting wheat, so it didn't really matter.

"Where are those horsemen?" Luthien muttered. He could hear trumpets blowing outside, and the fall of thousands of marching feet set the ground trembling where he stood. He remembered that, and the fear it brought, so vividly; from Kiderun, from Gidren Field, and from a dozen lesser battles faced during his five years in Tura d'Madai. Faced and survived. He didn't think he'd see the end of this one if reinforcements didn't come before the cavalry appeared.

He was twisting back and forth, trying to watch the gate and the streets of the city at the same time, when the watching townsfolk parted and Reis came through with some fifty Guardsmen at his back. All of them had spears, and Luthien almost gasped in relief. "We need you in the tunnel. Riders are on their way."

"Do it," Reis said curtly to his aide, and the man barked orders in a leather voice any serjant would have been proud of. The fifty men hurried past Luthien to take up places by the seven already there, forming their line slightly further forward so they couldn't be pushed out of the tunnel so easily.

"Heard there was a problem here," Reis said laconically. He jerked his head towards Raigal, still hacking at the door with his great axe. Splinters of wood lay all around him. "Someone seized the gatehouse?"

"And broke the winch," Luthien agreed. "If you can find another axeman I'd love you for it."

"One will be along," the general said. He was impressively calm. "The men assigned to the Gate of Angels will be here as soon -"

He broke off, his head turning towards the gate. The trembling of the ground had worsened, become a rhythmic drumming that set Luthien's bones vibrating. He took a step forward and drew his sword. He'd sworn once that he would never do that again.

"Here they come," he said.

*

The cavalry were Basilicans, the All-Church's own military Order, given the honour of being first into the fray. Usually they were seen as weaker than the other Orders, less well trained and less eager to do God's work besides, cut-throats and thieves as many of them were. Or had been, until given the choice of a long drop and sudden stop, or ten years in the Shavelings. But they roared in without a pause, hooves echoing in the gate as the spearmen screamed defiance and the lines met with a thunderous crash.

The Guard were good though. Riyand had always been a wastrel, but Reis was not, and he'd made sure his men were properly trained and equipped. The line of spearmen bowed under the impact of horses but didn't break, not at any point, and suddenly the echoes were those of screaming horses spitted on sharp points, and the cries of men tumbled from their saddles. One rider was flung right over the top of the spearmen to hammer down on the stone in a clashing rattle of iron. He slid almost to Luthien's feet, his neck twisted so badly that his eyes stared emptily over the back of his shoulder.

"I think I'd be of most use in the fight," Luthien said. "If I can leave the command to you?"

"Go," Reis agreed, not taking his eyes from the struggle.

Luthien took one step and then paused. "Haven't you got that door open yet, Raigal? All your muscle must have turned to fat since you came back from the desert."

"I see your mouth works as well as it ever did," the huge man called back. He swung the axe again and another thick chip flew out of the oak. "Blood of the God! Are you going to talk or fight?"

Luthien grinned to himself and went forward.

He'd known since the day he faced Mandein that he had lost nothing of what he had been, all those years ago. All his speed remained, all his strength, all his balance. They came naturally to him, with hardly any need to exercise or train. He would have been better if he'd done those things, but still, he'd been good enough to dispose of the assassin, world-renowned swordsman though Mandein had been. And Luthien had been surprised then, caught wearing his Elite's robe and sandals on his feet, completely unprepared.

He was armoured now, and ready. As he had been before, at all those battles: Gidren Field, and Kiderun, when the Madai had called him the Scorpion's Sting and fled from his face.

He slipped in among the spearmen and killed a Shaveling rider with his first blow, a serpent-quick thrust up under the ribs that found the beating heart and split it precisely. The cavalryman started to shriek and then simply toppled backwards, falling over his horse's hindquarters. Luthien twisted to avoid a kick from the horse, slashed his blade across its throat, and then moved backwards out of range as it screamed and began to lash out in agony. A flying hoof caught a dismounted Shaveling in the side of the neck and he went down like a rag. Luthien sprang over his still-falling body to deliver a fast lunge that nearly took another Shaveling in the throat, forcing him to lurch back in the saddle so violently that the horse reared and turned sideways, colliding with those on either side.

It was a dance, a lethal game of guesswork and speed. You had to know not where you needed to be but where you *would* need to be, in the time it took your heart to beat a single time. Luthien had always been better at that than anyone else he knew. There was no arrogance in that thought, no boasting: he couldn't cook an omelette, or paint a picture with watercolours on canvas, but he could do this as well as any man alive.

But perhaps he wouldn't do so for long. His leap had taken him high enough to see into the tunnel, and behind the Shaveling cavalry another regiment had already begun to enter, closing off the riders' retreat. The grey shields with their crimson cross were unmistakeable. They were Glorified; *always at the back,* Luthien thought with a soldier's contempt, *always behind someone else when the fight is on.* But their presence meant the Shavelings couldn't break away. They had to win or die, and even if the defenders killed them all they would face a new, fresh enemy at once, with no rest or respite. It was a clever move. Calesh had said all along that the All-Church general was clever.

More defenders were rushing into the line, a mixture of Guard and citizens all jumbled up together, with almost no order. A few men wore the black and white surcoat of the Hand of the Lord, including a man with a puckered scar down the left side of his neck who Luthien was sure he ought to know, but couldn't put a name to. The pair of them were pushed together in the press and fought side by side from then on: the scarred man had a weak chin and looked too slender to make a warrior, but he fought like a ferret in a sack.

After a long time the defenders began to drive forward. There had to be three hundred men in the line by then, enough to allow those who'd been there from the start to fall back and gulp at much-needed air. Luthien stayed where he was, and after a brief feral grin the scarred man did too. Leutar; that was his name, a friend of Baruch's. He ducked under a wild sweep from a Glorified's sword and rammed his own blade into the man's chest, as cleanly as Luthien could have done it himself. Thin or not, the man could fight.

The Glorified were nearly done. Only a couple of them remained, those fighting a retreat back through the tunnel to the plain outside. Once they were clear more soldiers would come, probably cavalry first, in the hope that the defenders had broken all their spears. Luthien dropped back a few paces so he could see the gatehouse door. "Raigal!"

"Nearly in!" the big man bellowed. There was another axeman on the other side of the door now, swinging in counterpoint to Raigal's blows. The door itself had a hole in the middle and the iron bands were bent and scarred, but they still held. As Luthien watched an arrow flashed out through the hole and clanged off shields held a few yards ahead, protecting a small knot of men ready to rush the gatehouse. Reis was watching it all, eyes narrowed.

This was going to be close. Luthien turned back to the battle, pausing to tug a shield from the arm of a man who wouldn't need it anymore. There would be fighting to do yet.

*

Raigal's axe thudded in to the door and sent a foot-long piece of wood flying back into the gatehouse. Curses and scuffing feet told of the men inside forced to scramble aside as the door groaned, then fell backwards. Raigal pulled his axe back and flattened himself against the wall just as three arrows flew out of the gloom. Two rattled off the shields of the men waiting to storm inside.

The third struck the other axeman, who had swung his blade before realising the door was broken. It took him in the eye and he fell without a sound, dead before the flights stopped quivering.

"Go!" Reis bawled.

The knot of soldiers dashed forward, keeping their shields high to deflect any further arrows. Another volley clanged against metal and then the troops went past Raigal in a rush, into the darkness of the gatehouse. Someone screamed. A Guardsman in blood and gold livery came out backwards with a wood axe embedded in his forehead, his eyes shocked and hurt.

"God-protect-my-blood-and-bones," Raigal said, all in one breath. Then he wheeled around the door jamb and threw himself into the room beyond.

His axe was all but ruined, the blade notched and chipped from hacking at the iron-bound door for so long. There wasn't really room to use it anyway, certainly not to swing it, but it never crossed Raigal's mind to toss it away. A figure came at him and he slammed the head of the axe into his throat, feeling the crumple of cartilage as the man's voice box collapsed. Raigal punched him in the mouth and he flew backwards into the wall with a final crack.

It was hard to tell how many men were in the room, or who they were. Someone had snuffed out all the candles and the only light came from the doorway, and even that was often blocked as figures wrestled back and forth or danced around one another with swords. Someone bumped into Raigal from the side and he thumped him hard without looking, not even sure if he was friend or foe. He was looking for the wheel that controlled the portcullis. That was what mattered. Close the gate and Mayence would stand, at least for today. Leave it open and the city might fall as fast as Parrien had.

He shuffled to his left and tripped over a body, flailing his arms to keep his balance. One hand caught someone a blow to the back of his head or his shoulder; it was hard to tell which. Raigal's breathing came in hoarse gasps, half due to the effort of his axe-work and half to tension. To one side someone made a wet bubbling sound and fell over.

The wheel was there, just ahead. Raigal stepped towards it, slithering in blood and what felt like a loose slice of flesh, and as he laid his hands on the spokes something hot went into him from behind.

He roared and spun around, reaching out in the darkness for his assailant. The knife was pulled out and Raigal tried to guess where the man's arm was and catch hold of it before the blade went in again. What felt like a pint of blood had already spilled over the back of his left hip, though he knew it would be less than that. It hurt like a bitch though. He managed to catch hold of the other man's jaw, but he missed his arm and the knife was driven in again, this time ripping through Raigal's side and bringing another pint of blood gushing out.

"Whoreson!" Raigal hissed. He caught the man's knife arm and shifted the grip of his other hand, settling his fingers around the man's throat. He was an ordinary-looking bastard, plain as you like, and normally Raigal was sure he'd be able to snap the man like straw. But he was tired, and losing a lot of blood as well. And none of that mattered, not at all: a soldier who gave up when he was tired or hurting would die soon enough. Raigal growled angrily and tightened his grip. The ordinary man wheezed and tried to wrench his knife hand free.

Raigal let his grasp loosen... and then as the man broke free he tightened his fingers and *twisted*. He felt bones snap in the man's wrist, and felt too the scream of pain caught behind that closed throat. The knife clattered on the floor. Raigal brought up his other hand and locked it around the man's neck, squeezing as hard as he could manage. Spots danced in front of his eyes. He roared out loud and pushed with his thumbs, compressing the windpipe even further.

The man thrashed. His hands clawed at Raigal's without effect, and his feet kicked and pummelled just as uselessly. Gradually the struggles slowed. When they stopped Raigal squeezed once more and threw the dead man out of the doorway, then leaned wheezing against the wheel. He was too tired for the moment to remember why the wheel mattered.

A shadow in the doorway became Reis, holding a lantern high. Yellow light spilled over a room torn to splinters, bits and pieces of cupboards and chairs carpeting the floor alongside a dozen bodies. Most were dead, though a hitching gasp like a faint snore meant at least one of them must not be. Raigal was beyond caring. He didn't think he could stand without help.

"Get off that wheel," Reis said brusquely. "I need to see what they did to it."

Raigal levered himself away, staggered a step and then hunched over with his hands on his knees. "I need... attention... here."

"In a moment," Reis answered, and then swore bitterly. "Damn them! They've broken the whole system. Every cog I can see is smashed. There's no way we can close the gate now."

"So?" Raigal panted. "Cut the... chain."

"Cut inch-thick iron? Not even you can manage that. We need a blacksmith." He strode to the door and shouted orders, and footsteps darted away. "Now let's get you some help. Looks like someone stuck you a good one."

"Two good... ones," Raigal managed. He didn't think anything vital had been hit, actually, but that wasn't much consolation when blood was pissing out of him and he couldn't get enough air in his lungs. He let Reis help him outside, blinking a little in the sunlight, and sat heavily on someone's shield to rest.

"Did you manage it?" Luthien asked. He seemed to spring out of nowhere, to Raigal's dazed eyes. "Can we close the gate?"

"Not yet," he said. "Sorry. Was too slow."

Luthien shook his head. "Not your fault. It's mine, really. I knew that man had come to Mayence with Mandein, but I forgot all about him. Well, there's no changing it now. I have to get back to the line." He hesitated though, and his voice changed. "Will you be all right?"

He was feeling better as breath came back to him, and he said, "God's Blood, yes - when wasn't I?"

Luthien smiled and was gone again, back into the wall of defenders that blocked the tunnel under the Gate of Angels. He would be safe there, if anyone could be: no one had ever managed to lay a blade on Luthien. Sitting on the shield Raigal might not be safe, if a stray arrow came his way, but it was too much trouble to move. He pressed one hand against each of his wounds and waited for a physician to come, and left his fate to God.

*

Arrows were falling inside the wall now, though not many of them as yet. There would be more: Luthien was grimly certain of that. He could hear the thrum of bowstrings from atop the wall as the sentries returned fire, and once a man tumbled down from the battlement to land in the street with a crack.

None of that was his problem.

"That was good work," he told the soldiers behind the gate. They had been resupplied with spears, taken from a stack piled up for exactly this sort of emergency, and now presented a thicket of points to anyone who might try to force entrance to Mayence. But they were bloodied and already tired, and that *was* his problem. "You can all be proud of yourselves. When they come again just keep doing the same things, and we'll be all right."

"Where's the Hand?" someone called out, from inside the ranks. "Where's the Hand of the Lord?"

That was Luthien's own question, in fact. It seemed an age since Baruch had darted off to rally the Order, when Raigal had said he'd have them *turned out in no time.* Their absence was worrying, but Luthien tried not to let that show. "They're on their way. The Preceptory is halfway across the city from here."

"We got here in time," a voice muttered.

Luthien nodded. "We did, and we can be proud of ourselves for that, too. Is anyone going to sidle away because the Hand isn't here yet?" He surveyed the ranks of spearmen, who this time remained silent. "No? Then let's concentrate on holding this gate. Once we get the chain cut and the portcullis down we'll be safe. We just have to wait until then."

"That might take -"

"Riders!" a watchman shouted from the tower. "Riders coming!"

"Front rank kneel!" Luthien ordered. He claimed a spear and joined the line, squeezing in on one knee between a man in civilian clothes and a palace servant in green and red. "Second and third ranks lower spears, and brace!"

He could hear the rumble of hooves already. Bows thrummed again from above but that wasn't much use against armoured cavalry, unless you hit a vital point. The spearmen took their positions well though, most of them having practiced military drills over the past month. They waited, and suddenly the hammer of hooves began to echo as the riders entered the tunnel.

"Steady!" Luthien shouted. He had time for the one word and then the cavalry came, storming down the tunnel to smash into the waiting forest of spears at a full gallop.

An instant before the impact Luthien drove forward and up, thrusting the spear in front of him. Then he was in the belly of the beast, surrounded by a great roaring of men and metal and horseflesh, with hardly enough room to move. The point of his spear went inches over a horse's head and the rider's momentum took him onto it, so hard that his armour was punctured and the steel went deep into his chest. He was punched out of the saddle and for a moment hung in the air, arms and legs thrashing, before his weight took over and he plunged in among his comrades crowding in behind him.

Spearmen had been hurled backwards, like water spraying over a stone. For a moment the line itself vanished under a tide of horses, only to then reappear as cavalry fell too, over a dozen of them felled in the first charge. Riderless horses plunged and kicked in the middle of the morass, as dangerous to their own side as to the defenders. The horsemen were Glorified again, Luthien saw. Probably they'd just happened to be closest, when the All-Church general realised the Gate of Angels was open. So much for their habit of being at the back.

There was no time for thought after that. No time for anything except staying alive, if he could, in the middle of a screaming press of men hacking and stabbing at one another. There was no room for finesse. Abandoning the spear, Luthien crouched behind his shield and cut at any horse or Glorified soldier who came close, trying not so much to kill as to wound, or at least drive away. Even so he managed to find the throat of a dismounted Glorified who shoved towards him from the right, and even when dead didn't fall because the crush held him up. He was heaved from side to side with his head flopping loosely until at last he vanished from sight. Moments later Luthien killed another man, with a straight thrust under the ribcage, and this time had enough room to kick his body back into the rest of the cavalry.

Not many of them were still mounted now. The fight had become sword against sword, with horses downed and spears broken in the first exchanges. Luthien was standing on bodies to fight now, which meant another problem because not all of them would be dead. He stabbed downwards when he could: the dead wouldn't mind, and it stopped anyone yet living from knifing Luthien in the knee or thigh from below. It was hard to balance as well. The crush lessened, as fighters spread out across the carpet of corpses.

Luthien found himself facing a wounded Glorified and dispatched him with a cut to the throat. This was where he excelled; in an open fight, with space to move. He was unmatched here. He was thinking that when hoof beats echoed in the tunnel again, and he began to turn in the realisation that the defence wasn't ready for another charge at all.

Then suddenly men cried out in relief, and the last surviving Glorified turned to flee. They had no chance, of course, not with more cavalry entering the tunnel. But behind them was the Hand of the Lord, five hundred men in tight-packed lines with spears in their hands, just back from the piled bodies. Someone barked an order and the first rank knelt, just as Luthien's men had done but with better discipline, and he laughed in delight.

"About time!" he shouted, spying Baruch behind the ranks. It must have been him who'd shouted that order. He was gesturing with wild arms, and it took a moment for Luthien to remember he was standing right where cavalry were about to thunder by in about a second. He threw a glance down the tunnel and got out of the way in two jumps, just as a stream of riders in plain coats erupted from the gate with their spears angled low for the attack.

"Streets are packed with people," Baruch said as Luthien joined him, without waiting to be asked. He had to shout to be heard over the din of battle. "It took us half an hour just to get out of the Preceptory and onto Waggoner's Way. After that I had the horns blown and told the men to walk over the top of anyone who got in the way."

"I'm glad you did," Luthien said. Now his part of the fight was over - for now, anyway - he had time to realise he was badly out of breath, and spattered with blood and dirt besides. Perhaps thirty of the spearmen had gathered behind the Hand's lines with him, most of them standing with hands on their knees or just lying on the street, exhausted. He hoped more had survived, but he doubted there would be many. Not much time had been spent training city folk to withstand cavalry charges; everyone had thought they'd be behind the wall, defending it against ladders or siege towers, if the All-Church tried those things.

Off to one side Raigal was easing into his shirt, wincing against the bandages that covered his middle. He saw Luthien looking and shrugged. "It's not as bad as it looks. The wounds were shallow, but they bled like bastards. And it hurts if I move too much."

"Looks like you're done fighting for now, then," Luthien said.

Raigal put his breastplate on and reached down to fasten the side clasps. "Let's hope I'm not needed again."

"That's two of us wounded now," Luthien noted, turning to Baruch. "It must be your turn next."

"I'll try not to disappoint you," Baruch said. "*Left side, you're sagging! Push forward! Push!*"

The area in front of the gate was a roaring mass of fighters, beating against the solid black-and-white wall of the Hand of the Lord. Even an inexperienced eye would have been able to tell which side was the best trained. The Hand kept to its ranks with a practiced discipline, while the men ranged against them struck and fell back in little clusters, as their courage waxed and waned. More All-Church men had fallen than Dualist, and many more were still falling, adding their bodies to the piles. But they could afford the losses, and worse, the Hand had been forced to form lines away from the corpses, in a wider part of the plaza. Luthien thought there might be as many as a thousand attackers inside the gate now. He sighed and shifted the shield on his left arm.

"Any sign of Reis's blacksmith?" he asked.

Raigal leaned on his ruined axe. "Two of them are in the wheelhouse now, trying to work something out."

"Tell them to work fast," Luthien said. He made himself ignore his aches and went back into the fray.

Ten

The Perfect Mistress

"This is futile," Ailiss said.

Calesh didn't bother to reply. The Lady had said the same thing twice already, as the little band made its way from the Manse to the Gate of Angels. There were three of them altogether, himself and Farajalla with Ailiss riding beside them. Twenty Hand soldiers had formed a guard to escort them as soon as they set out.

They were needed. People thronged the streets, though all through the preparations it had been made clear that they were to stay at home when the siege began, to stay out of the way of the troops and volunteers. None of the preparations had foreseen the wall being breached so quickly though, and panic did strange things to civilians. Calesh didn't blame them. Everyone knew the citizens of Parrien had been butchered when that town fell, and nobody expected things to be any different in Mayence.

But the escort kept people away from Ailiss. Hardly any of them had seen her before; she was a legend and a rumour both, a name whispered in dreams and in beds, when lovers came together. A talisman, held bright against the dark. Men and women alike cried out in joy when they saw her, and some pressed against the encircling ring of cavalry and stretched out beseeching arms. Ailiss smiled at them all, and lifted a hand to acknowledge them, but she didn't slow down.

The riders kept people away from Calesh too, and without that he wasn't sure he could have made it to the wall. He could only ride by hunching over, trying to crush the pain in the side of his chest, and any sudden movements filled him with flares and flashes that left him half numb. Panicked city folk bumping into his horse wouldn't have done him any good at all. Even allowed a smooth, slow ride, he wasn't quite sure how he'd managed to stay in the saddle.

When he'd mounted up in the courtyard, he'd had to sit perfectly still for two full minutes before the haze across his eyes lifted. When it did he'd found Fara watching him, of course.

"If you can't do better than that," she said quietly, "I'll put you back in your sickbed if I have to carry you there myself."

"No need for that," he replied, in a horrible whispery voice that he hardly recognised. "And no time for it either. Give it up, love. There are larger things at risk here than my life."

"There is no larger thing than you," she had answered.

But that wasn't true. Mayence was a larger thing, more important by far than a captain in the Orders, however much fleeting fame he might have lucked his way into. The Dualism was a larger thing by *far,* dwarfing everyone who prayed to its god and fought for its temples; Calesh, Riyand, Reis, even the Lady herself. It had been passed down through changing cultures as centuries slipped by one by one, adding into millennia as the past became half-believed legend. If he died then he died. It was a soldier's fate, much more often than not, and he had been prepared for it a long time.

He remembered Farajalla was pregnant then, and had to look away from her before he found the will to flick the reins and get his horse moving.

There is no larger thing than you. He had always felt that way about her, ever since the first day, in the sunlight of the courtyard at Harenc. Now he felt the same intense love for the child she carried, *his* child, though it had hardly begun to grow as yet. It was a savage thing, that love. He wondered what cruelties it might drive him to, if she and the child were taken away, or lost.

He heard the fight by the gate as soon as they were out in the streets. Battle was always loud, mostly due to the clang and clatter of steel. Now it sounded like an accident in an armoury, breastplates and helmets falling on the stone floor and rattling there, or rolling in echoing metallic circles. There were shouts too, but those were harder to make out against the background calls of frightened citizens passing rumour back and forth. Calesh let the horse carry him slowly closer and tried to breathe as deeply as his wound would let him.

They were just turning onto Waggoner's Way when Amand cantered up beside him, Gaudin riding beside him and a hundred Hand armsmen at his back.

"I should have known you'd climb out of your sickbed," the commander said. Farajalla snorted as Gaudin went to join her and the Lady. Strange, how the tall man seemed to guard both of them now, rather than just the one.

"I should have known you'd learn of it the moment I did," Calesh replied. He reached across to clasp his friend's forearm. "News?"

"That idiot Riyand led a sortie out of the Gate of Angels," Amand said crisply. "Three hundred Guard, I'm told. They stayed too long and were caught, though I don't know the details about how or why. The worse news is that someone got into the gatehouse and broke the wheels. The guards can't drop the portcullis or close the gates."

Calesh felt a clutch at his throat. "Who's there?"

"All your three friends," Amand said, "and general Reis as well. Baruch took five hundred Hand, but they're not alone."

"They're not enough," Calesh muttered. He hoped more men had joined those few, because otherwise the gate would fall in short order. "All right, take the women to the south gate and -"

"I'm not leaving you!" Farajalla said fiercely. "Put the thought out of your mind, husband."

"You are expecting a baby. You should -"

"How can you have the nerve to throw that at me?" she hissed. "You're so hurt you can hardly ride, and it took ten minutes for you just to put your armour on. If you're not delicate then neither am I. I'll leave if you do, but only then. I go where you go."

He closed his eyes, but he didn't have time to argue with her. "Amand, take the Lady and Gaudin to the south gate and wait for me there. Gather two thousand of the Hand as well. They couldn't fit into the fight for the gate, and if it's lost we'll need them to escape."

Ailiss reined her horse closer to Calesh. "Remember my vision. The city is doomed, and you cannot change it."

"You admitted that visions are sometimes wrong," he said.

"I also said it was rare," she reminded him. "Don't forget that. See for yourself if you must, but don't wait too long. The road to the mountains will not stay open while you dally."

"I won't dally," he promised, not sure if he would or not. "Go. Amand, be sure to keep her safe."

"As my own life," the bony man nodded. He turned his horse and led the majority of the soldiers away, leaving Calesh and Farajalla with only the twenty men they'd started with. He looked at her and opened his mouth.

"Don't," she said.

He didn't speak. She was going to stay with him, whatever he did: he could only make her leave by leaving himself. And he couldn't do that. Even with the risk, he couldn't. He'd come all the way home to fight for Sarténe, leaving the desert and all the places he knew, the ancient cities and age-draggled hills that had become his home. He had to at least try. Even if Ailiss had said visions were never wrong, he would have had to try.

They rode down Waggoner's Way in silence, except for the shouted questions of the crowd. As they approached the plaza they saw men on rooftops firing arrows down towards the gate, and so they knew the struggle was still ongoing even before they reached the barricade and could see for themselves.

*

He would be down there. Of course he would. Calesh had once said that he did everything with his whole heart, whatever it was. When Luthien had been Elite he had been as dedicated as anyone could be, and now he was a warrior again he would be the same.

Ilenia wished he wasn't. She had ached for him for years, fought against her body's longing with hopeless despair, because she knew Luthien would never break his oath and come to her in love. Then he had, if not for her - and now she wished he hadn't, that he was still Consoled, because that would mean he was away from the fighting and safe.

If any of them were safe.

The Gate of Angels was going to fall. She could see it from the windows of the Manse, at least a little. Buildings hid most of the plaza, but in the corner left visible men kept forming lines and then rushing into the fray she couldn't make out. Once they'd been driven back into it, fighting madly against unseen enemies, but after a few minutes they'd rallied and pushed back, shoving the All-Church men towards the gate again.

It wasn't going to matter. Another thing Calesh and Reis had both said, and Luthien as well, was that numbers nearly always told in the end. The All-Church had managed to get hundreds of men inside the wall, maybe more than a thousand by now, and that was too many. It wouldn't be possible to drive them out. Mayence was going to fall.

"I am leaving," she said.

Behind her Cavel twitched in surprise. "My lady?"

"I'm not your lady." She turned to face him. "I never was, in truth. I might have been Riyand's bauble but I was never his wife, and you know that. I only had a small place here. Now he's dead I have none at all."

She wondered if she ought to feel grief that Riyand had been killed. She didn't though. There was nothing where emotion should be: no sorrow, no relief, not even vindication. She'd always known he was a fool and he'd died like one. She had often thought he would.

"Tell me," she said to Cavel, still standing by the door of her chambers, "what did you think of him, seneschal? Truly?"

"Of whom, my lady?"

She fixed him with a stare. "You know very well. Riyand."

"I think," Cavel said, rubbing his bald head with one hand, "that I admired his father very much."

Ilenia almost laughed. That was a typical Cavel answer to a thorny question, avoiding the obvious trap and yet making his feelings perfectly clear. He had kept faith with Riyand for his father's sake then, much as Reis had done. *Protecting the*

131

cub out of respect for the wolf, Reis had called it, or something very like. Riyand had repaid them with one folly after another, bringing war down on Sarténe and then doing nothing about it until Calesh Saissan took control from his hands. Now her husband had thrown away his life in one last stupidity, and this one had brought down the city as well, with all Sarténe to follow.

She thought, if God truly loved his Believers in this Dualist land, that He might have allowed the plague to take Riyand and spared Bohend, his brother. In all her time in Mayence she'd never heard anyone speak badly of the elder sibling. Perhaps she would have been happy, married to him. Perhaps now she would be looking out over a city at peace, with three children gathered around her skirts and joy in her heart, or at least contentment, instead of this emptiness.

"I am leaving," she said again. "There's nothing for me here even if the city stands, and I doubt it will. Come with me, Cavel."

The skinny seneschal shook his head slowly. "I will stay, my lady. For me, there is nothing if the city falls."

"I told you not to call me that."

Another shake of the head. "You have been a source of some pride to me, since you came to Mayence. Virtually the whole city knows how lonely your life has been. Yet you've never once confirmed the rumours, or added to the gossip. You have been the perfect mistress of the Manse. I could not have asked for better."

"Then come with me."

"No," he said, with finality. "I have a perfect mistress of my own, my lady, and she is Mayence. I have lived here and I will die here. I was quite adept with a sword, as a younger man."

"Cavel, that was a long -"

"I will not presume to try to tell you to stay," he interrupted gravely, "or persuade you that your duty lies in the city. Please don't attempt to sway me from my course either."

She looked away from him. Cavel was an old man now; they had celebrated his sixtieth birthday during the winter, before the priest had been murdered by the river, and war had begun to throw its shadow over Sarténe. If he died he would not have lost the best years of his life, as many in the city would do. Whether men on the walls or women huddling in cellars with their children, a lot of people would die with most of their lives unlived. But Ilenia couldn't think in such cold terms; or at least, she couldn't do so of Cavel. It seemed she was fonder of him than she'd ever been of the husband she had been given to.

"Then I'd ask you to give me privacy so I can change my clothes," she said. She was careful to keep her gaze away from him. "A lady's gown is hardly suitable for flight from the city."

"Will you go to Luthien?" Cavel asked.

That brought her eyes up, despite her determination to keep her face turned away. The seneschal was watching her with a smile on his thin lips. "You knew? How long ago?"

"I didn't know until now," he replied. "I suspected, only."

That was typical of the man. Even now, with the clash and hammer of battle only a few streets away, Cavel was still unable to stop thinking, his mind whirring and ticking over one problem or another. He would have taken some small measure of satisfaction in being right, Elenia knew. Even now. He might pick up a sword for the first time in forty years, but he would still die as the man he'd been since he last put one down as a youth.

"I'm glad you found someone," he said then, still smiling. "You deserved whatever love you could find, my lady." He hesitated, then added, "Ilenia. Go to your man, and go in love."

He turned and left her then, closing the door behind him with a neat click. She felt the sting of tears in her eyes and wiped them away with the heel of her hand. There wasn't time for weeping. She'd had plenty of time for it these past nine years in Mayence, and had even succumbed at times, though less often as time went on and she became reconciled, if not happy. There had only been happiness since Luthien had broken his oath and came to her with blood on his green Elite's robe. Cavel was right: that was where she had to go. Not to where Luthien was, which would be in the heart of the fight, but to where he would be once it ended. She only had to work out where that was.

She was clattering down the servants' stair, at the back of the Manse, when she passed a window and through it saw rank after rank of Hand cavalry riding down the street. They were all armoured, of course, and carried spears in their right hands and shields on their left, but the thing she noticed was their saddle rolls. All were fully packed, the way they would be when the men departed on a long ride. She stared for a moment and then ran the rest of the way to the stables, to find a horse and be after the soldiers before they passed out of sight.

*

It was over.

That had become undeniable ten minutes ago, really, but still Calesh delayed. Battles that looked certain to be lost had been won before. Sometimes Fate played a card and the game changed, the tide turned, and seemingly inevitable defeat was turned into a victory. He'd seen it happen, more than once.

He had done it himself, killing Cammar a Amalik at Gidren Field, and sending the Nazir infantry fleeing in panic. The feared Nazir, never beaten in battle before, no matter who they faced. Before Amalik fell the Madai had been exultant, scenting triumph in the air, the way armies did. Afterwards they were silent, cowed, ready to turn and slink away the moment a Crusader so much as turned their way.

So he waited, watching as the All-Church army slowly forced its way in through the Gate of Angels, and he hoped for a miracle.

He and Farajalla were sitting on their horses more than a hundred yards from the gate, west of Waggoner's Way. From there they could see straight into the plaza, to the mounds of corpses which lay over it now like a macabre fall of snow, teased by the wind. The men still fighting did so atop the bodies of the dead, stumbling often as a foot went through a gap, or turned on an arm that rolled limply away under a man's

134

weight. Good men died that way, on both sides. Battle like this was about luck more than anything else.

That made it about numbers, and the All-Church had more. Their soldiers had pushed into the plaza until everything from the struggling front lines to the tunnel was a tight press of bodies, all waiting their turn to fight. In a way they were already fighting though, adding their weight to the pressure that had forced the defenders back one agonising step at a time. It was that which had made the difference. The Dualist soldiers just couldn't match it.

Reis was trying. On the far side of the square he was fighting like a dervish, or one of the toys in Tura d'Madai with a key in the back and filled with springs and toothed wheels. Start them off and they walked around, or danced, until the springs wound down. The marshal's spring seemed to be infinite, a never-ending fount of energy that drove him on and on without a pause. All-Church soldiers came up to him, but only for as long as it took them to die. He was so splashed in blood that the colours of his surcoat were all but lost.

Calesh longed to be in the fight, sharing the risks with the men he had led to this. It was madness really and he knew it, because only a fool *wanted* to be in the midst of such a screaming tumult as this. Someone like Elizur Mandein, who lived for killing and thought battle was all about personal glory. But it was useless to wish: Calesh knew he wouldn't last three seconds in a mêlée. He didn't think he could even stand for long under the weight of his green-copper armour.

"Husband," Farajalla said quietly.

He closed his eyes for a moment. She didn't say anything else, but she didn't have to. Farajalla could see it as well. *It's over.*

He opened his eyes to see his three friends moving towards him, all of them spattered and smeared with blood. In Raigal's case much of it was his own, and the big man winced as he walked, though he tried to cover it. Luthien and Baruch seemed to be unhurt, though there was a shadow in Luthien's eyes that Calesh hadn't seen before, and didn't like. Probably he was still grieving for his broken oath. Every blow he struck must feel like a betrayal of God.

The cordon of soldiers around Calesh and his wife parted as the three men came up to them. They stopped and looked at each other.

"We've lost," Baruch said, as blunt as ever. "We can draw this out for another half an hour, with luck, but then the gate will be taken."

Calesh looked towards the struggle. He started to draw a long breath, steadying himself before he spoke, and had to stop when the wound in his chest speared him with knives. "I know."

"Then we need to find a way out," Luthien said. "There's going to be a slaughter here, I'm afraid. Just as there was at Parrien."

He could say that it was their moral duty to stay and fight to the end, and die here if necessary. He even believed it, at least a little. But Calesh had seen too many battles, too many captured cities, to believe in such chivalry anymore. When the game was lost you saved what you could, and prepared for the day when things might be different. He couldn't see how they might be, not now, not here. But that didn't matter. You played the game to the end, theirs or yours, and never complained when the dice fell wrong.

"I should have cut Riyand out of command altogether," he said.

Raigal Tai raised his eyebrows. "There's nothing you can do about that now, and it's not like you to waste time on regret. Blood of the God, Calesh, don't go limp on us now."

He almost smiled. What stopped him was the echo of his earlier thought; *save what you can, and prepare for the day when things might be different.* Farajalla put her hand on his. She'd stayed close enough to touch him ever since they left the Manse, but she'd been spiky with anger at him and this was the first time she had done so. He did smile then. Just a little.

"Amand is waiting at the south gate with two thousand Armsmen," he said. He couldn't give his voice its usual crispness: there was too much slush in his chest for that. "We'll join him and head for the Raima Mountains. The rest, we'll decide as we go."

"You can decide it from a carriage," Farajalla said. "You're not fit to ride mountain roads. Or any roads, for long."

He shook his head. "There's no time to find one, and anyway, a carriage is too slow in the mountains. The All-Church would be on us in no time. No, Fara," he added when she tried to interrupt. "I agree with you; I'm too weak for this. But there's no choice." He glanced back at his friends. "Come on. We'll find horses for you on the way."

They had nothing to collect, no belongings they needed to fetch. Everything that mattered was already at Adour: the books of the Dualism, and Raigal's wife and son. Farajalla should be there too. Calesh willed himself not to look at her as he turned his horse with slow care. He wondered if they had all known defeat was inevitable, at the back of their minds, since the All-Church army had crossed the Riel more than a month ago. Perhaps that was why they could simply turn and ride away, leaving nothing behind to grieve over except the city itself, and the dreams that were falling with it.

As he finished turning an arrow struck him high on the left shoulder and skidded off his armour with a high-pitched whine. He hunched instinctively, then gasped as the movement brought the chill knives lancing out from his wound again. A glance back showed archers on the city wall, men in crimson coats with white crosses on the front. The Justified had showed themselves at last, and typically they chose to fight at one remove, while others hammered at each other in the morass below. Another man took aim as Calesh watched.

He went over before he could fire, shot through the throat by a man of Mayence on a rooftop. A moment later Luthien had slung his shield over his back and sprung up behind Calesh's saddle, using his own body to shelter the other man. "Time to start moving, don't you think?"

Behind them a horn blew, three quick blasts and then a pause before the tattoo was repeated. Calesh didn't have to look to know what it meant: Reis had reached the same dismal conclusion that they had, and was sounding the retreat. There was nowhere to retreat to, of course, no haven Mayence offered which might stop the All-Church soldiers once they were inside the walls. All it did was buy time, a few moments or hours before the end came. Reis must know that. He was conceding the city, and with it the war.

As they rode away the street curved slightly, and Calesh caught a brief glimpse of Guardsmen falling back onto Waggoner's Way. Companies of All-Church men made to follow them but were delayed by arrows from the roofs, which forced them to form shield walls before they advanced. It wouldn't be long. He saw a group of a dozen men push into the gatehouse, and a moment later could have sworn he heard a scream. Then a building moved across his view and he couldn't see any more.

He faced forward, telling himself to order his thoughts and forget what was done. It couldn't be changed. His task now was to rescue what he could, for whatever purpose it might serve. He had spent a lifetime thinking that way, moving on from an event as soon as it was done, treating victories and disasters just the same. The last fight never mattered when you were about to enter the next one. He knew that. He'd known it for years.

But there was a tightness in his chest that had nothing to do with the wound, and he couldn't seem to stop wishing he'd been able to fight, just to see if he could have made a difference.

Book Four

The Wolves

Behold, I send you forth as sheep in the midst of wolves.

Matthew 10:16

Eleven

The Desert Horn

"God is smiling down upon us," Sarul said. His voice
carried, even over the shouts and clamour of battle half a mile
away, and the tramp of thousands of feet. Men heard, and they
looked around. Some of them closed their eyes and murmured
prayers. He noticed that.

"God is smiling," he repeated. "You can feel it in the
sunshine on your face. You can see it in the ease with which
we have entered this city, just as we entered Parrien. We are
blessed, that He has chosen us to be the instruments of His
will in this cleansing."

They believed him. He could see that in their confident
smiles, the high colour of their skin. The soldiers were
Justified, of course, and Sarul had never really trusted that
gang of cutthroats and murderers, many of them as heathen as
the Madai they fought in the desert far away. But such men
could be brought to God, by long exposure to sermons and
parables while on campaign. And in the meantime they were
useful; yes, very useful at times.

Useful men tended to be dangerous. The All-Church
had realised as much not long after the Orders first formed, the
Justified with their assassins and the Glorified building a navy,
and both with growing companies of fighting men. In the face
of them the hierarchy of Coristos had worried they might be
overthrown, that the chiefs of the new armies would decide
they could hear the voice of God as well as any dried-up old
cleric in a palace. So they had founded the Basilicans, an
Order of the Church's own, to counter the threat. Two hundred
of those white-coated men stood in a ring around Sarul's tent,
being erected on a slight rise behind him. He would have
trusted no-one else to guard him.

He didn't trust them much either, in truth.

Trust was foolish. A century ago the All-Church had
trusted Sarténe, and allowed it to raise its own cadre of
soldiers as another bulwark against the two larger Orders.
Another way of reaching a balance, so the military leaders

worried about each other and had no time left to plot against the priests. It had made sense at the time, and in the years after seemed to be wisdom itself, as the Hand of the Lord excelled itself again and again.

It had all been lies. The Hand was worse than a serpent in the garden, because you could at least see the snake and know it for what it was. Instead the Hand had been like a scorpion among stones, unseen until its sting was felt. That had very nearly been the case. If it hadn't been for that fool of a priest getting himself murdered in the spring, the clergy of the All-Church might not have seen the disease in Sarténe in time, and then it might have spread too far to stop.

Sarul had wondered, in his darker moments, whether it had done so anyway. Amaury had been uncomfortably blunt about the difficulty of laying a long siege in this high, hilly country, where every field had been burned and all the livestock cleared. But they need not have worried. God was watching over His servants, and doors opened under their hands.

But it was a reminder of the need for vigilance, always. No country was pure, just as no man's heart was wholly free of sin. That was why priests were needed, after all. Why they always would be.

Amaury was off somewhere closer to the walls, doing whatever military things needed to be done. He was efficient, Sarul had to admit, but he didn't like the general's direct manner, or the sarcasm that sometimes insinuated itself into his words. He was both capable and unafraid of an Arch-Prelates authority, which to Sarul was a dangerous mix. Perhaps Amaury could be rewarded for his success here with a posting that removed that danger. Commanding attacks on mountains forts in Alinaur, or leading cavalry raids in Tura d'Madai. Not many men lived for long doing those tasks.

But that was for another day. Sarul watched another company of soldiers enter Mayence through the so-called Gate of Angels, his heart exulting within him. He looked up at the sky again, and lifting his voice he said again, "God is smiling down upon us."

*

The yard was full of men, some of them still helping one another to buckle on armour plates. A lot looked old, men who'd served their years in Alinaur or Tura d'Madai and then spent half a life at home, never thinking they would fight again. A lot more were too young to have gone on campaign at all. Their armour didn't always fit, and some men had no breastplate or mail at all, and no time to search through the storerooms in search of it.

But they were here, not fleeing for whatever refuge they could find. Perhaps they knew it didn't matter.

Ando had come to the Preceptory looking for a group with which to fight. For a short while after Riyand had been overwhelmed he'd felt as though he was choking, but that had passed; he hardly felt anything now. His arms and legs moved dreamily, barely connected to his body. Someone had caught his arm as he came in and Ando didn't feel it at all.

"What's it like outside?" the man asked. When Ando only looked blankly at him he gave the musician a shake. "Well?"

Ando knew the fellow from somewhere. Knew the scar on his neck, mostly: it wasn't the kind of thing you forgot. He frowned, worrying at it until the name came: Leutar. One of Baruch Caraman's friends in the Hand of the Lord, and a man who'd fought in the desert but was still in his prime. That made him unusual in this company.

"Bad," he said at length. "It's bad out there."

Leutar stared at him. "Did you take a blow to the head, or are you just simple? What's *happening?*"

"The All-Church has broken in," Ando told him. A dozen nearby men had stopped to listen, and he heard the hiss of their indrawn breath. "At the Gate of Angels. They're in the streets."

"We're done for," one of the listeners said in a horrified voice.

Ando nodded. "Yes."

"I see you mean to take one or two of them down with you though," Leutar said, with a nod to the sword Ando held. "It makes as much sense as anything. We can't run, that's for sure."

"We can try!" someone shouted. "We'd have a chance that way. If we stay to fight we have none!"

"That's true," someone said, from the door to the Preceptory.

Everyone turned. Ando wasn't sure why, afterwards; the voice wasn't loud, or particularly strong. But there was something, a tone of command maybe, that pulled men around to see Darien standing there, strangely striking with his white hair flowing over his neck. It was a moment before Ando realised the old man was wearing armour.

"If we fight, we will die," Darien said. "But others might live because of the courage we showed. Women, children perhaps. We men of the Hand of the Lord have always accepted the bargain we made: to act with honour, even at the cost of our lives."

He looked at them, the still men standing in the yard, and said, "I have not always been worthy of that ideal. Especially not these last years, when I've shamed my rank, and myself. I won't shame it today. I'm going to fight. I won't order any of you to follow me, though. Go, if you wish to. Find your families, and find safety of you can. Nobody will blame you."

There was a silence. Ando swallowed hard. Nobody moved for long seconds, and then a man near the gate unclipped his breastplate and let it fall with a clatter to the stone. He walked out without a word, or a look behind. Another man glanced shamefacedly around before he followed. And that was all: nobody else moved. Ando swallowed again.

"Thank you," Darien said gravely. His cheeks were red from drinking, but years of brandy had done that: he might be sober as an Elite now. "Thank you all. I don't deserve such loyalty."

"Yes, you do," Leutar replied. "You led fighting men in Tura d'Madai, and you led us here in Sarténe. We don't forget, Marshal."

"Thank you," Darien said again. The ends of his magnificent eyebrows twitched, as they always did when he was excited. It was the only sign he gave. "Shut and bar the gates. Bar the windows as well, even on the upper floors. We make our stand here."

"We're not going outside?" someone asked.

Darien shook his head. "In the streets we would be overwhelmed. Numbers count there. And in any case, the All-Church's military Orders will come to us here, as fast as they can. You all know how they hate the Hand of the Lord." He smiled thinly. "Almost as much as we hate them."

There was a ripple of laughter, and Leutar said, "Not a tenth as much as we hate them!"

Darien grinned, and then suddenly the smile was gone and he was the Marshal again. "The windows won't bar themselves! Get to it, and then stand guard at each window in pairs. Everyone else at the front and rear doors. Move!"

He had been a captain once, as Leutar said, a leader of warriors under the desert sun. It had become easy to forget that, in the ten years Darien had spent half-drowned in brandy. But it showed now, and men hurried to obey. The courtyard emptied quickly, to the sound of boots rattling up the stairs inside and the gates being swung shut.

Ando was only a few yards from Darien. He watched him for a moment and then said, "You sounded like Calesh just then."

"Once I *was* Calesh," the old man answered. "Twenty years before he even came to Tura d'Madai, I was what he would become. The proud captain of the Hand of the Lord, fighting heathens in a cause we never believed in, just to trick the All-Church." He shook his head. "Sometimes I think that pride is what undid me. I couldn't adapt, once I came home."

"A lot of men can't," Ando said.

Darien shrugged. "So? I was a Commander of the Hand. I was expected to do better. I expected it of myself." He began to turn away, and then paused. "Put that in a song, poet, if you like."

"Would you like that?"

"The aged Marshal, given a chance of redemption," Darien said. He smiled his thin smile again. "Yes, I'd like that."

He turned and went inside the Preceptory, leaving Ando standing alone in the courtyard. Latches were clattering closed all over the face of the building, as the soldiers shut it up as tightly as they could. Ando looked up the sheer stone façade and wondered how long they would last. Redemption was a fine thing, but this was a death trap.

And that was not for him. Ando had wanted to kill and be killed after Riyand was slain, but Darien had reminded him of what he was; a poet, and a singer. Not many like him would survive the wreck of Sarténe, but Ando had been at the heart of events here, and could tell tales nobody else knew. He wanted to, he realised. If he could somehow slip the net he would write the story of the fall of the Dualism, disguising it somehow so the Basilica didn't recognise it for what it was. He was good enough for that. He was sure of it.

A memory surfaced then, Calesh Saissan in an inn at Parrien: *you could improve those lyrics with an axe.* But that wasn't true. Ando had been spoken of as one of the finer talents in Mayence even before he'd met Riyand. It wasn't just the Margrave's patronage which had made him so well known. He'd written before Riyand and he could write now he was gone. And he would, because writing for him was a way to keep the darkness away, and with Sarténe (and Riyand) gone he'd need that more than ever.

He slipped through the big doors just before they closed. The street outside was already more crowded than it had been before, crammed with people pushing and jostling as they fought to get away from the encroaching army. The fact that there was nowhere to go didn't seem to matter. Panicked people simply fled, and left the *where* to chance, or to God. Most of them were heading for the bridge, and the domed Hall of Voices beyond it. Ando hesitated.

The All-Church's military Orders will come to us here, as fast as they can, Darien had said. They would go to all the centres of authority in Mayence, including the Manse, and also to the Hall of Voices. They would burn the flags and smash the bronze sculptures into shards, and it would be best to be as far from that as possible when it happened.

Grimacing, Ando turned against the flow of people and began to force his way forward, towards the west wall.

*

Market Road was thronged with panicked people, all fleeing to God knew where. Men carried baskets and crates with the sleeves of shirts hanging out, or bags stuffed so full it seemed their seams must split. Women everywhere had their arms wrapped around children, holding them in a grip tight enough to choke. All of them were roaring and bellowing, all trying to push their way out of Mayence before the hammer fell. Calesh saw one mother with a babe in the crook of one elbow and two older boys folded in her other arm, all of them being pushed back and forth by the heaving of the mob. She stumbled into a man with a crate on his head and the fellow went down, breaking the crate so china was strewn everywhere, smashing on the stones. His mouth opened in a cry of dismay Calesh couldn't hear.

"We're going to shove through," Baruch said to the soldiers. "Keep the circle tight; Marshal Saissan is in no condition to be barged around. And don't stop. Not for anything."

"These are our people," Luthien said.

"And there's nothing we can do to help them," Baruch replied. "Not anymore. We've done all we can."

They had, but it wasn't enough. Mayence was going to fall. It already *was* falling, as the chaos in the street showed. Calesh could hear a rising tide of noise from behind too, as All-Church soldiers forced their way deeper into the city. He didn't look around.

In truth he wasn't sure he could, given the soreness in his chest and back. Though *soreness* wasn't really the word. He was in quite a bit of pain now, and he didn't even try to protest at Baruch's assertion that he should be protected from the jostling crowd. The best he could do was hang onto the saddle and hope like hell that Fara didn't notice how bad he was.

She reined her horse close to his as the party started forwards. That was normal enough, but he didn't like the concern in her eyes as she studied him, and not just because it meant she'd noticed already. It wasn't good for the men to know he was struggling either. A captain had to be strong, so tough that the soldiers he led exchanged stories of his silence when in pain and his steady courage when in battle. Now, more than ever, he had to show that strength. He shook his head slightly when Fara opened her mouth, and for a wonder she hesitated and then, shaking her black braids, closed it again without speaking.

And reined her horse still closer, watching him keenly from the tail of her eye as they rode.

"Can you handle a trot?" Baruch asked then, from his other side. He spoke in an undertone, but still, Calesh gave him a thin frown.

"Of course I can," he said. His voice was still no more than a papery whisper, rasping in his throat.

Baruch simply nodded. "At the trot!"

They moved onto Market Road. Raigal Tai cantered forward to take a position at the front of the group, a massive man on an even huger horse acting as the point of the arrowhead. Townsfolk heard the clatter of hooves and looked around, their faces suddenly white with fear. Some of that terror receded when they saw the black and white of the Hand of the Lord, but it probably shouldn't have done. The Hand men were riding away from the fighting, and that could only mean one thing. Calesh thought he saw realisation of that dawn in a few expressions before the horsemen shoved into the throng.

People were pushed aside, tumbling into one another with sudden screams of dismay and surprise. The men of the Hand were their own sons and brothers, people who had been born in Sarténe or even here in Mayence itself: they weren't supposed to behave like this. Certainly not when enemies were already in the city. Even with bodies strewn in the street behind the cavalry the citizens ahead still stood and watched riders approach, without any attempt to get out of the way. They probably wouldn't have been able to, given the thickness of the crowd, but they could have tried. Some of them were vacant-eyed, men and women who had already given up hope, and had given themselves over to whatever horror might be visited upon them. Even by their own soldiers.

Save what you can, Calesh thought. He clung to it as a woman tried to grab his stirrup, missed, and was knocked over on her back as Baruch's horse came thrusting up alongside.

Save what you can, and prepare for the day when things might be different. If they ever are.

He stopped noticing much after that, because the pain in his chest was biting deeper every time his horse's hooves struck the stone of the road. He couldn't hide it anymore. It was all he could do to stay mounted, and he hunched over and gripped as hard as he could with his knees, willing himself not to black out. There was no time for that. He was aware of Farajalla speaking to him, but the words were distant and he wasn't sure what she said.

"Help us!" someone shouted, very close by, and Calesh stirred a little. "You're the Hand of the Lord. Help us!"

Luthien angled his horse over and let it barge into the speaker, a swarthy man whose skin was parchment white under several days of stubble. He staggered backwards, tripped over something and fell on his back in the middle of the heaving throng. Someone trod on him an instant later and then the crowd closed over him, before he had any chance to get up. Calesh grimaced and looked away. He felt sick now, and not just because of the wound.

They were slowing down. He took a careful breath and sat up a little, trying to see up the street to where Amand should be waiting with more of the Hand. It was no good though. He couldn't sit straight enough, and in any case there was a wagon not far ahead, piled with crates and cases in crazy teeter-totter stacks. It blocked his sight, and must be why the riders couldn't maintain their steady trot as well. The crowds around the wagon were thicker than ever, people crushed together like starlings on an autumn branch, without the space to twitch a wing.

Baruch was cursing, and ahead of them all Raigal Tai had begun to swear in the northern way, just as he had when the four of them first met. A man grabbed at his leg and Raigal hit him with his shield, a casual backhand blow that lifted the man off his feet and hurled him away. He took half a dozen others down with him when he fell, and the mob poured over them at once, forced into the space by the press of bodies all around.

"The devil take this," Farajalla muttered suddenly. She leaned over and reached down to Calesh's belt. Fuzzily he

148

wondered what she was doing, and then he saw her hand come away with the ivory horn of Cammar a Amalik, which he'd won on a desert field long ago. She put it to her lips and blew.

The sound was high and clear, a note meant to carry over the crash and thunder of battle. It carried over the shouting mob just as easily and for a moment the street went quiet, heads turning to look for the source of the call. Then the yells began again, and the cries of those crushed in the morass. The riders had all but stopped moving now.

"Well," Luthien said, "that's torn it. All-Church soldiers will have heard that horn, and they'll come to see what it was."

"What would you have me do?" Farajalla demanded. "We're stuck here. If we don't do something we'll still be sitting our saddles in the middle of the street when the Justified come to kill us."

He sighed. "I know, lady. Forgive me."

"Blowing the horn doesn't move us another yard," Raigal called back from the front of the group. The arrowhead had become a circle now, blunted by the pressure of the crowd. "We can't clear - get *off!*" he snapped, as a man caught his arm and tried to pull him from the saddle. With Raigal that was like trying to lift a house with one hand. He punched the fellow in the head and he collapsed like a sack of wet laundry. "We can't clear the street. There aren't enough of us."

"No," Farajalla said. There was a thread of relief in her voice that made Calesh lift his head as she pointed up the street. "But there are of them."

He looked.

Riders in black and white were forcing their way past the wagon on both sides, driving the throng back. One of the piles of crates wobbled and then toppled over. The townsfolk roared as dozens of horsemen rammed into them, opening a space in the middle of Market Road. Somewhere to Calesh's right he heard glass break as a window cracked under the weight of bodies; a moment later a door splintered closer to hand, letting people pour into someone's house like a rising autumn flood.

It wasn't enough. There were too many people and not enough space, and the arrival of a hundred Hand cavalrymen only made things worse. People crushed too tightly together began to cry out in pain and then desperation, as air was driven from their lungs. Calesh closed his eyes so he didn't have to look. He wasn't sure how much of the pain in his chest was from the wound, and how much from horror at what was happening to Mayence. To the people he had come home from the desert to save, if he could.

All lost now, whatever he did. Lost because of the rashness of a fool, and Calesh's failure to deal with him when he could have done. That thought might choke him if he dwelt on it for long.

"If I bring forth what is within me," he quoted, reaching for some kind of salvation, "what I have will save me." He couldn't remember what the words meant, but they were important. He was sure they were.

Farajalla put her hand over his.

Then the Hand riders had reached them, pushing the crowd back on either side to create a space lined with a double rank of horses. It swayed even so, bending under the sheer numbers of townsfolk pinned behind it, still calling and gasping as they struggled. Among the soldiers came another person, this one a woman, sitting astride a horse in the male fashion. Calesh frowned at her for a few seconds before he remembered who she was.

"I suggest you come quickly," said Elisande. Her golden hair seemed to glow too brightly for the day. "Your man Amand has secured the gate, and the road outside is clear, but it might not stay that way."

They moved forward without further words, riding into the open place won by Amand's men. As they went the four friends moved together again, forming a rough triangle with Calesh and Farajalla in the middle. They did it unconsciously, out of habit and friendship and trust. *Giant, wise man, soldier, king,* Calesh remembered muzzily. Ailiss had said that, a long time ago. He wasn't sure it was true, or what it meant if it was.

Thought faded, becoming little more than an awareness of pain, and dimly of movement. He didn't notice when they rode under the south gate and left Mayence for the last time.

Twelve

Brief Respite

There had been a time, long ago now, when Reis and the old Margrave used to share a bottle of wine on the terrace overlooking the city, at the end of a working day. It had been an occasional pleasure, something done when time and mood allowed: once a month, perhaps, or a little more in the summer. The air was clear so high up, even above the streets and markets, and when the wind blew from east or west Reis had been able to smell the sea. From the south, the sharp hint of mountain snow; from the north, or on still days, the air was redolent with the scent of oranges. Especially in the summer.

"Watch over him," Jérome had said. It was an autumn night, with the first shivers of cold in the air over Sarténe. Earlier in the year there had been plague, as sometimes happened when the weather warmed and diseases burst back into life again. Jérome's eldest son had died. The Margrave bore new lines now, etched deep into a face paler and more gaunt than the one Reis knew, and had loved.

"I will," he'd replied. There was no need to ask who Jérome meant. Both men knew.

"You're the only one who can," the old man said. He swirled wine in his glass, staring down at it. "Cavel would be willing, but he's almost as aged as I am, and he works harder than a merchant's mule. He won't be able to guide Riyand for long. It has to be you."

He had nodded, though Jérome still wasn't looking at him. It didn't usually matter and didn't now: they knew one another very well, after most of a life spent working side by side. Jérome running the city, and keeping the All-Church at bay with deceit and misdirection, whenever their priests came sniffing for reasons why the collection plates were empty and the pews unused. Reis running the Guard, in case deceit failed. It never had, while Jérome was Margrave. The man was as sly as twelve foxes.

"Riyand is a good son," Jérome said quietly. He didn't lift his eyes from contemplation of his wine. "A good son, and a gentle soul. But Sarténe today isn't a place for a gentle soul. Certainly not in the High Seat of the Manse. He won't make a good Margrave."

Reis said nothing.

"We can offset some of that by finding him a clever wife," Jérome went on. "Strong, too, so she asserts herself here. I've already asked Cavel to start looking, though I don't hold out much hope. One noble's daughter in twenty learns to be clever, and no more than one in ten to be strong." He shook his head. "Mostly the load will fall on you, my friend."

He nodded again and this time Jérome did look around, one of those new lines forming a crease between his eyes.

"Am I being unfair to you?" he asked, and then answered himself before Reis could speak. "Perhaps I am. But there's no one else, and so I have no choice. I'm sorry for it. If that helps."

"Being sorry always helps," Reis had said. "But you've nothing to be sorry for. None of this is of your making. And if you're being unfair, it doesn't matter. Did you think I would watch your son fall on his face, and do nothing?"

Jérome had smiled a little, but the grief behind his eyes didn't lessen. "Thank you for that."

Simple words, simply spoken. There was rarely any need for more, between two men who had been allies and comrades through so many years. But Reis had known, watching the man he knew grow old from sorrow for his lost son, that those years were drawing to an end, as all things ended. He knew as well that the years which followed would have less pleasure, fewer moments of ease shared with a trusted friend.

The Adversary was always working, always trying to turn the hearts of men and women from light towards the dark. It was just a truth of the world, whichever god you believed in. Black sat alongside white, as on the banners and shields of the Hand of the Lord. Sometimes white was stronger, and you laughed or sang; when black rose in power, all you could do was step carefully and wait for the balance to change.

Reis knew how to be wary. He thought it would be enough.

It hadn't been enough. Men were piling furniture against the barred doors of the portico, buttressing them against the inevitable assault of the All-Church's soldiers. Bangs and hammering came from all around, as other men slammed shutters across windows and nailed them in place. That wouldn't be enough either. It was going to end, all of it, here in the Manse.

A dozen Guardsmen lurched past, all carrying a table from the kitchen, one of the solid oak monsters on which the cooks chopped and sliced and where they arranged the dishes before sending them out to the dining hall. The board of the table was a good two inches thick. The men set it down and then began trying to tip it on end, so it would rest against a set of wide window shutters and hold them closed. Reis opened his mouth to tell them not to waste their time, then stopped himself. It was as good a use of time as any. Who knew, it might even buy the defenders another moment, before the butchery began. A moment was all a man needed to speak his last prayers to God.

Reis didn't feel like praying. There was a makeshift barricade behind him, where the portico fed into a wide corridor running to the reception hall beyond. He thought he would go to God there, if he could manage it, and let his sword speak his last words for him.

He could hear city folk shouting outside, a roar of sound that he felt through his boots. People were fleeing with no idea where to go, so that tides of citizens flowed every which way and sometimes crashed into each other, clogging whole streets with a press of struggling bodies. Reis had seen that, as he rallied the soldiers he could find and led them up the steps of the Manse. When the invading soldiers found them there would be a slaughter, as there had been in Parrien. As there would be all across Sarténe, now. There was nobody left to prevent it. The land would burn from mountains to sea, and whatever the Dualism might have become would wither in the fire.

A young man rushed up to him and saluted, right fist to left shoulder, but so sloppily that Reis was sure he'd never done it before. "General, sir! There are enemy soldiers in the garden."

"I expect there are," Reis said. He studied the youth for a moment. There was a sword on his hip, but Reis would bet it had been taken from a fallen trooper. "You're not a Guardsman, are you?"

"No," the man admitted. "I'm a butcher. But blood and innards don't bother me, and I can fight, sir!"

"Blood and innards bother me," Reis said mildly. "Although I don't think they will for much longer. If you're not a soldier then why are you here, when you don't have to be?"

That was met with a disbelieving stare. "I'm a Believer, sir. I've followed the Elite and the God all of my life. I won't abandon my faith because it's convenient. Besides," he added, almost as an afterthought, "my sister was in Parrien. Her two boys, as well."

Heaven help us, we're all insane, Reis thought, *we Believers just as much as the All-Church Faithful. So certain we're right that we'll die for it, and from there it's not such a large step to killing for it, the way the All-Church does. Would we have been any better, given time?*

He didn't think any of that showed in his expression, perhaps because he understood. The youth was going to stand and die for his sister as much as for God. "What's your name, lad?"

"Guillaume," the other replied.

Reis nodded. "Well, Guillaume, it's good to have you with us. Keep an eye on the soldiers in the garden and report back when they break into the building, all right?"

"Sir!" Guillaume retorted, but he didn't move at first. "Sir... wouldn't it be better to defend the upstairs? They couldn't get at us so easily there."

"They wouldn't need to," Reis said. "They'd pile timber at the foot of the stairs and set it alight, and wait for smoke and flame to do their work for them. Go on, lad. Watch the back for me."

This time Guillaume darted away, the unfamiliar sword rattling on his hip as he went. He was hardly out of sight when there was a hollow boom and the main doors shuddered, dislodging a divan that had been flung on the pile of furniture serving as a buttress. It tumbled to the floor with a thump, just as the doors boomed again. Shutters to one side rattled as they were tried from outside.

"It will start now," a voice said behind Reis. "There were archers on two rooftops across the street, but they're dead now. The Justified found a way up and cleared them away."

He turned to find Cavel standing there, leaning on a sword and smiling thinly. Reis blinked in surprise. "I thought you'd fled."

"To where?" the old seneschal asked. "There are no havens anymore, my friend. This is the last."

"Even so," Reis said. He didn't know what he could add to that though, and stopped before he made a fool of himself. Something heavy hit the doors on the far side and two chairs broke free of the pile and fell with twin clatters on the tiles.

"By the way," Cavel said after a moment, "the Preceptory is on fire. I saw it from an upstairs window, before your men closed the shutters. There are a lot of All-Church men in the streets there though. I think some of the Hand must still be fighting, even with the fire."

Reis felt his lips twist. "They won't be for long."

"No," Cavel agreed. "Not for long. But then neither will we, here."

A set of shutters cracked under a blow, from a hammer or heavy club of some sort, Reis thought. A Guardsman in blood and gold stabbed his pike through the hole and someone outside cursed, but that wasn't going to work for long. As soon as enough ingresses had been created the All-Church men would let their archers come forward, and clear the defenders without coming close to them. Reis couldn't answer that: he had too few bowmen, and hardly any arrows. He'd have to order his men back behind the barricade of tables, and wait for the assault.

"Tell me," Cavel said. "Did you think it would come to this? When the priest was killed by the river, I mean. Did you think it meant the end of Sarténe, and all we tried to build here?"

He looked at the old man for a moment. Cavel had been Jérome's friend even before Reis, working with him at least as closely. If the Margrave had been as sly as twelve foxes then his seneschal had the quick mind of a lizard, and was slipperier than a whole convention of priests. The All-Church had known for decades that there was heresy in Sartène, as they called it, but they'd never known quite where or how widespread. Jérome and Cavel had kept them looking in the wrong places. It was only when Riyand came to the High Seat, with his predilections and his monumental stupidity, that things went wrong.

"Yes," he said quietly. The doors boomed again, and the one on the left cracked near the middle under the impact of the unseen ram. "I thought that if you couldn't negotiate a way out of it, then the All-Church would attack, and that would be the end of us."

"And when the Hand of the Lord came home?"

"The same," he answered. "It was brave of Calesh, and he's a gifted captain. Better than I am. But they were never going to be enough. I think Calesh knew that himself, in truth."

"So do I. He brought the Hand home knowing it." Cavel moved to stand beside Reis and leaned on his sword again. "And I thought the same, by the way. That Sartène was doomed from the day the priest was murdered."

"Great minds think alike," Reis murmured. Three windows had broken shutters now, and more were shuddering under repeated blows. A chorus of shouts beyond the main doors preceded another ringing boom, and the heap of furniture was pushed back a few inches. It wouldn't be long now.

"And fools never differ," Cavel agreed. He should have looked ridiculous, a skinny old man with a sword too big and heavy for him to handle properly, but he didn't. There was a dignity about his calmness which made it impossible to think of him so. "By the way, when I was upstairs I saw a large number of the Hand by the south gate. I think they might slip out. All-Church companies haven't cut the road to the mountains yet."

156

"Let's hope they do," Reis said. Perhaps it wouldn't all end here in the Manse after all, then. He couldn't honestly see what a few hundred men could do against the All-Church, with no means of support and nowhere to run, but strange things happened in war. If the Hand could reach Alinaur they might be able to hide in the high sierras, or take a mountain fortress and hold out there for years. He didn't think it was likely. But then, fooling the All-Church for all those years hadn't been likely either, yet Jérome and Cavel had managed it. Perhaps this wasn't the last haven of the Dualism after all.

"Let's hope they do," he repeated. He raised his voice. "There's no point defending the door and windows anymore. Get back to the barricade. We'll make our stand here."

Most of the soldiers obeyed at once, but some hesitated and looked back at him in surprise. Those would be the rookies, Reis thought, or else men who'd seized a sword today for the first time in their lives. One paid for the delay: a spear came through a hole torn in a shutter and took him in the throat before he even knew there was danger. That brought the others scurrying hastily to the overturned tables, shields held behind them to ward against arrows that never came.

Soldiers did though. With no one to defend them the apertures were quickly overrun, the shutters torn aside or simply smashed. It was a motley crew who crowded inside, Glorified and Justified mixed in with Shavelings, and as many men again who wore no badge Reis recognised and must belong to mercenary companies, here to make a profit from the agony of Mayence. A dozen or so bore a red rose as an emblem on their chests, which Reis thought was idiocy because blood would obscure that in the first moments of a battle, and after that they wouldn't know who was friend and who was foe.

At any rate, the intruders were a disjointed mess, and if Reis had had any archers they could have cut down scores in the first minute. But he didn't, so he just formed his men into a triple line across the corridor, putting Guardsmen with large kite-shaped shields in the front rank. The All-Church troops saw them and began to jeer at once, shouting that they were going to burn in torment for their heresy and their crimes. One or two of the inexperienced defenders went white, but none of them left their places.

"I wish we had an Elite," Cavel said.

Reis nodded. He did too, but one couldn't come now. "I must go to the front, Cavel. May God walk with you."

"And with you," the seneschal replied. "He won't walk with us long. But for every song of joy there must be a song of sorrow, must there not?"

"So I'm told," Reis said. He supposed he and Cavel had had their years of joy. For them this ending was cruel, but they had years of happiness to set against it. There were men in the ranks across the corridor who were little more than boys, like young Guillaume, with hardly any of their lives lived. For them there were no wives and never would be, no children, no memories of pleasant evenings on the terrace with wine, and the scent of oranges. His heart grieved for them, and there was no time to sorrow for it.

He shouldered his way to the front of the line. He'd never cared to general from the rear, though there were times when it was necessary. It wasn't now, with everything lost. The All-Church men saw him and let out yells of delight and contempt. They were forming proper companies now, he saw, men of each Order gathering together in semi-organised clumps.

In the moments before the charge came there was a sudden outbreak of noise from the back of the Manse, towards the gardens. Crashing steel and shouts echoed up the passage, magnified by the stone. Reis knew what it meant; the attackers had breached the wall, and for some reason Guillaume hadn't come to let him know. Probably the youth was dead.

There was no time to sorrow for that, either. A regiment of mercenaries to the left suddenly hurled themselves at the defenders, perhaps energised by the clamour deeper in the building.

Half a dozen men went down on each side almost at once, driven onto enemy swords and spears by the jostling crush behind. Reis was nearly one of them. He was twisting to avoid a lunging spear when someone bumped him from behind, very nearly pushing him back into danger. The iron point plucked at the fabric of his tabard and then slid past, and

Reis killed the spearman with a quick thrust to the throat. He fell forwards over the table, hanging there with his head on one side and his feet on the other.

Reis killed a second man, then a third, this one a rat-like little man with a beard that wasn't much more than stubble. By then he was well back in the corridor. The defenders had been pushed back by weight of numbers, though they'd killed more men than they'd lost. That wasn't going to matter. Reis ducked a wild sword sweep, the blow of an untutored idiot playing at hero, and killed the idiot with little more than a flick of his wrist. It opened a red line across the man's throat and he staggered back, choking horribly as he gasped for air before his own people pushed him over and trampled over him.

Cavel lunged past Reis, his shirt flapping absurdly on his thin frame. He held his sword out in front of himself, straight-armed, and took an oncoming Justified in the groin. The soldier gave a strangled yelp and went down all on his own, to be trampled as well. A second Justified, an officer, leaned casually over and thrust his sword through Cavel's throat and out the back of his neck. There was a great spray of blood and Cavel fell.

Reis hardly felt grief for his friend. There had been too much to sorrow for today, too many pains to deal with. The heart could only take so much before it went numb, and stopped feeling anything anymore. He engaged the Justified captain; there were a lot of the white-coated men in the struggle now, but they might break off if their leader was killed. Justified often did, they were known for it. Reis had never fought them before, nor been part of the same army, but stories got around and a good captain always listened.

Calesh Saissan would know that, he thought. Bones in his wrists ground under the impact of the other man's blade on his own. The man was strong, driving Reis back by the sheer force of his blows. *Escape if you can, my young friend. For the Dualism, and for yourself. There may be songs of sorrow sometimes, but there can always be another song of joy.*

The captain pushed forward again, shield held before him like a weapon, a ram to batter Reis and wear him down.

He angled his own shield, so the other man's deflected off it and his momentum brought him stumbling a step forward. Reis killed him with a chopping blow to the back of the neck that cut through the mail coif and almost severed his head. Blood sprayed across his legs as the man collapsed.

He looked up to find only a handful of Guardsmen still fighting. The corridor was full of Justified, several of them converging on where he stood by the wall. Reis realised suddenly where he was and knew, without looking around, that behind him was the mural of Calesh killing Cammar a Amalik at the battle of Gidren Field. It made him smile, strangely.

"There are worse places to die," he said aloud, and then the Justified were upon him.

*

Someone had smashed the staircase, blocking access to the roof where thirty people had taken refuge. It would delay the All-Church soldiers for a time. Not for long.

Below, corpses were scattered across Market Road like spilled refuse. Men, women, children; it didn't make any difference. The invading troops had cut them down as they fled, or as they tried to fight, using broom handles or kitchen knives to fend off trained fighting men. Chance had favoured them, now and then, and uniforms were dotted among the dead: the white of Basilicans, the crimson cross of the Justified, and the grey cloaks of Glorified. They were all here, the Orders of the All-Church, here ravening among the slain.

But Ilenia could see fewer than ten dead soldiers. All the rest were civilians, people of Mayence. Sometimes women had been spared, and gangs of soldiers had dragged them into buildings, already tearing at their clothes as they went. Once they'd thrown a girl of about fourteen down on a man's dead body, right there in the street, until a man on the next roof fired arrows down and killed two of them. The archer had been shot himself a little later, but the soldiers dragged their victims out of sight after that anyway. Ilenia had heard their screams. She thought she'd hear them in her old age, if she managed to survive this.

Although she knew, really, that she wasn't going to.

"Do you think she got out?" the man next to her asked, for perhaps the tenth time. His expression was wrenching, the mouth slack and the eyes too wide, with horror lurking in their depths. "My Anaïs?"

"I'm sure she did," Ilenia answered, also for the tenth time. Numb lips made the words feel strange, or perhaps that was because they were a lie.

She had been perhaps one minute too late. When she came within sight of the south gate it was to see the Hand withdrawing towards it, a cordon receding down the street with a small knot of people inside it. Ilenia was too far away to make out details but she saw that one of the group was black, which made her Farajalla and meant Calesh and his friends must be nearby. They were a hundred, maybe a hundred and twenty yards from her.

They might as well have been in Tura d'Madai, or the Distant Isles across the ocean.

Ilenia had known they wouldn't hear if she shouted. The noise in Market Road was too great, a constant bellow of sound that had physical force, so she was sure she could feel her eardrums vibrating with the strength of it. She'd dug her spurs in and urged her mare forward, trying to close the gap and telling herself there was hope, there was a chance, even if it needed one of the party to look back and see her. Apart from the Hand themselves she was the only person in sight on horseback. If they looked, they would see her.

Nobody looked back, and as the Hand drained towards the gate she abandoned the horse. It was worse than useless in the crush, too large to squeeze through gaps but not large enough to force a path through, not alone. Ilenia had what she needed, jewellery for the most part, stuffed into pockets and a small hip bag that she wore under her coat, so as to avoid the eyes of cutpurses. If there were any about, or plying their trade if there were, and if so she had a knife tucked into the back of her belt. At any rate, she didn't need the horse. She left it and hurried ahead on foot.

But that was no better. The crowd was simply too thick, the people within it too desperate and afraid. They pushed blindly at one another, sometimes one way and sometimes another, like currents in a mad tidal swirl. When one person changed direction others followed suit at once, and suddenly there was a stampede in a random direction that caught up anyone nearby and swept them along. Then someone else would move away and the surge would flow back. It took a bare minute for Ilenia to lose track of where she was. It was less than that before she knew she wasn't going to escape.

Once the throng parted slightly, a momentary gap opening right in front of her, and she could see the south gate again. The Hand had vanished by then. Instead citizens clogged the gate, all struggling to get through the narrow tunnel under the wall. And then - she saw it happen - they were suddenly struggling to get back *inside,* and she knew in an instant that the All-Church must be outside the gate, and the road had been cut.

She started looking for a refuge then, but escape from the throbbing mass of people was impossible. The best she'd been able to do was to reach this building, a squat block of apartments three stories high with a wooden staircase running up an outside wall. There was a ragged canvas shelter in one corner, against the low wall, with a few meagre possessions inside. Some poor, dispossessed soul had been calling this rooftop home. Ilenia wondered if his closeness to the gate had meant he slipped out in time.

"Anaïs," the man next to her said. "My wife. Do you think she was able to get out?"

No, she didn't think so. She didn't think anyone would escape, not for more than a few days. The hills around Mayence would be crawling with All-Church men within days, if they weren't already. The only people with half a chance were the Hand of the Lord. Ilenia hoped they'd made it. There was no chance for the Dualism at all if they hadn't.

"I think so," she said.

They didn't know who she was, the people on this roof. She'd chosen simple riding clothes when she left, and taken a plain but sturdy mare, the kind of animal that was better at bearing foals than running races. Not the sort of mount Riyand would have chosen at all. Ilenia was surprised to feel a stab of sympathy for him with the thought. He was a fool - had been a fool - and no kind of lord at all, but still, he'd been her husband.

Not her lover though, except for a few fumbling efforts when Riyand had tried to do his duty, however distasteful he found it. She'd had to wait for that until Luthien came to her, with blood on his green robe, to say that his oath was broken. Ilenia had been privately, selfishly glad of that. She still was. She understood how the man beside her felt, with his need to believe that his wife had escaped, and was safe. Come to that, she supposed she was better off than he was. She'd seen Farajalla inside that Hand cordon, and if she was there then Calesh Saissan must have been, and almost certainly Luthien as well. He must have got out. Ilenia was sure of it.

She wished she could have seen him again. Escaped with him, even, and gone to live on a farm somewhere, or in a small house in a far-off city where they would live as artisans, unknown and unremarked. She would have been happy living such a life with him. Nearly a decade married to Riyand had taught her that wealth and comfort made very little difference if you were unhappy, but if you were in love then nothing mattered at all. Palaces and hovels were all the same then. She knew she might be being romantic, but it was a pleasant thought, and romantic or not she *did* believe it.

There were crashes from below now, inside the building. Soldiers must have found a way in, and were now trying to smash through the roof. It wouldn't take them long. She thought of the raped women again, some of them pleading, the rest shrieking as they were dragged away.

She took the knife out of her belt and looked at it. Someone had given it to her as a present, when she first came to Mayence to be married to Riyand. It wasn't the sort of gift a lady would be given anywhere else, but this was Sarténe, and things were done differently here. She couldn't remember who the present had been from, now. But she'd kept the knife, a slender thing with an inlaid wooden handle and narrow blade, as a reminder of happier times. She had thought she would be happy, when she first arrived at this city.

She *had* been happy, in fact, but only in the last days, and only with Luthien. There'd been nothing else. An empty life, a wasted decade, except for the brief respite of love. She prayed that Luthien had escaped. If any man deserved happiness it was him.

The man beside her had turned slightly, his eyes on the knife in her hand. He still bore that shocked look, as though his brain hadn't quite caught up with what had happened.

"Anaïs won't have escaped," he said. "Will she?"

Ilenia looked at him and shook her head slowly. Something in him seemed to crumple. She unsheathed the knife and slid it between her ribs, into the heart. There was no pain, just a peculiar coldness that felt strange next to the wet warmth of blood over her hands. There were still crashing sounds from below, mixed now with shouts of triumph, and then there was nothing at all.

Thirteen

Easing Hurts

Calesh wasn't going to be able to go on. By the time the column of Hand riders had crossed the plain south of Mayence and reached the first hills, two miles away, he was hunched over so far that his chin rested on his chest. He'd had to put both hands on the saddlebow to stop himself swaying. Farajalla was already riding as close to his side as she could, and she saw it plainly.

"Don't steady him unless he's about to fall," Luthien said. The small man had braced Calesh on the other side. "The men don't need to see that."

"Do they need to see him sickly and weak?" she retorted. "Brittle like old glass? With that wound, a fall might kill him."

"Then we won't let him fall." Luthien pushed his glasses up his nose. "But for now, let him ride. The horse will keep going, even if Calesh sleeps."

There was something strange about his tone, a tightness Farajalla hadn't heard in his speech before. She was clever, not as much as Luthien was, but enough to notice such things. His expression might be calm, his words serene, but underneath he was in pain, probably grieving for the fate of his city. Well, there would be a good deal of that among these men, and more grief to come as well, once the All-Church began to follow.

They *would* follow, of course. Farajalla had no doubt of that. Several companies had already been sweeping around to block the south road when the Hand of the Lord rode down it; another hour, of half as long, and they might have surrounded Mayence completely. But the pits and traps Calesh had ordered dug had delayed them just enough. As the Hand slipped past Farajalla had seen All-Church scouts ahead of the regiments, poking the ground with pikes as they inched forward. The infantry had seen the Hand as well, sending up a chorus of shouts and blown horns to warn others of their escape. Word of it would be running through the attacking army already. There was not much time.

Ailiss rode with Gaudin at her side, as he always was. Just behind them Amand and Baruch made another pair, neither of them talking. Behind Farajalla came Raigal Tai and Elisande, he on a truly huge horse and she on a small palomino, its coat as golden as her hair. That was it. Nobody else had made it out of Mayence; not the other officers of the Hand, not Reis or Ando Gliss, and not even Cavel the seneschal. She thought he might have got away, in fact; he was such a shrewd man that it was hard to see how he couldn't. Perhaps some of the others had made it out, too. But if so they'd taken other roads. For now all that remained was this little band, nine people out of everyone she'd come to know in her short time in Sarténe.

"Do you remember Elorium at all?" she asked Luthien.

He looked at her across Calesh's slumped form. "I remember it well. I think of it every day."

"We used to have a small apartment near the fruit market," she said. "Calesh and I, that is. It had a terrace on the south side, what they call a solarium, where the sun always fell."

"Do you miss it?"

That had been their first home together, after they were married. Their only home, until the message came from the Basilica and Calesh called the Hand of the Lord to the ports. It had been part of the Hand's Preceptory in Elorium, a medium-sized apartment on the third floor, above the map halls and conference rooms, and the stables below them. Farajalla hadn't cared about that. There were always two guards in the corridor outside the apartment, where the Order took precedence, but on this side of the door it was her home.

She'd loved the parlour, where they received friends who came to visit. They had a considerable number of friends. Gulusa who ran the fruit market, and his wife Tudert, always ready to share a piece of gossip she'd heard earlier in the day. She had taken a shine to Farajalla, and several times invited her out to a wine shop or clothier's, showing her the city. Yattay had visited, the cobbler trusted by the Hand to make their boots and as such an important man. Farajalla never saw his wife - some Madai believed women should not be part of social visits - but Yattay often arrived with two or three of his children bubbling around his knees, and for an hour the little flat would be filled with laughter and games. Once Vadalin had come, the cobbler Farajalla remembered from Harenc, bringing a rare tinge of homesickness that hadn't left her for days.

Diolus Syra had appeared every month or so. He shouldn't have been a friend, really. As Warden of Elorium for the new western king it was his job to co-ordinate the four military Orders, with each other and with the forces of the King; he ought to have been impartial, even a little distant. But he was a cheerful, garrulous man Farajalla had found it impossible to dislike, even after she heard rumours about his liking for boys in the bedroom. She'd never encountered a homosexual before, at least knowingly. It hadn't made any difference; Diolus was pleasant, witty, and fearsomely good at his job. She wished they could have told him the Hand was leaving, before they left for the coast.

But before that there was talk and laughter in the parlour, and relaxation in a tiled bathroom with its own piping, a luxury she had never dreamed she might enjoy. She'd bathed every day, luxuriating in soap and warm water, and the oils she bought at various stalls in scattered markets, tiny vials that filled the room with heady scents. There had been love in the main bedroom, sometimes fierce and sometimes languid, and sleep with Calesh breathing softly beside her. And there was a second bedroom, waiting for the child they both yearned to have, Calesh with an unspoken desperation that had frightened her a little before he told her about his lost brother, and she began to understand.

There had been the solarium, oranges eaten in evening sunshine, the air rich with the scent of dates and hot desert sand. Calesh beside her again, sometimes for a whole evening when work allowed, and time slowed so much it seemed the days would never fade.

"Yes," she said. Luthien was still looking at her, waiting for a reply. "I still miss it."

"You've only seen Sarténe in war," he told her. "I wish you could have seen it before this happened. In Elorium you can feel the age of the city, its history, like a weight in the air. It's rich with experience. But Mayence was rich through opportunity, the sense of what it might become, in time." He started to look back and then visibly checked himself, facing forward again. "You would have been happy here. I'm sure of it."

"So am I," she said. "My husband told me so."

The road began to slope upwards, following a valley which climbed steadily towards the Raima Mountains further south. As the horses' gait changed Calesh swayed in his saddle and mumbled to himself, then fell silent once more. Farajalla watched him uneasily. She thought his wound might be bleeding again, under his copper armour; he was certainly pale enough.

They crossed a small river, twice in half an hour as it snaked back and forth across a valley far too large for it. It wasn't much more than a stream, nestled between gravel banks at the bottom of a steep-sided ravine. In spring the flow would be greater though, filling the bed to the top of the banks with foam and rushing water. Amand dismounted at both bridges, for some reason, clambering down the bank as the riders filed past above him. He rejoined the leaders later, his gaunt face grim, to give Baruch a brief nod. That piqued Farajalla's curiosity, and usually she'd have studied them or else just asked what they were doing; both men had always been open with her, right from the start.

But that would mean leaving Calesh, which she wasn't prepared to do. Not while he remained in his current state, more asleep than awake and losing colour almost by the yard.

An hour after leaving the plain they reached a small town, just three parallel streets crossed by a series of alleys and one broader avenue. They had to cross the river again, and on the far side met what looked like all the townsfolk gathered together, dry-washing their hands and carrying worry in their eyes. Farajalla's mind flashed suddenly back to Harenc as she'd known it growing up, a little burg with an outsize castle and a little stream to water its fields. The clothes were different, but otherwise these people were much the same as those, far away in the desert. Farmers with the same concern for crops, and pests; millers tending their wheels; smiths leaning in the doorways of their forges.

They were facing the same fate, too. Harenc had been sacked when the All-Church came, then burned again when the Madai took it back, fifty years later. That second time everyone found in the town had been killed. It was her own people who'd done that, Madai butchering Madai. She'd never really understood it, and Calesh couldn't explain it very well, except to say that war did strange things to men's minds, and their hearts.

The riders drew rein, pulling to the side of the street so the rest of the cavalry could keep moving past them. Amand dismounted again and scrambled down the stony side of the ravine, to peer at something under the bridge. By then Elisande was speaking though, and Farajalla turned away from the skeletal Captain to listen.

"Mayence has fallen," the golden-haired Elite said bluntly. She paused as a babble of questions arose, but answered none of them. Several of the townsfolk had put their hands over their faces, so their eyes peered out between fingers. "The All-Church will be here soon, perhaps even today. You must flee. They will kill everyone they find."

"But these are our homes," a woman near the front protested. "Where will we stay, if we go?"

"With family, if you can. If not, you can pay for lodgings for a few nights, I expect." Elisande swept an arm to indicate the whole town. "All this is going to burn anyway."

"I can't leave my crops," someone shouted.

Raigal Tai's big horse pushed forward abruptly, pawing the ground as he hauled angrily at the bit. "Are you a fool? Soldiers will come down this road," he pointed with an outflung arm, "and they'll steal your crops and livestock and burn what they leave, or else drive it off. And they'll kill you too, if you're here. Blood of the God!" He shook his shaggy head. "You can rebuild a home, or plant new fields another spring. But not if you die here. Well, I can't help a fool who won't listen. We have to go."

"Not just yet," Ailiss said.

Farajalla hadn't even seen her dismount. But she was on the ground now, moving neatly towards where Calesh sat hunched in his saddle. Gaudin was beside her again, his white robe grimy now, though he gave no hint of weariness. His mistress did: Ailiss looked drawn and old, as frail as her advancing years said she should be. Her skin looked like ancient parchment, patterned with fine lines that looked like incipient cracks.

"Help him down," she ordered. "And be gentle. He is not strong."

Farajalla bit back the urge to deny that. Her husband *was* strong, as tough and hard as any man could be. Too much so, sometimes. If it wasn't for his will to act, to always be *doing,* he wouldn't be as obviously weak as he now was. She watched in silence as Luthien and Raigal Tai lifted Calesh out of his saddle and braced him, each with an arm under his shoulders to hold him up. His head lolled on one shoulder, and his eyes were closed.

Ailiss stepped up to him, a tiny woman next to any man in armour, and utterly dwarfed by Raigal Tai. She reached up with one hand and placed her fingertips against Calesh's forehead, with her palm over his nose. Gaudin steadied her as she stretched to whisper in his ear, words that Farajalla didn't catch.

"What did you do?" she demanded. She scrambled down from her saddle. "What did you do?"

"Eased his hurt," Ailiss replied. She'd aged yet further in those few moments, her eyes becoming deep-set glints in nests of wrinkles, and her voice was faint. "Be easy, girl. You know I would never harm him."

Calesh was still hanging between his two friends, apparently unaffected. Or nearly so; Farajalla was almost sure his colour was a little better, and he was breathing more easily. She went to him and slid her arms around his waist. "I can hold him, thank you."

Raigal let go with a hesitant frown, Luthien with a smile. It was all right for him, with no one he loved to worry over. His gaze shifted away from her almost at once though, and suddenly his stance was all alertness. "Baruch?"

"Trouble," the stocky man said shortly. He flicked the reins and his horse cantered away, back towards the edge of the town. Farajalla turned her head to watch him. Amand clambered out of the ravine, evidently finished with whatever he'd been doing, and the two men exchanged quick words and then came hurrying back. Baruch began calling orders and officers relayed them along the line, bringing ranks of Hand Armsmen to a halt in the street.

"All-Church," Amand said when he reached the group. Farajalla had known him for three years, but this was the first time she'd seen him less than perfectly turned out, unless he'd just been in a battle. His tabard was muddy and there was even a small tear on one side. "At least three companies, all cavalry."

The townsfolk exchanged horrified looks and began to scatter, running for their homes. Farajalla's heart plummeted. "Calesh can't ride yet!"

"Of course I can ride," he said, right beside her, and she whipped around to stare at him in shock. "Why would you think I couldn't? And by the way," he added, smiling, "not that I don't like your arms around me, but are you sure this is really the place?"

She gaped a moment longer, then leaned forward and kissed him on the lips, doing it thoroughly. "It's good enough for me."

"Then it's fine by me too," he said. He looked around. "We seem to be in a town. Have I been unconscious?"

"For an hour or more," Ailiss put in. "And you will be again, before long. You need rest quite urgently, Calesh, and when the weariness comes on you again there will be nothing I can do to stop it. But I bought you a little time."

He frowned at her. "You look exhausted."

"Don't worry about me," she said, turning away. "My time is almost over in any case."

He stared at her retreating back, then turned questioning eyes to Farajalla. She put a hand over his mouth before he could speak. "Don't ask, because I don't know. But hear me, husband; when you begin to tire again I'm going to insist you stop working and rest, and you *will* do so. I will drape myself around you and scream before I let you ignore me again."

"Then this really isn't the place," he quipped, and she couldn't quite smother her laughter, however hard she tried to seem stern.

"Amand," Calesh said. He disengaged from Farajalla's arms. "Is there fire-oil under the bridge?"

"Two barrels," the cadaverous man answered. Farajalla understood, abruptly; that was what he'd been doing underneath the bridges they passed. Even while Calesh and the others had planned for the best, they'd also prepared for the worst. This was their escape route, and they would blow it behind them so the All-Church couldn't chase them down.

"Then I want -" Calesh began.

"Have you considered," Amand broke in, his voice quite calm, "that we can't all fit into Adour?"

Farajalla couldn't remember him ever interrupting Calesh before. It must have surprised her husband as well, because he just stood there with his mouth half-open, a tiny line between his eyes.

"The road south has been cut," Amand went on. "The other Orders had enough men in Alinaur for that. We can't get through the passes, so that means there's only one possible refuge: Adour. And it's too small. It might hold eighty people, at a squeeze. It can't hold more."

"There are two thousand Hand of the Lord here," Calesh said, finding his voice. Raigal Tai and Luthien had turned to listen. "I'd back them in an even fight against twice their number of anyone else."

"Three times," Raigal rumbled.

Amand nodded. "I won't argue that. But it won't be an even fight. You know what warfare in Alinaur is like. Every road is guarded by a fortress on a crag, and that's what we'd have to overcome, if we went south." Amand raised his voice a little, actually raised it, when Calesh tried to cut in. "Besides, there are considerably more than twice our numbers waiting for us. Three times at least. You saw the reports, Marshal; you know it's true."

Calesh stepped away from Farajalla. She watched him go, alert to the change in his posture, the too-erect carriage that spoke of emotions held in check. "What do you suggest?"

He knows, Farajalla thought. That swooping in her belly had returned. *He already knows.*

"If only eighty can stay in Adour, then only eighty must go," Amand said calmly. "The rest must buy them time to reach it."

"No," Calesh said.

"I spoke to the captains before we left Mayence," Amand went on, remorseless. "We agreed we would do this, if it was needed. Any Armsman who wished otherwise were given permission to depart before we left the city." His thin lips curved in a tight smile. "I'm pleased to report that nobody left the ranks. Not one man."

"They're the finest soldiers in the world," Calesh said. It was then that Farajalla knew he was going to let it happen, and she had to look away so none of the men would see the tears in her eyes. Her gaze fell upon Baruch, who'd ridden back and now listened from a little distance away.

"I know they are," Amand agreed. "And it's you who made them so, as much as any man. The failure here in Sarténe was not your doing. You mustn't blame yourself for it."

Calesh shook his head. "I know it wasn't my doing. But still I blame myself for it. I failed."

"You *were* failed," Amand corrected him. "No man can do everything himself. You were let down by another man's folly."

"And our failure isn't certain yet," Luthien said, his voice soft. "The Dualism survives. It still might."

"Belial take the Dualism!" Calesh snarled suddenly, and several of the soldiers gasped in dismay. "What does a belief matter, against the lives of friends? What does a *faith* matter?"

Amand bowed his head, and Luthien said, "When it's the right faith, it always matters."

"I'm sure the All-Church would say exactly that," Calesh retorted. "And yet you broke your oath for me, Luthien. You had that choice and you opted to save your friend."

"I did," Luthien said. He'd paled slightly, but his tone remained steady. "That act made a difference. It was not the same as this."

"It feels the same."

"But it isn't," Luthien insisted. "You've trusted me in questions of faith for eleven years, Calesh. Trust me again."

"I can see five companies now," Baruch interjected, from the edge of the group. "Justified first, and the Glorified at the back, as usual. We don't have any more time for discussion."

Amand nodded. "It's been the honour of my life to serve with you, Marshal Saissan." He saluted, right fist to left hip, and looked down at Farajalla. "It was an honour to know you too, lady. Keep him safe."

"Always," she said. She hesitated, and then went forward and, swinging on his stirrup, she kissed Amand lightly on the lips. When she pulled back it was to see the first open astonishment she thought she'd ever seen in him. "Thank you. For being a friend, all these years."

"I'd have stayed ten times as long for a kiss from you, lady," Amand said. His expression grew serious as he turned to Elisande. "We have very little time, Elite, but will you pray over us?"

She was very pale, but she nodded. "I will."

The men of the Hand within earshot dismounted, to kneel beside their horses in the dirt of the road. Those further away saw them and followed suit, rippling down the line in both directions. Most of them wouldn't be able to hear Elisande, but they would know she had spoken. That would have to be enough.

"The Light that shines over all things, shines over you now," Elisande said. Her voice when raised was strong; more soldiers would be able to hear than Farajalla had thought. "The Lord sees you. He knows your repentance, and He forgives you your sins. His spirit dwells within you, as it always has."

"You are his true Believers. Whatever hardships may come, whatever cruelties the years bring, that remains true. In the *Unfurling of Spirit* we are asked; what is our strength, that we may hope? The answer is this: God is within you, and if you bring him forth, what you have will save you."

She lifted a hand, turning so the palm was held towards each section of the column of men. "You have suffered me to speak, and this shall be your consolation. Go in beauty."

Farajalla realised she was holding Calesh's hand, though she couldn't remember taking it. A moment later she grasped that he wasn't really aware of her, and she turned to find him staring at Baruch.

Who had just risen from his knees, his gaze already fixed on his old friend from the desert.

"No," Calesh said, his voice a whisper.

"I'm married to the Hand," Baruch answered. The corner of his mouth curled in a sardonic smile. "That was always a vulgar joke, but it's true. The Order is my life. What did you expect me to do?"

"Please come with us," Calesh said.

Baruch shook his head. "You have been my brother. But we both have other loves, and I love the Hand as you love Farajalla. You know I have to stay."

This time Calesh only looked at his feet. His fingers tightened around Farajalla's, and she gripped back in silent support. Baruch took a few steps forward and folded Calesh into a hug, but still Farajalla kept hold of his hand, so he had to embrace Baruch with one arm.

"Look after yourself," Baruch said to Raigal Tai, when he stepped back. "And that child of yours."

"There aren't enough All-Church soldiers in the world to hurt my son," Raigal said. He seemed about to say more but then turned away, coughing into his hand.

Baruch seemed to pretend not to notice. "You get that history written, Luthien. You must know the text by heart already, and I'm damned if I spent the last six years listening to you witter on about a book that's never going to be finished."

"No story is ever finished," Luthien said.

Baruch laughed out loud. "A typical Luthien comment! Well, I never expected you to change. I hope you never do."

He turned and went back to his horse. The rest of the Hand had already remounted, waiting for Amand's order to cross back over the bridge towards the advancing Justified. The gaunt man didn't speak though. He was watching Baruch, and when the other commander looked back Amand gave him a brief nod of respect. After a moment Baruch returned it, a faint smile playing about his lips.

"Listen up!" Amand bellowed suddenly. If Elisande's voice had carried Amand's was an outright boom; Farajalla thought people in Mayence might be able to hear him. "If this is the end of our story, then let it be an end for musicians to play of, a hundred years from now. Make sure your swords are loose and your prayers are spoken. This is the last dragonnade of the Hand of the Lord, and God willing, we will see our second Gate of Angels in one day!"

The Armsmen answered him with a roar. There were no swords raised in dramatic poses, no horses made to rear and paw the air. These were fighting men, plain and practical, with none of the romance in their souls that had led Ando Gliss to write his silly battle songs, or the Margrave to have a mural of Calesh painted on his palace wall. Farajalla knew that from the years in Tura d'Madai; she'd known it even before she met Calesh. The Justified might divert themselves with women pulled from the streets, or the Glorified indulge in illicit drinking, but the Hand of the Lord simply did their work, without fuss.

So she thought, until she saw that every one of the soldiers lifted a fist to his shoulder in salute to Calesh, as they rode past.

He jerked beside her just as she noticed that. The motion was so slight, so quickly covered, that Farajalla would never have noticed it if her hand hadn't still been in his. But Luthien noticed, on Calesh's other side, and he put a hand on her husband's arm.

"You can't join them," the small man said softly. "They're doing this to give you a chance."

"I know that," Calesh said.

Luthien looked down the road, to where the Justified companies had begun to spread out in battle lines as the Hand came back down the valley towards them. "I left Ilenia in Mayence. It would have done no good to go back for her. All I could do was ride on, and pray for her."

Farajalla felt a fool. She had thought Luthien had no one he loved to worry over, but she'd forgotten Ilenia. Somehow people always seemed to. Luthien's smiles had hidden his pain, they weren't because he didn't feel any. And he had nobody here to comfort him. She wondered, with a sick feeling in her belly, whether Calesh would have ridden to his death here if not for her presence at his side, and she thought he probably would.

Then she wondered if he would have stayed just for her, or if it had been the baby growing inside her which made the difference. She knew she would never be so cruel as to ask him that.

They were a mile north of the town, climbing up a road already narrower and more uneven than before, when an explosion behind them sent a billow of black smoke into the air. Twisting in her saddle to look, Farajalla saw the red glow of flames beneath the cloud, and knew the oil had been fired to destroy the bridge. She couldn't see the fighting though, and Calesh didn't try. He rode with his mouth set in a flat line, Luthien on one side and Raigal on the other, and none of them looked back.

Fourteen

The Road to Adour

He was trying not to think about Ilenia.

It had been so long since Luthien had let himself feel, allowed his emotions to flow freely through him. His life had become defined by control, but restraint, all the things an Elite was supposed to impose on himself. It had been his own choice, and he didn't regret it, even now.

But he remembered feeling Ilenia's eyes on him across the room, when Ando was reciting perhaps, and her husband sat listening with a glass of wine and a smile. The gaze had excited him, *thrilled* him, though he knew he could never do anything about it. Physical love was one of the things an Elite gave up when he took the Consolation. And yet he had gone to Ilenia after the assassin tried to kill Calesh, with blood on his robe and shame warring with desire in his heart, and he had laid her on a divan and himself down with her.

He remembered *that,* with a pulse of blood inside.

But he shouldn't be thinking about Ilenia. She was gone, almost certainly dead in the city. He could have gone back for her; most men would have done, he knew. They would have let their emotions override sense and plunged into the chaos in Mayence, and would have been killed too, without even seeing the woman they sought. Luthien knew how foolish it would have been, but he'd had to fight to stop himself turning his horse on the road.

Stop thinking *of that!*

He studied his companions, knowing nobody would notice him doing so. Hardly anyone had spoken all morning, the third since Baruch and the soldiers had gone back down the road. They rode now without looking at each other, heads down or eyes unseeing. Even Raigal Tai, riding at Luthien's side, was lost in thought and silent. He had been for hours.

Ailiss, Gaudin and Elisande made a small group on the other side of the track. The Lady was tinier than ever, somehow drawn in on herself as though despairing, or simply exhausted. Gaudin's expression of permanent concern had deepened, if anything. Beside him Elisande looked almost as worried, and never strayed far from the old woman who led the Dualism. She might not know that Farajalla was the Lady's chosen heir; and if she did, it would probably make no difference to her. Elisande had always been devout, if in a quiet kind of way. Sometimes the fiercest passions were the most silent.

As his had been, for Ilenia -

He jerked his head around to look at Calesh and Farajalla, riding on the same horse. She refused to let anyone else hold him, even for a moment. Calesh was unarmoured now, the weight removed to spare the horse. Besides, it had taken over an hour to ease the armour off last night, Calesh conscious but breathing fast and shallowly, his flesh the colour of sour milk. He wasn't conscious now; he leaned back against his wife, his head on her shoulder while she held him steady, guiding the horse with her knees. Concern had worn lines into her face which hadn't been there a week before.

She had reason to worry. Luthien didn't know how Calesh had kept going for as long as he had. His friend must be made of stone, or the strange, too-hard copper of that armour he wore. Men who survived the desert were always hard, indifferent to wounds or fatigue that crippled lesser men; Luthien was himself, even after his years in the green robe. Some things never left you. But he had never seen anyone as tough as Calesh. The man was incredibly tough, resilient beyond belief. The four of them were all brothers to dragons, all sturdy and strong, but Calesh was tougher than weathered rock.

Not the four of us, a whisper in his mind reminded him. *Three. Baruch is gone.*

Ilenia was go -

Behind them all rode fifty men of the Hand, just about all that were left of the whole Order. There were another twenty in Adour, and perhaps another hundred or so further south, in Alinaur. Or perhaps not, if the All-Church had hunted them down by now. They probably had.

These fifty had been vital though. Yesterday afternoon the party had encountered a Glorified scout, nosing his way northwards through the pass. He'd slipped away before they could catch him, whipping his horse back towards the All-Church forces which must be coming up from Alinaur. Early this morning there had been two more. Luthien had wondered if the group would be able to reach Adour, or if the advancing army would cut it off.

But the little party of refugees had arrived at the turning first, apart from a knot of Shavelings who had sat their horses and watched, making no effort to intervene. That was wise, since there had only been a dozen of them, but Luthien had yearned for them to be foolish and attack. He needed to kill someone, to take a life in revenge for all the sorrow inflicted on him, and the people he loved. That horrified him when he dwelled on it, but he supposed it was natural. Grief turned easily to hate. Half the history of the civilised world seemed little more than repeated proof of that fact.

He looked back at Calesh and Farajalla again. She was pregnant, of course, and Luthien knew how much that would mean to his old friend. Even in the desert Calesh had sometimes talked of settling down. They'd all had their favourite topics: for Luthien it had been faith, for Raigal his longed-for home in Rheven, and for Calesh it was finding a wife and raising a family in a little house somewhere. He'd never cared where that house was, Tura d'Madai or Sarténe, or the far north where the winters lasted most of the year. All that mattered was new lives to quieten the dying cries of his brother, cries Calesh still heard in his dreams.

There would be more cries now, in Mayence, and more to come here.

*

They were met at the gates of Adour by Kendra and Segarn, the boy toddling a few uncertain steps while his mother balanced him. That was all, but Raigal Tai gave a great shout of pride and delight and bounded up the rocky trail to join them, folding his wife and son into a hug that almost smothered them.

It was very hard not to smile. Hard, but not impossible, especially through the clouds of exhaustion which weighed on Farajalla's mind and body. She needed to sleep quite badly.

Calesh was a dead weight against her, and much as she hated to think of him that way the phrase kept coming back to her, circling around inside her mind.

"It's the children who matter, isn't it?" Luthien said, reining up beside her. He pushed his glasses up his nose with one finger. "In the end, it's always about the children."

She eyed him through veils of weariness, this clever friend of her husband's. Calesh had told her about him back in the desert, of course, showing her something of the man whose name so terrified the Madai, so she'd always known he was intelligent. But knowing wasn't the same thing as understanding, not with Luthien. He was uncannily sharp, as adept at reading people as he was at parsing truth from an ancient book of histories. There was an odd expression on his face now, as he watched Raigal and his family. *Intense, and yet analytical*, Farajalla thought vaguely, and then gave it up. She wasn't going to be able to make sense of him now. Give her food and ten hours in bed, and she might be able to puzzle through what he was feeling, behind those enigmatic eyes.

"I suppose it is," she said.

"He's walking!" Raigal bellowed from further up the trail. "Did you see, Luthien? He's walking!"

"A feat to stand with the heroisms of the Age," the little man smiled.

Segarn was eight months old. Farajalla thought that was about right for a child to take his first steps, and for a moment she couldn't understand why Raigal Tai was making such a fuss over it. Then she remembered she was pregnant herself, there was a baby growing in her belly right now, and she realised with a jolt that she'd be exactly the same, clucking over her child's every fall and beaming when he (or she) managed to cross a room without falling.

Calesh's limp body slid sideways and she caught him quickly, noticing only then that her hand had fallen to her stomach to feel the slight curve there, almost too slight to feel. Unless it *was* too slight, and the gentle swell was only her imagination, her need to believe.

"We should get inside," Ailiss whispered. She was hardly any better off than Calesh, and her voice was a frail reed, barely audible. "The All-Church could have archers in the rocks."

Farajalla nodded, but for a moment she only stayed where she was and watched Raigal tickling his son. Luthien kneed his horse into motion and then stopped again a few yards in front of her, looking back with a quizzical expression as the other riders streamed around them.

"What?" he asked.

"You're right," Farajalla said. "About the children. They're the ones who matter, because they have futures while we only have pasts, and those full of blasted hopes. Our stories are nearly over."

He smiled at her, like a tutor pleased with a quick-witted student. "No story is ever wholly finished."

He had said as much to Baruch, three days ago on the road above the bridge. The last words spoken to an old and dear friend. He could remember them now, and speak them again with amusement playing around his lips, though the grief must be raw in him. He was an extraordinary man. Farajalla thought she could spend ten years with him, a lifetime in fact, and still feel she'd only glimpsed the shallowest waters of his complex soul.

She couldn't do even that much when she was so exhausted. With a click of her tongue she started her mare moving, and carried her husband up the trail into the fortress of Adour.

*

"I assume," Sarul said, in his most sarcastic voice, "that it's more bad news you bring me?"

The Arch-Prelate had not been very far from rage for a week now. In truth he never was very far from rage, and Amaury had learned to walk carefully around him at all times, however serene the clergyman seemed. Fury could explode without warning. The day after Mayence fell Sarul had ordered a groom beaten for making his horse's girth straps too tight; had ordered thirty lashes with the triple whip, in fact, which killed as often as not. Amaury had managed to avert that by having the youth sent to duties back by the river Rielle.

With luck, Sarul wouldn't even remember the incident, or notice that one face had been replaced by another. He rarely did.

Mayence's sudden, shocking fall ought to have put him in a good temper. It had pleased Amaury no end: he'd planned for a long, tortuous siege, with his army sitting helplessly outside the city's intimidating walls. That would have grown nasty when winter came. Instead the fool Margrave had led an assault and left the gate open, and All-Church soldiers had got inside. The subsequent fight had been ugly, as savage as battles in confined spaces usually were, but it was better than the disease and hunger that ravaged siege camps in bad terrain.

"I told you the city would fall," Sarul had said that evening. In the streets men had still been fighting, winkling out the last stubborn pockets of resistance. "God has held His hand over us in blessing, general Amaury. You should have more faith in His will."

"I will try, Arch-Prelate," Amaury had answered.

He wouldn't try. Mayence had fallen not because of God, but because of an idiot and some luck, nothing more. Plain human stupidity changed battles, simple as that. But it was best not to argue with Sarul. He took the slightest sign of dissent as a personal challenge, and went on to harangue and lecture in that wonderful voice of his, all thrum and resonance, until the opponent slunk away beaten. Or seemed to be. Amaury had mastered the art of seeming cowed without being so, at least some of the time.

All the same, trying to command this army with Sarul nagging at him had been a *nightmare,* worse than anything he'd ever known. Leaving the endless squabbles of Rheven dukes for the greater campaign of a Crusade had appeared good sense at the time, but back then Amaury had expected to be going to Tura d'Madai, to fight infidels in the desert. He hadn't even *known* there were infidels in Sarténe as well. He certainly hadn't known his every move would be scrutinised by a deranged cleric with a mania for control.

Just after Mayence fell he had shaved his beard. He'd always worn it, right back to when he was more boy than man, but it just wasn't worth the constant harassment it earned from

Sarul. Amaury's face still felt odd without it, especially in the wind.

"Some bad news," he said, making his tone as neutral as he could, "and some good, I think."

"Ah. One of those days." Sarul turned from the window of his tent. (A window! In a tent! Amaury had never seen such a thing in his life.) "Sometimes the voice of God is clear in me, general. As clear as good spring water, or a cloudless sky. Other times it's all I can do to make out what He is saying, what He wants me to do. Drawing sense from the voice on those days is like pulling teeth."

"I'm sure you will manage, Your Grace," Amaury said. He was still aiming for bland words, blandly spoken, but Sarul shot him a glare that ought to have fried him on the spot.

"Your news?" the clergyman asked waspishly. "Or do you mean to stand there all day and leave me in ignorance?"

You will still be in ignorance when you stand at the gates of Heaven itself, Amaury thought to himself, *because you have never learned to listen.* None of that showed on his face though - a trick any general knew, one he'd learned long before he met Sarul - and he said, "The fugitives have turned off the road. They're heading for Adour."

"Adour? What is Adour?"

You don't listen, Amaury thought again. He'd told Sarul about the fortress at least three times. "It's a stronghold in the Raima Mountains, Your Grace. Very high, very tough to break. According to the stories nobody ever has."

"Then I hope that is the bad news," Sarul said. His voice had gone from barely-suppressed anger to silk smoothness, as suddenly as light flares from a match. Amaury hated it when that happened. It meant another mood swing was even more likely than normal.

"It's the bad news," Amaury agreed. "The Hand of the Lord had to lay siege for two years before it fell, I think, and they never even tried to get over the wall. We may be there a long time, I'm afraid."

"But they can't go anywhere else," Sarul noted. He nodded as he spoke. "You must think an issue through, general. This group of renegades is the last of the heresy. There are other followers, of course, but with the leadership gone they can be brought back into Mother Church, in time. These few are the last focus of a misguided faith. Once they are surrounded in Adour their fate becomes certain." A smile began to play around the corners of his mouth. "I actually think this is good news."

So did Amaury, in fact, but he'd become wary of presenting information to Sarul as good when he was so likely to be contradicted. Offer it as bad and the cleric would probably find a way to see it as good, proving you wrong; that was better than the other way around. Amaury hid a sigh. Sometimes it was depressing to be proved right again.

"The second news is better," he said. "A delegation is on its way from the Basilica. I received the news an hour ago."

Sarul's smile disappeared. It was so hard to read this man; however subtle Amaury had become, he still sometimes got it wrong. He'd expected the cleric to be pleased by this information, but instead he was scowling like an angry child. "Who is in this delegation?"

"Only one man was named," Amaury said. "One of your fellow Arch-Prelates. A fellow named Irrian."

Sarul spun on his heel, turning to face the window again, but not before Amaury had caught a glimpse of rage breaking through the frown. Obviously he wasn't exactly friends with this Irrian, then. There were factions inside the Basilica of course, everyone knew that, but Amaury wouldn't have thought a rival would be sent to Sarul now, just when the heresy was about to be crushed. Congratulations seemed more likely. He didn't understand, and decided not to think about it. Let the clergymen squabble if they wanted to: he would keep his mouth shut and be the good soldier, and give no grounds for complaint at all.

Except that when Sarul turned back to him he was smiling, a wide grin that filled his whole face. "Didn't I just say it, general? Didn't I? That sometimes I can see God's will so clearly?"

"You did," Amaury agreed cautiously.

"Antanus must be dead," Sarul said. There was exultation in that magnificent voice, a fact he seemed to realise as he rubbed his hands together in glee. "Such a shame to lose our beloved Hierarch, of course. The Faithful are leaderless today, adrift without guidance in the world. But Antanus has been called home to Light, and blessed peace forever. It is the rest of us who must find a way to continue without his wisdom."

That was how Amaury felt. Just the thought that the Hierarch might be dead made him feel queasy, as though he'd eaten a bad apple and his gorge was full of sour stomach acid because of it. But if Sarul felt that way then Amaury would eat his saddle, with the bit and bridle for afters. The man was obviously pleased that Antanus was dead; he'd forgotten to hide his delight, at first. There had been rumours that Sarul wanted to be the next Hierarch, or even that he was sure to be, and Amaury thought he might just have had those stories confirmed.

"My ministry will begin in cleansing fire," Sarul whispered. His face was alight. "God's will is in me, general. It has always been so, I believe, but today… I can almost feel His touch."

There was nothing to say in response to that. Nothing safe. Sarul was transported by his own ecstasy right now - that, and not God's touch - but his mood could change in an instant. You could never speak freely, never allow your face to show what you truly felt, when you were with him. Amaury wondered how many servants the man had dismissed, or ordered flogged or worse, because they ironed a crease badly at the wrong time and his temper had snapped.

"You are wrong," Sarul said. "About Adour. We will not be there a long time." He spread his arms out wide, like the God-Son in his final agonies, his lips still curved in that enraptured smile. "God has willed it so. The fortress will fall as easily as Mayence, or Parrien before it."

Amaury doubted that. The two cities had been lost because of fools, and wherever people gathered together there was always a surfeit of fools. There wouldn't be at Adour. It was a Hand of the Lord castle, filled only with trained men, most of them veterans. The Hand didn't tolerate idiots. The hare-brained were weeded out in training and any remaining halfwits got themselves killed soon enough. Nobody at Adour was going to leave a gate open.

And there was still Calesh Saissan, as well. He might have lost his army, and his base of operations besides, but a man didn't lose his talent because of one setback. Saissan still had his cleverness, and all the craft and experience gained through years of hard command. He'd managed to slip out of Mayence just before it fell, despite being wounded if the reports were true; that alone spoke of how canny he was. If he could slip out of Adour too, perhaps join the remaining Hand soldiers in Alinaur, he could still be a threat for years.

Amaury was still appalled at what had happened in the valley north of here, when regiments of Glorified and Justified caught up with the fleeing Hand. The fugitive Order had turned and ridden back *down* the road, smashing into their pursuers and breaking them into pieces. Four full companies of cavalry - two thousand men - had been reduced to splinters in half an hour, and the survivors hunted back down the valley until they found refuge behind the first battalions of pikemen coming up behind. Even those had found themselves in a ferocious fight, struggling hand to hand with riders when their sturdy lines really ought to have been able to hold. Amaury had arrived on the scene to find pockets of men fighting all over the vale, sometimes Hand soldiers embattled by All-Church men, sometimes the other way around.

Sarul had not been pleased.

"What is the point," the Arch-Prelate had demanded in *a voice that shook with rage, "of a commander who is not even* present *when an important engagement is being fought?"*

And all that, half a day of chaos and confusion, had been caused by the Hand of the Lord *without* its fabled captain. Saissan was still loose, still able to plan and act. Amaury wouldn't believe him finished until he saw the body, and then only if it didn't move for a day or two.

Sarul's criticism was viciously unfair, of course. Amaury hadn't been with the pursuit of the Hand because there was still fighting in Mayence, a fact the clergyman knew perfectly well. But fairness wasn't one of Sarul's concerns. He wanted what he wanted, right now, with no excuses. All you could do was keep your mouth shut during his rages, and try to speak such sense as he allowed when he was calmer. Which wasn't much.

This man was going to be Hierarch of the All-Church. Amaury was a man of the Faith, had been since his cradle, but he had real difficulty imagining why God would pick out a monster like Sarul to be His hand on Earth.

Still, God chose who He chose, so Amaury only said, "Perhaps you're right, Arch-Prelate. Adour may fall in a day, if God decides so."

"Exactly," Sarul agreed. He didn't even frown at Amaury's cynicism, though he often did so, even when none was meant. Probably he was too far lost in his own joy to notice.

Amaury slipped out of the pavilion, not without a sense of relief. A few steps later two of his aides fell into step on either side of him, their expressions carefully blank. They must have heard every word of his exchange with Sarul, but they wouldn't admit it. Neither of them spoke until they were well out of earshot of the tent.

"Did he take the news well, sir?" one of them asked finally.

Amaury gave him a look from the side of his eye. "Better than I expected. I survived, at least."

"So what now?" the other said.

"Now," Amaury muttered, "we pray that Sarul is right, and Adour will fall as easily as a child's spinning top. Because if it doesn't, we're going to have our siege after all, and up in those mountains it's going to be appalling."

Fifteen

Rats in a Barrel

Calesh was still asleep. He'd learned the soldiers' trick of sleeping at every opportunity long before Fara had met him, that sunlit day in the courtyard of Harenc. But he'd never slept like this, for two days and nights without stirring, like a man standing on the brink of death with no more effort in him. She didn't think anyone ever had.

She remembered him coming home from Malakar, the savage battle in the south of Tura d'Madai, when the Crusaders had stopped the Madai breaking through the border forts. It had been a week-long campaign, in fact, the westerners pushing the Madai together and then annihilating them, and everything had depended on speed and timing. Only the Hand of the Lord could be trusted with that part of the operation. Returned soldiers said Calesh had hardly stopped to eat in those seven days, let alone to sleep. He'd come back to Elorium with a hectic look in his eye, striding along on momentum alone, and two hours later had collapsed into bed and scarcely moved a muscle for eighteen hours.

But he'd breathed at least, enough that Farajalla had been able to notice. She couldn't see his chest move now, unless she crouched down by his bed so her eyes were level with his prone body. She had to hold his hand in both of hers, sometimes for an hour, just to be sure she could feel the slow pulse of blood through his flesh. Every time she let him go she was afraid he would die; every time she strayed from his side she half believed she'd return to find him cold, his hands limp on the linen. And so while Calesh slumbered an inch from death, Farajalla barely slept at all, and weariness ate at her and tried constantly to pull her into rest, while fear fought to keep her awake.

"You must live," she said, several times. *""You're going to be a father, my love. Would you let your child grow up without you?"*

She was talking to herself as much as to him, of course, and anyway that wasn't what she meant. Not all of it, anyway. *Would you let me go on without you?* She couldn't say it like that, though the thought never left her during those two days, skulking at the back of her mind only to push into the light whenever her attention wandered for a moment.

She and Calesh had been given a small room inside the fortress wall, just to themselves. Three Hand soldiers had moved out to allow them the space. Fara had difficulty understanding how they had managed in such cramped conditions; there were three narrow cots, a small wooden seat, and that was all. Soldiers learned to deal with such things, she supposed. They were forced to share crowded tents when on campaign, so this wasn't much different and perhaps even a little better. The walls and roof were solid, at least.

Three times a day someone brought food, bread and fruit for Farajalla and broth for Calesh, which she fed him herself. He wasn't aware of her but he'd swallow when she dribbled soup between his lips, though she had to hold his head. She tried not to think of the sicknesses that left men invalids and then carried them away, though that too loitered around the edges of her awareness and then ambushed her with dread once again.

She was sitting on the middle bed, holding his hand in hers again, when his fingers moved. Farajalla had been nodding, not really awake, but that slight motion was enough to bring her back to awareness with a lurch, and she jerked her head up to find his eyes were open, and on her.

"I won't let him grow up without me," Calesh whispered.

A smile broke from her. She opened her mouth to say something witty and the vision came, spilling across her vision like water over glass. It was there and gone in moments, a second perhaps: when it passed she found Calesh still looking at her, a hint of puzzlement around the corners of his mouth. Her hands trembled. The man she loved noticed, of course, and his fingers wrapped around hers and held them tight.

"Tell me," he murmured, and she did.

*

"There," Raigal Tai said.

He was leaning on the battlement, his great bulk filling the gap between crenellations. It always seemed a wonder to Luthien that the stone didn't crumble under his weight, and send the big man tumbling to the rocks below. "I don't see them."

Raigal grunted. "Put your glasses on, then."

He did, and the figures at the mouth of the valley came into sharp focus. Well, sharper focus, anyway. Luthien had started to wonder if his eyesight had worsened since he'd had the spectacles made, all those years ago in Elorium. Reading by lamp light in the evenings was difficult again now. Last night he'd tried to write down some of his thoughts about the struggle in Sarténe, and had abandoned the effort after half an hour.

He remembered his ideas, of course. That the war here was only a single page in the long history of the Hidden House; that the Dualism itself was little more than a chapter, in fact, and the beliefs and principles would live on. *Perhaps not,* his rational mind interjected, and Luthien grimaced as he acknowledged the truth of that. If everyone died here in Adour then the Hidden House would die with them, its ancient secrets lost forever. It had become a real possibility.

The three men at the end of the valley were proof of that. They were scouts only, small men with bows but no hand weapons, and plain cloth garments instead of armour. But they were the harbingers of a larger force to come: the first white snowdrop that whispers of approaching spring, Luthien thought to himself. The simile made him smile, despite everything. It took more than war and defeat to rob words of their power to please.

"So," Raigal Tai said presently. He didn't shift his weight, or even look around. "What do you think?"

Luthien shrugged. "I think they'll find very little they can use. This valley is as bad as it can be for a besieging force. The mountains slope right down to the river, so there's nowhere to place catapults or ballistae. The slope outside the walls is steep and littered with rocks, so ladders can't be placed there. In short, I doubt the All-Church will break in, however hard they try."

He thought they *would* try, if he was honest. The general leading the enemy army was very good - Calesh had realised that straight away - but he wasn't wholly in command: at least, Luthien didn't think he was. The Basilica would never have allowed a campaign of this importance to be led by a mere soldier. There would be a cleric involved somewhere, probably a senior one, always pushing the fighting men to do more and faster, regardless of casualties. If the dead were promised Heaven as a reward for their sacrifice, then what matter if they died? Luthien had seen that attitude in Tura d'Madai, time and again when the All-Church priests came to whip up fervour for the fight.

With the last remnants of the Dualism at bay, cornered here in this fortress in the Raima Mountains, the clergyman with the army would be frothing with eagerness. So would half the soldiers, in truth. They would assault the walls, Luthien was sure of it, however slim their chances. They would scramble over mounds of their own dead to make one more attack, until even the priests realised it was futile and called them back.

"I know all that," Raigal said, breaking into Luthien's chain of thought. He'd turned from his perusal of the valley now, finally. "It's why we chose Adour for our last stand, after all. I was asking what you think our chances are."

Sometimes being clever was a drawback. Blissful ignorance was impossible when you could see what was coming, as inevitable as the tide or the curving circuit of the Moon across the field of stars. And you couldn't hide when asked a question like that, not from a friend. Raigal would know if Luthien lied, and he wasn't going to lie.

"Zero," he said.

The huge man nodded slowly. "That's what I thought, too. They can't get over the walls, but they'll sit outside them until we starve."

"Right through this winter and the next one too, if necessary," Luthien agreed. "Adour is not Mayence. The weather will be colder and the winds stronger, but the All-Church needs fewer men to pen us in. A thousand would do it. They could leave twice that number here and supply them easily, even when snow is piled ten feet deep in the pass."

"Then it's over."

"Yes. It's over."

They stood there for a moment in silence. Both men looked back at the mouth of the valley, and the three riders still scanning the terrain before them. Under different circumstances it might have made sense to place archers to have them shot, but not here, when there was nothing for a scout to achieve and the All-Church could simply send more anyway. Adour was as ready as it could be made for the siege. The larders were full, quivers of arrows were piled in every corner, and the horses had been turned out to wander the valley and find what fodder they could. Everything had been done in time.

None of it would matter.

"I thought Calesh would save us," Raigal said finally. "Him, and the Hand come back from Tura d'Madai. Didn't you?"

Luthien took his glasses off and stowed them in their wooden case, closing it carefully. "Sometimes."

"You weren't sure?"

"The All-Church had four or five men to every one of ours," Luthien said. "Even if that wasn't enough, they could call on more. Historically that sort of numerical advantage nearly always tells." He smiled. "I can quote you the years and the wars, if you like."

"God save me from that," Raigal growled, and they laughed together on the wall.

No, Luthien hadn't believed Calesh could save Sarténe. Not really. But there was something about the man, even after all these years; a light, perhaps, that dimmed all others when he walked into a room. When he'd heard Calesh was home Luthien had felt a quickening of his blood, seen a brightening of the colours of the world, against all logic and common sense. Usually he'd thought the Dualism would lose. But there were times when Calesh had shaken that belief, had made it seem that anything was possible as long as the people of the province believed and worked as one, and trusted in their God.

That had not happened; and wouldn't, now. But still, Luthien could admire the strength and courage that had brought Calesh back to Sarténe, throwing himself into harm's way for the sake of a country he'd spent his adult life trying to forget. That was part of the man, of course. There was nobility in him, and bravery, and a speed of decision which was almost frightening. Farajalla had recounted the story of how Calesh had issued orders within an hour, after word came from the spy in the Basilica of what the All-Church planned. He'd been right to do so; any delay would have meant the other Orders might receive instructions to block the Hand, to arrest its members or at least keep them in the desert.

And that, too, would not matter.

The Dualism had needed another decade, he thought, perhaps even a little less. The first, careful missionaries had been sent out forty years ago, to establish Dualist cells outside Sarténe if it could be done. Most had failed. Some had been exposed and hunted, then usually killed. But a few had succeeded, creating small sects in Falmark and Alinaur, and in Rheven where a youth named Raigal Tai would soon begin to grow to manhood. Once established, these cells had always grown. Ailiss had once told Luthien that there were over a thousand Believers in Alinaur, two or three times as many in Falmark, and more all the time.

Ten more years, and that number might have been too large for the All-Church to destroy. The round Dualist temples would have been springing out of the ground itself and Crusade would have been impossible, because the armies called by foreign lords would have included Dualists themselves.

It all came down to Riyand, in the end. To his stupidity, allowing the All-Church an excuse for war; to his inability to see the danger in time; to his folly in trying to sally against the arriving army when there was nothing to gain and a huge risk to be run. Except that of course it came down to God, who had given Sarténe one gifted Margrave after another for over a hundred years and then, when it mattered, given it a fool.

"Perhaps we ought to have foreseen this," he said, thinking it through. "The Hidden House has been persecuted for hundreds of years, ever since it was founded, in the desert south of Tura d'Madai. For thousands of years, in truth. Every time it tries to step into the open it's crushed. We had no reason to believe it would be different this time."

"People always believe it will be different this time," Raigal said. "They like to think their own lives, their own days, are special."

Luthien looked at him, a grin tugging at his lips. "That was very nearly profound, my friend."

"I'll give you a clip round the ear," Raigal warned, and then chuckled. "It wasn't profound anyway. Every parent thinks his child is cleverer than anyone else's, or more handsome, or more talented. If you'd ever had kids you'd know it yourself, Luthien."

"I do know it," he answered. "I just didn't realise you did, as well."

"Segarn is going to survive," Raigal said. The amusement was gone from his face, replaced by a feral expression Luthien didn't like at all. "Somehow, he's going to live. Tell me how I can make that happen."

"Get him out before the All-Church arrives," Luthien said. "There are trails through the peaks west of here, high paths so dangerous that even goats avoid them. The Hand has mapped some of them, over the years, but the All-Church doesn't know they exist."

Raigal nodded. "Then you get him out, Luthien. Take him."

"What?" he asked, not sure he'd heard.

"Take him! I can't do it. I'm too big for a trail like that, and anyway the All-Church will expect to find me here. If they don't they'll start hunting. You have to do it. You don't want to fight anyway, you haven't for years, so do this for me. Keep my son safe."

He hesitated, his mind already holding this new idea up to the light to be examined from every side. It didn't take long. There was a flaw in Raigal's thinking, a fatal one, but that could be dealt with later. "I can't."

"Please," Raigal said. "Please."

"I broke my Consolation," Luthien said. "Broke my oath to God. I only have one vow left, Raigal, and that's to the Hand of the Lord. I won't leave men here to die for me. I'll stand, and share their fate. But there's someone else who can take Segarn away for you."

Mouth open to argue, Raigal Tai stopped and thought, and gradually his brow cleared. "Calesh?"

"Calesh," Luthien agreed. "Farajalla is the Lady's named heir, and she *must* escape this trap if the Dualism is to continue. If the Hidden House itself is to endure, in fact. That means Calesh must go as well, to guard her. Maybe one or two others. Segarn and Kendra can go with them."

"Not me," she said from behind them.

They turned, the giant and the wise man, to find Kendra standing at the entrance to the tower behind them. As always it was hard to think of her and Raigal as a pair, because of the difference in their sizes, like an eagle and a sparrow put in the same cage and told to be friends. She was standing very straight though, looking her husband straight in the eye, and Luthien bowed without expecting her to notice him at all.

"Dear," Raigal began, and she cut him off.

"We both stay," she said. How long she had been listening to them Luthien didn't know, but she obviously understood what they'd been saying. "You because they expect you to be here, Raigal. Me because the All-Church knows Farajalla is here, and they'll hunt her just as much as they'll hunt you, if they enter and find you gone."

"But they know Farajalla is black," Raigal said. "Even the common soldiers won't mistake you for her."

The flaw in the plan, Luthien thought. He felt tired to the bone, as weary as Calesh slumped against Farajalla as they rode, but there was a little more yet to do. Just a little, before he could rest. "I can explain that."

They both turned, waiting on him, though he thought they both knew already. Their expressions barely changed as he laid it out for them, which confirmed his•guess. After a while Kendra moved to take her husband's hand, her own vanishing in his bear-like paw, and Luthien saw they were both crying silent, silver tears.

It was then he realised he was, too.

*

Gaudin opened the door, of course. When he saw who it was he gave a slight nod and beckoned for them to enter.

Luthien led them in, and so he was the first to see that Ailiss was lying on a divan, propped on such a thick pile of cushions that her upper body was halfway to upright. She smiled at him, then at Raigal and Kendra as they followed him in. Luthien thought she looked exhausted, a woman whose body is at last beginning to find it hard to draw the next breath, and whose blood has begun to grow slower and cooler in her veins.

She wasn't alone. Farajalla sat on the edge of the divan, the *Book of Breathing* open on her lap as though she'd been searching for a reference, or perhaps just reading to the older woman. Across the room, also reclining on an enormous stack of cushions, was -

"Calesh!" Raigal Tai bellowed. The stone walls shook under that yell and then threw it back, making both women flinch and Calesh chuckle weakly. "You dog! When did you wake up?"

"Barely an hour ago," Farajalla cut in sternly, "and I'll thank you not to agitate him, Raigal Tai. Calesh is here on his word of honour that he'll go back to our room the *moment* I decide he's over-exerting himself," she turned to him, "aren't you, my love?"

He nodded and said "Yes, dear," with a little smile.

Calesh looked weaker than Ailiss, even more tired than Luthien felt. Corpses had more colour than he did. Even his lips were pale, and there were threads of grey in the hair at his temples that Luthien was almost sure hadn't been there before. Not even a week ago, before the disaster at Mayence. But he was awake, and among them once more, and Luthien couldn't help the lift in his heart as he sketched a bow to the best friend of his life.

"Dare we hope you'll do some of the work this time?" he asked.

"Maybe a bit of it," Calesh whispered.

Gaudin appeared with a tray, set it down beside his mistress and retired to a corner of the room. Farajalla rose to pour hot berry tea without being asked, then handed round the cups. Nobody spoke until she was done. Luthien glanced from face to face and saw the same knowledge in each of them.

"We've all come to the same conclusions," he said, when Fara had sat down again. "Haven't we?"

"Perhaps," the Lady said. Her voice was even more papery than Calesh's. "What are yours?"

He frowned at her, suddenly and uncharacteristically out of patience. "You know very well what they are."

"Tell me," Ailiss said.

"Adour will fall," Raigal Tai said bluntly. He'd always been best at speaking plain truth, with none of the delicacy other men used. "Not soon, because there's not an army in the world can scale these walls. But it will fall, this winter or next, and we will all die."

Ailiss glanced at Farajalla, and the younger woman gave a nod. "Yes. That's what I've seen."

"Part of it?" Luthien asked.

She met his eyes. "Everyone here will be killed. The All-Church knows our leaders are here, the military men and the women who hold the secrets of the Hidden House. There are five people they want above all, of course."

"Of course," he murmured. Everyone knew the names: Calesh, Farajalla, Luthien, Raigal and Ailiss.

"The leaders of the army plan to parade those five before their soldiers," Farajalla went on. "And then execute them. I don't know how, but I'm sure it will be horrible."

"Burning," Ailiss whispered. Farajalla lifted an eyebrow and the ancient woman smiled. "Don't be upset that I see more clearly than you. I've had years of using these magics, but you've mastered them faster than anyone I ever heard of, even in the oldest records."

"The army will be here the morning after tomorrow," Farajalla resumed. "At that point a cordon will be thrown around Adour, and anyone still here will be cornered like rats in a barrel."

Those of us still here. Luthien heard the phrase and it made him smile, though it wasn't amusing at all. It was just that they really had all reached the same conclusions, the women through the gifts conferred by the books and the rest of them through plainer means. It was gratifying to realise that his intellect was a match for all the magics of the ancient world, if only sometimes.

"And so logically," he said, "it follows that whichever of those five can escape before the noose closes, should do so."

Fara nodded gravely. "It does."

"And further," Luthien went on, taking time to make sure his voice remained steady, "that those of us who remain take measures to ensure that the All-Church thinks its quarries were here, at the end."

There was a pause.

"Those of *us?*" Calesh asked, in a murmur from the far side of the room.

You might be weak, old friend, but you're as damnably quick as you ever were, Luthien thought. He took a deep breath. "I will stay. My choice. I left the woman I love in Mayence. I won't leave anyone again."

A different reason to the one he'd given Raigal, but just as true. Or more so. He saw Calesh absorb it, though the other man didn't speak. Luthien remembered their meeting on the road west of Parrien, weeks ago and in another world, when it had been Calesh who would not ask him to fight, though it seemed everyone else had. *I know what oaths mean to you,* Calesh had said. He understood, instinctively it seemed, just as he understood so much about so many men. Calesh couldn't grow any paler, but his mouth tightened all the same.

"I stay too," Raigal Tai said. "I'm too big for any deceit. The All-Church would know me just by my size, whatever was done to disguise me."

"I stay," Ailiss said quietly. "I'm too old to run anymore. Besides, my work is done, and my time over. It's time for the next Lady now."

"No," Gaudin said, from the wall.

His voice was shot through with anguish, and he stumbled more than stepped a pace forward. Ailiss had already turned to him, smiling wearily. "You knew this day would come, my friend. We've both known it was likely for a long time. What do servants of the Hidden House do, when the Lady dies or is lost?"

"You are not merely a Lady of the House," Gaudin said.

She shook her head, a tiny negation. "What do they do, Gaudin?"

He stared at her, an absurdly tall man with eyes hidden under strong brows, and didn't speak. Neither did Ailiss, and the moment stretched until finally, reluctantly, Gaudin said, "They serve the next Lady."

"You know who she is," Ailiss said. She pushed herself up from her cushions and Gaudin was there to steady her at once, though she beat at him weakly with her free hand. "My heart and hands, let me be, Gaudin. Listen, now." Her hand stopped flailing and fastened on his arm. "You've been my touchstone and my conscience, these fifty years in the Hidden House. I needed a helper but you've been a friend, and you know it. My dear, we've said all that need be said, many times. It's time for it to end now."

He bowed his head, and said nothing. Ailiss lay back against her cushions again and Luthien found himself turning to Calesh, without quite knowing why until their eyes met. Then he knew; he was seeing whether Calesh would accept it too, or argue as he had when Baruch left them back on the road to Mayence. Their gazes locked and held, and then Calesh sighed and looked away. Luthien felt a breath whoosh out of him.

"How will you do it?" Gaudin asked. He had knelt at Ailiss' side now, holding her hand against his cheek. "Fool the All-Church, I mean."

"Fire," Kendra said.

It was the only way. Luthien had explained it on the wall, though he thought he'd only been putting into words what she and Raigal already knew. Kendra could not pass for Farajalla, not to anyone with eyes, but one woman's bones were much like another's. Burn away her flesh and nobody would know the difference. The same trick would work for Calesh, as long as he left his distinctive green-copper armour behind. Someone else could wear it, or it could be left by the pyre. All that mattered was that it was found.

"It would be easiest if we could take poison," Kendra was saying. "But we have none here. So we'll have to kill ourselves with knives, or have others do it for us, until only a dozen remain. Those will burn the bodies of the dead, and then join them on the pyre."

"You will go," Ailiss told Gaudin. "The new Lady will need you, my friend, just as much as I have. Her husband will protect her from harm, but who will guide her through the traps of the Lore, if not you?"

Calesh and Gaudin looked at each other. There was an eternity of pain in that glance, grief for the lost and sorrow for themselves too, the ones damned to survival while their friends died for them. They had only a moment, before Farajalla crossed the room to kneel by her man and fold him into her arms. Luthien didn't think his friend was crying, but Calesh's hands came up to grip Farajalla by her shoulders, and the fingers were white as bone.

"The Lady will escape," Ailiss said. "The Hidden House will endure, and what has all this been for, if not that?"

It was for the truth, Luthien thought. Tears were close and he didn't dare look at his friends now, sure that would bring them on. *It was for good and for right, for a light in the darkness, for succour to the needy and comfort to the lost. And most of all it was for God. Always, for the Word of the Lord.*

Take that too literally, believe in it too strongly and with too pure a fervour, and you found yourself where the All-Church was. Killing people for the crime of finding God in their own way. Launching wars against innocents unfortunate enough to live in a city you called holy, though it was far away and mattered in itself to nobody but those who lived there. Spreading your gospel with threats and through fear, and then enforcing it with violence.

Or you found yourself in a castle in the mountains, preparing yourself to die so that your gospels could survive, be carried on somewhere else and by somebody new, so the whole savage episode could be played out all over again and written in the blood of the fallen.

Sixteen

The Gleam of the Spirit

They left the next morning, long before the sun came up.

Calesh packed slowly, and in almost complete silence. That worried Farajalla as much as his motionlessness had, over the previous two days. He was still weak of course, still pale and drawn-looking, but she thought he was past the worst danger now, where his wound and exhaustion were concerned. But this quiet disturbed her. She was used to a husband who was all spark and energy, his movements certain and his words swift. As he folded clothes into a backpack he struck her as an old man, wearied by too many griefs.

She didn't know what to say to him. That was new as well, a gap between them she didn't know how to bridge, for the first time ever. She'd thought it could never happen. But here she was, alone with her husband, her great love, with no clear idea what to say or how to ease his soul.

There had been stories about him long before she saw him for the first time, dismounting in front of the steps at Harenc. His three friends featured in most of them. Raigal Tai, Luthien Bourrel and Baruch Caraman; the giant, wise man and soldier to Calesh's king, making a quartet to echo those of legends from ancient times, in cultures all across the world. She'd known they shared a bond she couldn't touch and which would never break. Sailing to Sarténe, she'd worried she would lose part of her husband here, as he met his old companions again.

It hadn't happened. Calesh and his friends were at ease together again so fast that the six years apart might never have passed, but Farajalla had never felt excluded, never a whit less loved than before. The other three had accepted her - more than that, they'd *welcomed* her, making her a part of their lives the same way that Baruch's career was, or Luthien's decision to foreswear his former life and take the Consolation. Antiquity might tell tales of other bands of brothers, four men around whom legends grew - giant, wise man, soldier, king -

202

but these were the true icons, tied together by love and honour as much as the battles they'd fought, and the memories shared.

And Calesh was going to lose them.

Baruch was already dead. Luthien and Raigal Tai would stay in Adour and wait for the end, both for good reasons. Calesh knew that but it was killing him, she could see it in him, and so at last Farajalla found herself outside the circle of his heart, and she didn't know how to let herself in.

There were soft sounds from outside, in the courtyard. All day the men had stood in little groups, watching and waiting as the daylight wore away. She thought they would all be there, every man in the fortress, to watch as the four chosen to escape went over the wall and took all the hopes of the Dualism with them. Or of the Hidden House, rather: the Dualism was finished, in the form it had taken in Sarténe. The lore might resurface in future, perhaps a thousand miles from here or more, and a century from now, but it wouldn't be the same. It couldn't be. Nothing happened the same way twice.

She wondered if there were other worlds, as the philosophers sometimes claimed, places where life went on much as it did here except that every changed choice sent it down a different path. Places where Calesh hadn't been injured by the assassin, and had stopped Riyand before he could launch that doomed, foolish sortie from the Gate of Angels. Where the priest hadn't been murdered by the river Rielle, and the war had never begun; or where word had never been sent to the Hand of the Lord in Tura d'Madai, and the soldiers knew nothing of the attack until the other Orders arrested them in the night.

Places where a young serving girl had not been in the courtyard to see a captain swing down from his horse in the courtyard of Harenc, and had her life changed forever.

"I feel I should apologise to you," Calesh said. He buckled the straps of the backpack as he spoke, not looking at her. "For all this. For the sorrows we've found here."

She shook her head. "None of them were your fault."

"I was in command. I *insisted* on command," he added, and now he did look up, a wry twist on his lips. "Some of it must be my fault. Authority has no meaning without responsibility."

"You sound like Luthien," she said, and regretted it immediately as he flinched from the words.

I don't know how to ease his soul, she thought, and then quite suddenly she realised she did. *Other worlds than this.*

"What would have happened if we'd stayed in the desert?" she asked.

He hesitated, frowning slightly. "I suppose we would have been snatched by the Justified, once the All-Church gave the orders."

"And they would have executed us, wouldn't they?"

"All of us," he agreed. He was watching her intently now, shaken out of his silence. "Every man of the Hand."

She nodded. "I always find it hard to keep secrets from you, with that clever mind of yours. You already know what I'm going to say."

"Yes," he admitted. "That sorrow would have found us whatever we did. The die was cast here in Sarténe before I ever knew about it, and everything since then has just been fate playing out its hand. But, Fara -"

"And now *you're* going to say that leaves no room for people to make a difference," she said. "Aren't you? So tell me, husband, can you think of no difference you made by coming here?"

He'd begun to frown again. "No important one."

"Tell that to Raigal," she said, "when you take his son out of danger tonight."

"That isn't -"

"Tell it to Luthien, who broke his oath because he realised just how much he loved you. Tell it to Ilenia, who found time for love because of that. Or tell it to Japh, and Athar, and all the other young men who fought so hard because they were fighting for *you,* and you made them feel as though there was hope and light amidst all the darkness." She sighed. "Clever mind or no, Calesh, sometimes you can be damnably stupid."

He was smiling at her. She hadn't noticed until she stopped speaking, but then she did, and a moment later she'd crossed the room in two strides and seized his head in both hands so she could kiss him. His arms went around her waist.

She had time for one clear thought before the kiss broke: *I was never outside the circle of his heart, after all.*

"Why," he asked then, just a murmur in her ear, "would you want to keep secrets from me?"

She was nearly startled into a laugh. That wouldn't have been appropriate at all, given that there were eighty men outside preparing to give their lives so the two of them could escape. This was not a time for levity. Still, she kissed her husband again before she let him go, and felt the back of his hand brush her belly as it so often did, as though feeling for the child inside her.

*

The courtyard was almost wholly dark, with just one torch by the gates and another at the foot of the steps up to the tiny temple. The stairs zigzagged into utter darkness: no stars shone through heavy clouds, so there was nothing for the shape of the pinnacle to show against. The gloom was good, in truth. Any All-Church scouts sneaking outside would have trouble seeing anything of what was about to happen.

Farajalla didn't think any would. Her vision had shown four fugitives slipping away, but she hadn't caught any hint of pursuit. Neither had Ailiss. Danger might come later, but not tonight.

Everyone had indeed turned out to see them go. Most of them were the Armsmen who had ridden here from Mayence, shepherding their charges through the pass while their comrades died to buy them time. Farajalla realised with dismay that she didn't know a single one of their names. It seemed a poor reward for their sacrifice. But Calesh knew them all, stopping for a moment with each to press their hands and murmur brief words, the remorseful man of moments ago gone without trace. Here he was the leader of men, utterly sure of himself, able to tease a smile from the grieving and bring courage to the fearful. Farajalla just followed him through the press, letting men bow over her hand and sometimes weep a little, as they couldn't with Calesh.

"God go with you," they said, one after another; or "Forgive us, Lady, for failing you." One man told her she was his strength, and gave him hope, even now. She tried to imitate her husband, sharing a smile and what scant words of comfort she could find, though they sounded hollow to her ears.

"It's been a short road, since you came to Adour for the first time," loquacious Rissaun said, near the stairs up to the parapet. "You and the Lady together, do you remember?"

"You met us on the trail outside," she said, nodding. "One of the doors was stuck, and wouldn't open."

"It's been a nuisance for years, that door." He was dry-washing his hands, a habit almost as strong in him as the need to talk. "I've spent most of my life either in foreign parts or here at Adour, Lady, and I never thought I'd live to see Ailiss, or her heir. Thank you. Keep yourself safe, now."

"I will," she said. She moved on before tears could swamp her. She hardly knew Rissaun, had never met him at all until a month ago, but leaving him here wrenched at her throat. She only had one pace to compose herself before the next man, but that was old Haun, who claimed he was barely fifty but was probably two decades older, and looked like the husk of a withered tree. He was weeping helplessly, and couldn't do more than kiss the palm of her hand and then blunder away, crying like a child all the while.

The last man was Seran, looking at Calesh over the top of his squished, oft-broken nose.

"You're going to wear that?" Calesh asked. Farajalla realised his green armour was resting against the wall. "You'll pretend to be me?"

"We're close enough to the same size," Seran said. That blob of a nose made his voice thin and reedy. "Once the fire is through with me there won't be any reason for them to doubt that I'm you."

"Thank you," Calesh said simply.

Seran shook his head. "Thank *you,* Marshal. I wasn't there when you were fighting in the desert; my Crusading days were long before that. But I know what you did there. You sent men home alive when any other commander would have got them killed, and you sent them home in glory. There's not another captain in all the Orders could have done what you did. God bless you for it."

"Thank you," he said again. The words seemed to catch in his throat, so that for the first time he betrayed a hint of discomfort. For a moment Farajalla thought he would shake Seran's hand, but then he wheeled away and went up the steps beside the tower, up to the parapet. Farajalla paused long enough to kiss Seran on the cheek and followed him.

The last goodbyes waited to be said on the wall. Luthien and Raigal were there, and Ailiss with Gaudin by her side. The tall man's eyes were puffy, though it was hard to believe he had it in him to cry. Elisande was there as well, the shine of her golden hair missing in the darkness. Kendra stood by her husband with a bundle in her arms, and Farajalla felt her heart clench at the sight.

"No need for words of sorrow," Luthien said, before Calesh could even speak. "We're decided on that, my friend. What's done is done, and as God wills. It's better that we should thank him for our blessings, than mourn over the things that might have been."

"We don't seem to have had many blessings of late," Calesh said.

"Not true." Luthien was smiling, as usual, amused by something nobody else yet understood. He was always three steps in front of everyone else. "You were allowed to return home safely, Calesh, and we were all permitted to meet again, and share a meal and late conversations before the end. You will be allowed to leave safely as well, and in the future there will be other friends, other laughter. Don't let yourself think only of the grief. You're blessed, and you'll stand one day at the Gate of Angels into Heaven and know it."

"I will have hard questions for the Lord," Calesh said, "if that day ever comes."

Luthien's smile widened, the expression of a teacher pleased with a promising pupil. "Of course you will, and God won't mind. He loves curiosity. I'll wait for you there, Calesh, and we can go talk to Him together."

"All three of us," Raigal rumbled. He enfolded his wife in one bear-like arm and reached down to stroke a finger down his sleeping son's brow. "All four, in fact, because Baruch will be there already, and counting the days until we join him. And trying to organise the saints, I expect."

"Take care of my son," Kendra said. Her voice was tight with control and yet it still shook. She stumbled forward and handed the bundle carefully to Farajalla, then retreated wringing her hands. Raigal opened his arms and she flung herself into them, her sobs muffled by his bulk.

"Luthien," Calesh said. "I know you... your vow..." He took a breath. "Will you bless us, before we go?"

The blond man cast a sardonic glance at Raigal. "I told you he'd ask, didn't I?"

"Who better?" Calesh said.

"I would love to," Luthien answered. "But I'm not Consoled anymore. I broke my oath."

"You are Consoled if I say you are," Ailiss rasped from behind them. "And I do say so, Luthien. I don't believe God will hold you to account for defending a man you love from a killer."

"Even so," Luthien said, "I won't speak this prayer. Elisande must do it," he held up a hand as Calesh tried to interrupt, "because I will be kneeling by my friends, not standing before them. If you'll have me."

Calesh seemed suddenly unable to speak. He nodded though, and they went down on their knees on the wall, with Farajalla on one side with the baby in her arms and Raigal Tai on the other with Kendra still in his. There was a rustling sound in the courtyard and Farajalla saw all the men were kneeling, their heads lowered to receive blessing. It struck her that she would never do this again, not in all her life. She would be the Lady of the Hidden House, a dispenser of grace but never its recipient. She bowed her head.

"When I was a child I used to wonder what religion was for," Elisande began. Her voice was perfectly calm, betraying nothing of the tension and grief that afflicted the rest of them. "I used to think it was about wealth, because the All-Church priests gathered so much of it, and were still hungry for more. Then for a while I thought it must be about power, the ability to make kings dance as you wished, because the Basilica seemed to care for little else.

"But then I grew, and I began to understand what the verses in *The Unfurling of Spirit* really meant. One in particular struck me; *The land shall support the Good in men, for where men are Good, there the land shall be plentiful.* I thought I knew what it meant. All men have it within them to be cruel, or destructive, and where such men rule the land always withers away, in the end. But where there is peace, and understanding, there you find all the good things in life; music, laughter, food and drink."

All the things that are gone from Sarténe, Farajalla thought bleakly.

"But the truth is simpler yet," Elisande went on. "What is religion's purpose? It's to bring salvation to men and women on earth. As simple as that. We can dress it up in proverbs and verses, and study it from twelve different angles every day, and still it remains the same. All churches exist to bring salvation. They may get lost along the way, they might forget their purpose and blunder off into dreams of power or riches, but underneath it all they still have the same aim, the same dream; to save the souls of mortals.

"And yet we can save our own souls, by our actions. By our deeds. Sometimes we do so by a thousand acts of kindness through our lives, each one too small to be worth mention, but together they bring hope or cheer. Other times we do it by one great act, as Baruch Caraman and the Hand of the Lord did in the valley, when they gave themselves so we few could escape." Elisande paused briefly. "And as those of us here will do now, so fewer yet may flee. That ability, the willingness to sacrifice ourselves for others, is the gleam of the spirit of God inside us. If we bring forth what is within us, what we have will save us." She smiled. "The best-known words of the Dualism, those, and yet we forget what they mean. God is inside us all, and so we can never truly die.

"You have suffered me to speak," she said, using her fingers to make a pair of linked circles in the air. "And this shall be your consolation. Go in beauty."

Farajalla got to her feet. She was crying, she realised, slow silent tears that had trickled down her cheeks all unheeded until now. She thought others were too, Calesh among them. She could see why Elisande had been talked of as a rising star of the Dualism, not very long ago. The woman could persuade a stone and bring it to tears.

Then Ailiss was there, reaching up to wipe Farajalla's cheeks with gnarled fingers. "None of that, girl. Cry later, if you must, but not tonight. You must be well away before the sun comes up."

Farajalla tried to gather herself. Around her the others wiped their noses with sleeves or brushed at their eyes, which allowed her the moment she needed. At length she looked at Ailiss and nodded.

"Good for you," the old woman said. "I'm proud to have met you, Farajalla din Saleh. My years had almost run their course even before all this began, but I'm glad I had time to teach you a little."

"Don't," Farajalla said, raising a warning hand. "You'll start me weeping again if you go on."

"And there isn't time for it," Luthien said. A single forgotten tear gleamed on his jaw. "You have to go."

He, Calesh and Raigal looked at each other. It only lasted a second, but Farajalla thought she and Calesh must seem the same sometimes, when they shared a private glance in the midst of a conversation and nobody else understood it, or why they laughed. There was no laughter here though. Without a word the three men came together and hugged, their heads bowed as though in prayer once more, and then they parted.

"Go," Luthien said.

Calesh turned and went over the wall. A rope had been slung down to help him, but he was still too weak to go hand-over-hand, so Raigal lowered him and then looked at Farajalla. Kendra's sobbing became muffled as Fara wrapped one arm around the cord, keeping little Segarn snug in the other as Raigal paid out the rope. It wasn't long before her feet touched bare rock and Calesh was there to steady her. She was close to tears again and turned away, trying to fight them down, and only then noticed they weren't alone.

"Hello, Lady," Othaer said.

Even in the darkness he looked lopsided, his polio-withered arm tight to his side as always. He seemed a strange choice to be the fourth escapee, at least at first, but then Farajalla thought she could see the thinking behind it. Othaer was young, and apart from the bad arm he was strong, as you had to be if you worked with horses. He was as good a choice as any. Certainly she didn't think the All-Church knew who he was, or would notice he was missing.

Gaudin came slithering down the rope, one leg wrapped around it to control his descent. He let go and strode over to the mule without looking at anyone. Farajalla looked tactfully away. In a way this was harder on Gaudin than anyone, though Sarténe wasn't his home and Ailiss had never been his wife, or his lover. He had given her his whole life though, abandoned whatever dreams or plans he might once have had, to serve her and the Hidden House instead. That had been taken from him now, and it was everything. She had Calesh, and Othaer had his horses, but Gaudin was left with nothing at all.

"Let's go," Calesh said.

Segarn snuggled deeper into his blankets and put a thumb in his mouth.

*

Dawn found them high in the pass west of Adour, the fortress a tiny square marked on the broken ground far below.

Segarn had woken once, bawling hungrily until Othaer dug into the mule's packs and produced a bottle of milk and a cloth. Farajalla dipped the cloth and let Segarn suck it dry, which was easy enough, and he seemed not to miss his mother's breast. But it stopped them for half an hour, the break spent almost entirely in silence, each of them lost in their own thoughts. Gaudin stalked some distance away from the others and stood with his back turned, staring into the darkness with his fists clenched at his sides.

"You've been my touchstone and my conscience, these fifty years in the Hidden House", Ailiss had said to him, back in the castle. But Gaudin didn't look a day over fifty at best, and probably less. He couldn't have been serving the Lady when he was an infant so that meant something didn't add up. Farajalla had an inkling as to what that might be, but she wasn't sure, and she thought it better to wait before she spoke. Gaudin wasn't in the mood to be interrogated anyway. He needed time, and they had that, at least.

"There's no sign of the army," Othaer noted, looking down at the valley below them.

"There wouldn't be," Calesh answered. "Not for three hours at least. It takes time to get a camp packed away and the troops moving, especially in tight conditions like the pass. But by midmorning that vale will be crawling with Justified and Glorified. I don't want us to be silhouetted against the skyline when that happens, so let's not stand here gawping."

He went back to the mule and tugged on the leading strings, but as he passed Farajalla he touched her hand. Some things remained to them, despite everything. He hadn't touched her stomach but their baby was still there, still patiently growing towards the day of his birth, and that hadn't changed. *Thank God,* she thought; *thank any God, even the murderous tyrant of the All-Church faith, as long as the child is born healthy.*

Everything else was lost. The war, the land, the Dualism. It would be called heresy in years to come, in books written not by men like Luthien but by scholars in the Basilica, who would edit out the atrocities of the All-Church but emphasise the crimes of the infidels. That was how history accrued: one lie at a time, laid over the dust of the truth until it couldn't be seen anymore.

But there were books here too, bulging in the mule's packs, so perhaps the truth wouldn't be wholly buried after all.

"Come, Lady," Gaudin said from behind her. "We must go. The ship will be waiting."

She looked at him, wondering whether to ask how he knew, or what else had been arranged. But Gaudin could be trusted, utterly and forever, if anyone on this earth could. Farajalla nodded, and turning away from the fortress she followed her husband into the mountains.

Seventeen

The Light

The last of them were here. Luthien Bourrel and
Raigal Tai, and the damnable Calesh Saissan. The few
remaining Elite, priests of a filthy faith, spreaders of lies and
distortion. Not least, the Lady of the Hidden House was in the
castle too, driven from the mansion that had been secret for so
long, its name no more than a rumour and its location
unknown.

Sarul wanted to see her face, before she died. Perhaps
the mark of the Devil would be visible somehow, a stain on
her skin, or a taint that lay beneath her eyes like a shadow on
water. Perhaps her blackened soul would writhe as she burned.
It would interest him to find out.

He'd ordered his pavilion set up on one of the flatter
pieces of ground in the valley, which wasn't saying much. The
slope was gentle enough that he kept forgetting it was there,
but several times he'd missed his footing and nearly fallen.
Wind sneaked under the flapping hems of the tent as well,
where it hadn't been possible to drive pegs into the bare rock
to anchor them. Men had spent hours with chisels and picks to
gouge out holes for just some of the pegs. Well, they could do
the same again tomorrow, at least. A slope he could manage,
but Sarul was damned if he'd let himself be cold.

Adour lay beyond the main flap of the pavilion, half a
mile away and some hundred feet higher. There was no sense
in getting any closer: Sarul was no fool, and he knew the
danger of an opportunistic arrow fired from atop that thick
wall. But he was eager now, he couldn't deny that. There were
surviving Dualists away from here, of course, a few Believers
in scattered towns and villages, but the core of the heresy was
here, its heart and soul. Once Adour fell the whole stinking
apostasy would be over, with only the last cleaning up left to
do.

He was standing at the entrance to his tent, staring
hungry-eyed at the fortress, when Amaury came up and
bowed.

"The cordon is complete?" Sarul asked.

The general nodded. "One ring near the bottom of the surrounding slopes, and another higher up. Nothing can get in or out."

Amaury had stopped calling Sarul *Your Grace* quite as often, in the past few days. It was only part of a change Sarul thought he saw in the man. Amaury was more cautious now, less trustful of him. At the beginning he'd been wary but willing to go on faith. That wasn't the case anymore. Amaury now had the look of a man who finds himself in a room with a rabid fox, and no way out.

Well, that could be dealt with. Once this was finished he could be sent somewhere out of the way, possibly to the desert, although if Amaury spoke of his disaffection word would quickly spread, in Tura d'Madai. Maybe the north would be a batter bet. Let Amaury spend a decade shepherding missionaries through unmapped mountain passes, and see whether he still had the fire in him to criticise Sarul then. If he even survived.

"And our visitor?" Sarul asked, but he wasn't surprised when the general just shook his head.

The army had moved fast, racing to pen the heretics here before they could find a way to slip out of the trap. Even so, Sarul had expected Irrian to have caught up by now. The other Arch-Prelate had always been persistent. Sarul had a nasty suspicion that he was cleverer than he let on as well. Irrian was another man who could benefit from a posting somewhere remote. The north of Rheven might do nicely for him. There was nothing there but mist-wreathed forests and clans of barely-civilised brutes, and the boredom might drive Irrian insane. He wouldn't be able to do any harm even if it didn't.

That was for later. He still had work to do here, and it was time to focus on it once more.

"Send the emissary," Sarul said.

*

The remainder gathered in the courtyard that evening, after the envoy had come to the gates.

There were pale faces all around. Not just for what was to come, although that would have been enough, and quite understandable. The soldiers were still in shock. Luthien thought he might be himself, in fact. He felt strangely distant from events, as though everything was happening to someone else, a person living inside his body and moving it around while Luthien simply slumbered in the depths of his mind, hardly aware of what was going on.

The All-Church army had arrived an hour before midday. Pikes and spears, mostly, marching in neat companies that split off as they entered the narrow valley, one going left and the next right, so they divided around the fortress and encircled it. Luthien had been on the wall again, with Raigal and Kendra; the two hadn't parted at all since their son had been taken away. Almost everyone was up there, in fact, though not Ailiss or Rissaun. The talkative man seemed to have taken over the Lady's care now Gaudin was gone.

A company of cavalry had entered the valley, lances held upright, and suddenly Luthien had been sure he was going to be sick.

There were heads mounted on the tips of those lances. Every point bore a trophy, some mangled but most of them more or less whole, and streaked with dirt and grime. Luthien even recognised some of them. Alcalde was there, his black beard stiff with blood; he had taught the four friends their catechism, half a lifetime ago. Before the desert, even before they'd been summoned to the Hidden House, and met the Lady for the first time. Cavel's head hung there too, bald and somehow seeming gaunt even without a body.

A moment after he saw that Luthien leant over the wall and *was* sick, helplessly so, because the next head was Baruch's.

"Damn their hearts and eyes forever," Raigal snarled next to him. The words came through tears, though Luthien doubted his friend was aware of them. "By the blood of the God, they're cursed. Anyone who had a part in this monstrosity is cursed until the Heavens fall."

The big man had never been so eloquent in Luthien's hearing before. He wiped his mouth with the back of his hand, and then turning he went down the steps so he wouldn't have to look anymore. He couldn't; after all the suffering, in the desert and then here in Sarténe, it was this he couldn't bring himself to face. He stumbled into the courtyard and then his own tears came, and it wasn't much comfort to see other men weeping around him, sharing their grief with his.

Two hours later the emissary came.

*

"This is the last chance," Ailiss said. The men of Adour had gathered around her, eighty of them filling the small courtyard. A few were up on the walls, just in case the All-Church tried a sneak attack, though Luthien didn't think they would. Even those men didn't check outside very often. Their attention was almost all inward, to the meeting below them and the Lady who addressed it first, her voice a thin rasp in the air.

"The last chance," she said again. "You know what you've been offered. There's no fault in wanting to take it."

"Those who wish to leave may do so in freedom and peace," the envoy had said, calling the words out in a rich, sonorous voice. *"The Basilica has no desire to kill innocents. All it asks is this: those who depart must recant their heresy and come anew to the arms of the All-Church, and live the rest of their days in obedience to the Faith."*

The words had made Luthien's mouth twist. *No desire to kill innocents;* tell that to the thousands butchered in Parrien, or the greater numbers slaughtered in the streets of Mayence. Tell it to the souls whose heads were now mounted on lances outside the walls. It was too late for the All-Church to decide it wanted to forgive those of a different belief. It had been too late since the Crusades began, and soldiers sailed across the sea to fight and kill people they'd never heard of before, simply on the Hierarch's say-so.

"The Dualism is over," Ailiss said now. "There's little to be gained in holding fast to a creed which is lost. Recant, and you can live in peace. I won't ask you to refuse that."

"You won't have to," Kendra said.

Luthien glanced across at her in surprise. The small woman had barely spoken throughout the day, but now she stood with her lips set in a firm line. There had always been strength in her, of course; there had to be, in any woman who could live with Raigal Tai. It was visible now. She was white, and looked to have aged a decade in a matter of hours, but she stood straight and proud and every eye in the courtyard was drawn to her.

"I want no part of the All-Church," she said, as blunt as her husband. "I have no place in my heart for a faith which justifies every atrocity by the phrase *in the name of the Lord.* And I cannot believe their way is the right way, the right path to understanding God. But it's more than that."

"Yes," Raigal said, when she paused. "It's more than that. What trust can we put in the promises of the All-Church, after they massacred the people of two cities and put our friends' heads on poles?"

"I won't take the offer," Haun said.

"Nor will I," Seran added. He was wearing Calesh's plated green armour, which kept catching at the corner of Luthien's eye. When it did he would turn his head, always half-expecting to see his friend, only to find the man with the bulbous nose there instead, an interloper dressed in another man's clothes.

The chorus of refusals ran around the group, man by man, voice by voice. None of them spoke over each other, or raised their voices. None of them demurred. When Luthien's turn came he spoke the same words, quite simply: "I will not take the offer." And then the chorus moved on, speaking through another man's mouth as it made its way through the crowd.

We are all mad, Luthien reflected, listening to the same words repeated yet again. *All of us, as insane as trapped monkeys in those cages in Tura d'Madai, biting the bars as they fought to escape. Give us faith and we can find redemption, tranquillity, perhaps even a glimpse of the face of God. But give us religion and we find only zealotry and intolerance. We cleave to one creed and then disdain all others, hold them in contempt, even attack them. And when driven to it we die for trivial little differences in doctrine, and we do so because we think it shows how right we always were.*

He wasn't sure, just then, whether the Dualism was any better than the All-Church itself. He'd always said that the difference lay in the Dualism's freedom; all they wanted was to be able to worship as they chose, and of others wished for a different faith then they should be allowed it. But now, faced with a choice of compromise or death, every person in the castle had chosen to die. The terrible thing was that Luthien understood.

He couldn't be certain that Dualism was right. The rational, thinking part of his mind had always known that, and he'd accepted it long ago. It was enough that he believed it to be the best path to God available, so he was content to follow it and see how close he was allowed to come. But he knew, he was *certain,* that the All-Church was wrong. Nobody found enlightenment through ritual. The spirit of divinity wasn't revealed by dogma, or a rigid hierarchy of clerics who told others how to behave and what to believe. If God was anywhere then he was within people, in their hearts: perhaps their souls were actually splinters of the Godhead itself. God was immanent, not transcendent.

It meant that you could never truly force someone to believe in your version of the truth. And if you abandoned your own beliefs, then you betrayed nobody but yourself, and the God within you.

"I will not do it," he murmured to himself, as the last men were speaking their rejection of the All-Church's terms. "Whatever I may have given up, I will not surrender this."

Ilenia's head had not been on those lances, when the cavalry rode into the valley. He clung to that, a glimmer of hope that she may have got out. He would know, once he was dead, because if she had died too then she would be waiting for him at the Gate of Angels.

He was certain of that, too.

*

They prayed alone, all of them, through the evening. It didn't seem right to have Elisande lead them, or even Ailiss. *God is in our hearts,* Luthien thought again: a simple truth the All-Church always missed.

He couldn't find the peace he needed to pray though, so after a futile hour of trying he went back onto the wall, to look out over the twinkling sparks of the army's fires. He couldn't see the heads now. By the entrance to the valley he could make out a large white pavilion though, lit by torches at each corner, which he didn't think looked much like the sort of tent a general would have. His guess had been right, then; there was a cleric with the army, probably pulling the strings which made the general dance. It must have been him who wrote the speech for the envoy to deliver. Most likely he thought it would deliver him the prize of worshippers brought back to the Faith, people he could show off like trophies to display the power and rightness of the All-Church.

He wouldn't get that. He wouldn't get anything, except an empty fortress, and the dead.

At midnight they began to gather wood. There was always plenty to be found, even in a small fortress like Adour. The slats from men's beds, and the posts from their doorways; stalls from the stables, together with piles of straw for kindling; lintels and door jambs, the doors themselves, buckets and poles and batches of arrow shafts. They piled it all at one end of the courtyard, with two large barrels of cooking oil beside it.

Several times men had to step out of the work lines and stand alone for a time, breathing deeply and looking up at the stars, before they came back to help. It was very late when they gathered in the courtyard again, silent and calm. Ailiss was sitting on a stool well back from the pyre, seeming shrunken in the darkness, diminished by age and events.

"Light it," she said.

Raigal tipped one of the barrels over, splashing oil across the wood. When it was half empty he lifted it and threw it into the centre, where it gurgled thickly to itself and then ran dry. Seran worked his fire lighter, striking sparks until one of them caught in a tangle of kindling in a bowl. He carried it over to the pyre and tossed it on. For a moment it flickered feebly, then caught the oil and flames spread in a rush of air.

Nobody moved. They all stood there, watching the fire so they didn't have to look at each other. Nobody wanted to start, Luthien realised. It was one thing to accept death, even welcome it, but it was quite another to make yourself walk into its embrace.

Someone had to be first. He drew a breath.

"I will begin," Rissaun said.

He had always been a chatterer, ever since Luthien had first met him a dozen years before. Rissaun could talk about anything and everything, nonstop and without needing to breathe, or so it always seemed. But now he seemed to have no words. He bent to kiss the Lady on the cheek, grasped her frail hand for a moment, and then walked up close to the fire, his back to the others. He drew a knife from his belt. There was a pause then, just long enough for a man to steel himself, and then his hands moved and he fell.

Luthien and Seran picked up the body and threw it onto the fire.

Men died in battle because they couldn't stop thinking, or feeling. They would cut a man and then pause, horrified, and be spitted for it. A soldier had to shut those feelings off, make himself see the enemy as nothing more than pigs or cattle, with no real emotions or lives of their own. Luthien had learned to do it long ago. It made it possible for him to function now, lifting one body after another and throwing them onto the growing flames, even as the stench of roasting flesh began to thicken the air. Part of him was screaming, but it was a buried part. He saw a distant madness in Raigal Tai's eyes as he worked, and knew it must show in him as well, but it didn't make any difference.

Seran couldn't do it. His hand shook but he couldn't drive the knife home. He reversed the blade and handed it to Raigal, weeping, his hands held out in a silent plea for help.

Raigal bent over him and Seran's body went limp. The big man lifted it and flung it away like a rag, onto the crackling flames.

Then there were no more bodies. Luthien blinked, aware for the first time that his eyes were stinging with smoke. Four people still stood; himself, Raigal and Kendra, and Ailiss. They looked at each other.

"Come here," Ailiss said to him.

Luthien went. Everything was dreamy now, held apart from him by a thin layer of unreality. She took his hands.

"You must understand that it is needful for you to truly repent all your sins," she said. Her voice was hardly audible now, either through smoke or grief, or just weariness. "Do you so repent?"

His mind didn't seem to be working properly. "I don't understand."

She shook him gently. "This is the beginning of the Consolation. Listen, now. You must understand, it is needful for you to truly repent all your sins. Do you so repent?"

"You - you want to Console me?" he asked, unbelieving.

Ailiss shook him again. "Do you repent?"

"Oh yes," he whispered. He realised he was beginning to cry. "Oh, by my heart and eyes, I do so repent."

"Luthien Bourrel, you wish to receive the spiritual baptism of the Consolation, by which the Spirit of God will enter into you," she said. "Luthien, will you keep the Commandments of the Lord, to the best of your ability?"

He thought of his oath, broken once before, and knew there would be no time to break it this time. Tears ran down his cheeks. "I will."

"Then these charges are laid upon you," Ailiss intoned. "You will not lie in love with man or woman, you may not kill, and you may not lie. Never utter oaths or steal. Meat and wine will be forbidden to you, and you may commit no acts of violence, lest the Spirit of God leave you bereft. You must turn aside from those who persecute you, and disarm them with forgiveness. Do you vow to uphold these charges until your soul is called home?"

"I do," he said.

She nodded. "Usually you would kiss a copy of *The Unfurling of Spirit* now, but we don't have one here. Still, as Lady of the Hidden House, I think I can ignore that lapse. You are Consoled, Luthien."

He kissed her hands instead, both of them, and then stood up. His tears had stopped, strangely. He felt as though there was a light inside him, outshining even the yellow malevolence of the fire. He wasn't even sure his feet were touching the ground.

"Now," Ailiss said, perfectly calmly, "will you kill me, please?"

Luthien smiled at her. "Of course I will."

He did it cleanly, sliding the knife in under her ribs to find the heart, as smooth and precise as the best of surgeons. Ailiss shivered once in his arms and was still. He carried her body to the fire and laid it on, burning his hands a little in his eagerness to be gentle. It didn't matter. His hands had done almost everything now, all but the very last thing. He turned to Kendra and Raigal to find them on their knees, facing each other.

"I only stayed in Sartène because of you," he told her. "I planned to come back from Crusade and then go home to Rheven, to my hills and forests. But then I met you, and I stayed, and I don't regret a thing.

"Neither do I," she said, and then, "Our son is safe, Raigal."

The big man's back was to Luthien, but it seemed he might have smiled. A moment later his body spasmed and he slumped. Luthien caught him before he fell and Kendra pulled the knife free. If there was any emotion in her it was buried too deep for him to see, except for the whiteness of her face, like old pastry left forgotten on a shelf.

They couldn't haul Raigal onto the fire, so they laid him next to it and threw faggots on his body, so the fire would find them.

Luthien didn't remember how Kendra died. She might have killed herself, or he might have done it: he didn't know. He came back to himself beside the fire again, revolted by the reek of burned meat, with her small body in his arms, her head hanging over his elbow. For a moment he stood there, wondering what had happened. He didn't suppose it mattered.

He threw her onto the fire.

The Al-Church must be able to see the flames, he realised, or at least the smoke. They would be able to smell roasting bodies as well, and it wouldn't be long before scouts were sent to see what was happening. Luthien would have to be quick now. He picked up one of the knives scattered over the courtyard floor and went up the steps to the parapet, then paused despite himself to look out at the tall white tent one last time.

"You have not won," he said, not really speaking to himself, though he knew there was no one else to hear. "You will never win, as long as there are people who choose their own paths in life. And the books survive. The lore will appear again, one day, perhaps far from here. You've won nothing."

The tent simply sat there, unresponsive. Luthien watched it a moment longer and then turned, going along the parapet to a point above the fire. Flames licked almost as high as he was, feasting on wood and oil and cloth, burning away all of that and flesh too. The stench was appalling: he knew that, but at the same time was hardly aware of it. Smoke stung his eyes and blurred his vision as he moved to the edge and knelt down, leaning out into space. He reversed the knife and held it against his chest.

The fire was very bright. As bright as the light still glowing inside him, perhaps. *The Light that shines over all things.*

He slid the knife home. There was a brief, hot moment of pain, and then he felt himself falling forwards and consciousness left him.

Eighteen

A Square-Faced Man

Smoke had been seen rising from the castle during the night, a sombre plume against the starry sky. Before long the smell of it had covered the encircling camp; that, and the reek of burning meat. Sometimes a flicker of bright light could be seen, just a glimmer that peeped over the thick walls and then was gone again.

The cleric, the glowering bald one nobody liked, watched for a while and then demanded information.

Scouts eyed each other nervously when that order came through, none of them willing to be first to speak the obvious: that sneaking up on a fortress at night with no cloud cover was madness. Especially over this broken, treacherous ground. But nobody did speak it, so after a time they crept forward, easing themselves over the stones with the sinuousness of shadows. They made less noise than the wind on a still day. Still they expected to be shot at any time, a killing arrow flying out of the dark to embed itself in throat or chest before you heard the tell-tale whine.

No arrows flew.

Closer to the wall it was clear that something was very wrong. The stench of cooked flesh was overpowering there, and on the southern side the smoke gathered in thick cords roiling on the ground, like the web of some gigantic spider. More, there was nobody on the parapet. The scouts watched for an hour, wrapping scarves over their mouths and noses to keep out the worst of the smell, and no movement broke the monotony of the stone battlement.

Finally, near to dawn, a whispered consultation took place not far below the gate. Shortly afterwards a single man threw a grapple over the wall and scampered up it and out of sight. A few minutes later one of the main doors swung open and he stumbled out, a hand over his mouth and his eyes wide and staring. The senior scouts exchanged worried glances and went inside.

When they saw what awaited them there was a second, even more urgent bout of whispers. Risking death by an arrow near these walls, or on them, was bad enough. But this was worse, this was appalling, because someone was going to have to go and tell *him.*

*

A little after dawn Sarul stood in the courtyard of Adour, watching as body after body was carried off the pyre.

To Amaury, an authority by now on the mannerisms and giveaways of this intense cleric, the rigid stance told everything. Sarul was livid; angrier than when Saissan had taunted the army outside Parrien, more furious even than when he'd learned that the Lady of the Hidden House had fled her home before the Church assassins got there. He stood with his feet wide and his head down, like a bull enraged by flags and bells until he can hear nothing but blood thundering in his head and see only the glare of sun upon the sand. Exactly like a bull, in fact, because like Sarul the bull constantly thinks he has snared his target and will gore and trample it, stamp it into a bloody mush on the ground... and then finds it has slipped from his grasp, and he cannot see how.

A man's body was dragged away, still smoking slightly. It was burned beyond any possibility of recognition, all the clothes gone and most of the flesh, so that bone showed through in patches. But the size meant it could only be Raigal Tai. Sarul's hot stare followed it for a moment and then his head snapped back around with a click Amaury heard from three yards away.

"Crucify the bones," Sarul said. The richness of his voice made the words ring. "Do it now, in this valley."

Amaury hesitated. "Your Grace, that's impossible. Without flesh to hold them the bones will come apart."

Sarul wheeled on him. "Find a way! What, are you helpless? Bereft of ideas! Nail the bones up if you must, but *find a way!"*

Amaury signalled the men with the body to do as the priest said. There was nothing else for it, insane as the order was: insane as the man was, come to that. Amaury didn't doubt it any longer. This man would be a catastrophe on the Eternal Throne, with the red mitre on his brow and the power of the All-Church at his fingertips. He would know how to use the power, Amaury was sure of that, but he didn't think Sarul would know how to stop, or understand that there were limits to any power. A general's, a Margrave's, even a Hierarch's.

The next body was a woman, small and thin-boned, with the remnants of what might have been a fine dress melted to her form. Or what remained of her form. Amaury turned away to spit, trying to clear the cloying thickness in the back of his throat.

"Wait," Sarul told the soldiers. He crouched over the woman's body and turned her head in his long fingers, examining it from each side as though the corpse was a horse at a county fair. "You know who this is?"

Amaury shrugged, trying not to look but not be conspicuous about it. "Either Farajalla or the Lady, I suppose."

"She was Lady of nothing!" Sarul snapped. "Nothing but a few deluded fools, and a shack in the middle of the hills. But yes, this is her. She doesn't look so grand now, does she?"

"Not at all," Amaury said, while thinking that her *shack* had been big enough to sleep five companies of pikemen and have room left for pack horses, if the ruins the fire had left were any guide. And the *few deluded fools* had been so much of a problem that an entire Crusade army had been diverted to deal with them, with who knew what catastrophic results in Tura d'Madai where the troops had been supposed to go.

The next corpse was another woman - Farajalla, then - and underneath her, as though holding her even in death, was a body clad in armour of overlapping plates, like the scales of a fish.

"Saissan," Sarul snarled.

Amaury looked closely as the body was carried past. It was certainly the right size for Saissan, which was about as much identification as you could do with bodies this badly seared. That was his armour, too: there was nothing else like it among the nations, or even in the desert as far as Amaury knew. This was Calesh Saissan then, forced to defeat at last... except that seemed too pat to Amaury, too convenient. Like calling something a pig just because it has bristles. He frowned, wondering where his thoughts were taking him, but he didn't have the chance to find out.

"This is your fault," Sarul said.

Surprised, Amaury forgot his usual tactic of keeping quiet and meek. "How is it my fault?"

"You took too long," Sarul said. "I told you we should have made more speed up the valley from Sarténe. And I told you before then that you wasted too much time dithering in the Aiguille, before you brought the army to Mayence. Those delays have cost us, general."

"Delays?" he repeated. His voice cracked in disbelief. "This campaign should have lasted years, Arch-Prelate. Perhaps two, perhaps ten, but *years.* We've been extraordinarily lucky in that Parrien and Mayence fell through mistakes by the defenders, because without those we'd still be outside Parrien now, most likely, and making plans for a winter war."

Sarul flicked dismissive fingers. "I notice you don't address the delays in the hills. Is that an admission of guilt?"

Perhaps it was the scene around them, and the stench of it in his clothes and hair, but Amaury felt his control slipping further. "Those *delays* were necessary to secure my flanks before I brought the army forward. I'm sure you wouldn't have enjoyed being caught in an ambush in the Aiguille. I don't see any need to address the chatterings of a - a man who doesn't understand strategy."

He'd nearly said *of a fool.* He thought he might as well have done, because Sarul turned that basilisk glare on him anyway, all but quivering in rage. "So you say it's my mistake?"

"No," Amaury said, suddenly tired. He wanted to be away from here, far from Sarténe and the memory of this madness, and far above all from the lunacy of this priest. "No, I say we were lucky to achieve what we did. Sometimes you take what you can and call it victory, that's all."

"Perhaps," Sarul said, still glowering. "And I suppose this is a victory of sorts, after all."

Amaury managed to keep his mouth shut this time. But this was no victory, not by any standard he knew. They had come to destroy the Dualism and had done so, but they had no prisoners to parade through the streets, no converts they could cheer as they were welcomed back into the Faith. They had nothing but an empty fortress in a barren land, and if there was glory in that then Amaury didn't know where it might be found.

He made himself stay until the last of the bodies had been carried out. Sarul had left much earlier, to begin writing the letters announcing his triumph all over the world. The part of it which mattered, anyway. Amaury wished he could go too but these were his men carrying out this grisly task, and he owed it to them to stay and share the horror at their side. It took two hours, and by then most of the men doing the carrying had been sick, several times.

Outside he had to walk past rows of scaffold, hastily erected on either side of the little river. The burned bodies were being nailed up with their arms spread, though most had to be secured with ropes to stop them collapsing the moment supporting hands were taken away. That Amaury didn't stay to watch. There were limits, after all. Clearing the dead was always a vile task; there was no need to make it fouler by insisting on a pointless show of barbarity. He went to his tent, smaller and plainer than the Arch-Prelate's white monstrosity further up the slope, and sank down at his desk with a sigh that was nearly a moan.

He didn't even notice his visitor until the man said politely, "Good morning, general."

Amaury's head jerked up. "Who in hell are you? How did you get past my guards?"

"Even the best soldiers are tempted by a little money," the fellow said. He had a square, rather plain face, unremarkable even on this dreadful day. "As for myself, I'm Jayan, and now I have a question for *you,* general Amaury. Tell me, do you *really* want to see that monster Sarul on the Eternal Throne?"

*

He hated writing letters. Usually he had a scribe, or rather several scribes, but Sarul had thought it would look too ostentatious for him to take them on campaign with him. A Hierarchical Legate was supposed to share the travails of the soldiers, of course, and while that could be taken too far there were still some people who thought the effort was important. Besides, Sarul would be Hierarch himself in a very short time, and everyone else knew it just as well as he. There would be time enough for luxuries then. He could do without a scribe until that day, surely?

Now, trying to produce neat calligraphy on an unsteady desk, and with spots of ink already on his sleeve, he was beginning to regret it.

"Triumphal assertions already?" someone said at the door. Sarul turned his head quickly, already furious that someone had dared interrupt him, and saw that it was Irrian.

Normally the sight of the other Arch-Prelate was enough to sour his mood on its own. Having him turn up abruptly might ruin a whole day. Everyone in Coristos hid their thoughts and feelings behind a mask, but there always seemed to be something knowing beneath Irrian's hooded eyes, a joke that only he knew and wouldn't share. Sarul had never trusted him, right back to the day when Irrian had first come to the Basilica, twenty years or more ago. There had never been a firm reason for that, never a misdemeanour or sin that could be hung on Irrian, but still... Sarul didn't trust him.

But Irrian had been coming from the Basilica with news, Sarul remembered, even as he opened his mouth to shout. Good news: it must be. "Is Antanus dead?"

"Your concern for our Father on earth does you credit," Irrian said ironically. He moved deeper into the room. "Doubtless that's why so many of our brothers in faith wished you to lead us."

There it was again, that slightly too knowing tone, the words perfectly respectful but the meaning ambiguous when you scratched them only a little. Sarul narrowed his eyes. "Doubtless it is."

Irrian nodded towards the desk again. "So, *are* those triumphal letters you're writing, then?"

"I wouldn't call them that," Sarul answered. He was watching the other man carefully. Something was wrong here: Irrian was never this overtly sardonic. He preferred a tiny hint there, a nudge there, not this heavy layer of irony in everything he said. "But they relate our success over the heretics, yes."

"I doubt," Irrian said, after a pause, "that you have the least idea how durable this so-called heresy is."

*

Amaury stared at the square-faced man. "Meaning?"

"Sarul will be a disaster as Hierarch," the man called Jayan told him. He said it plainly, without any emphasis at all, which only made it more astonishing that he dared it in the first place. "You know it as well as anyone. How has it been, trying to control your campaign with him looking over your shoulder all the time? With him flying into a rage at the least of setbacks? He will be like that with everyone once he wears the mitre, general. Every bishop, every officer in the west will find his hand nudging them in the back, endlessly."

"I am not an Arch-Prelate," Amaury said. He'd lowered his voice, though if there was a tattle-tale within earshot it was already far too late. "I can't change the will of the clergy. What would you have me do?"

"Nothing," Jayan said, and he smiled. "Really. Just sit here, general Amaury, and do... nothing at all."

Amaury stared at him again.

*

Sarul scowled. "Meaning?"

"The Dualism is just the latest irruption of an old, old idea," Irrian said. "Or a set of old ideas, I should say. Concepts of good and evil, like those we have in the All-Church, but also a model of personal responsibility. "God is within you", they say. So we can't claim we acted out of our natures, or that voices in our heads told us to do this or that, because *God himself* is within each of us, and we're responsible for how we choose to behave."

"I don't -"

"Of course the Hidden House lies at the heart of it," Irrian said. "It began in Magan, did you know that? More than five thousand years ago, perhaps a good deal more. Certainly it's older than the earliest tales of Adjai the God-Son. The Hidden House was teaching resurrection of the spirit long before the Church taught rebirth of the Lord's body."

"So what?" Sarul broke in testily. "I don't know how you discovered all this, but it doesn't matter. The Dualism is finished."

"So what," Irrian repeated, and he laughed. He actually laughed, and Sarul felt his face redden. Nobody had laughed at him in years, since he was a novice most likely, and perhaps not even then, He couldn't actually remember, it had been so long. But Irrian was laughing at him now. Sarul ground his teeth together and swore inwardly that Irrian would suffer worse even than Amaury when he was Hierarch. He'd find himself posted to the worst place on the map, a distant country of snow-wrapped peaks *and* swamps riddled with mosquitoes. If such a place existed Sarul would send him there, and never call him back.

"So what," Irrian said again. "That's you in a nutshell, Sarul, do you realise it? You've wanted to be Hierarch since you were an acolyte. Everything you've done has been aimed towards that. You know Church law better than anyone, you excel at the machinations and manoeuvres of the Basilica, and you can quote Scripture as accurately as anyone in Coristos. But outside that you know nothing, because you never cared to learn. It couldn't help you so you ignored it. *So what,"* he said again, and snorted further laughter.

This had gone on long enough. "I don't know what game you're playing, Irrian, but I'm busy and I want to -"

"Antanus is dead," Irrian said.

Sarul stopped. His mouth froze mid-word and his brain stopped dead, stunned by the beautiful simplicity of those words, of his victory at last, and that was when he realised Irrian was standing much too close to him and he felt the thin blade of a stiletto knife go in under his ribs.

*

"Nobody will ask many questions," Jayan said. "The Basilica is full of people with reason to dislike Sarul. You can probably understand why, I expect. Even most of his supporters will be glad he's gone. Most of them hitched their stars to his when it seemed like a good idea and then found they couldn't let go of the tiger's tail." He paused. "Oh dear. I do seem to have mixed my metaphors, don't I?"

Amaury was still struggling to comprehend. "You're suggesting that we kill Sarul. Aren't you?"

"Oh, no," Jayan said with a smile. "Irrian will do the killing. All you have to do is look the other way."

He stood up. "I ought to arrest you right now."

"Yes, you ought." Jayan's smile widened. "Whether you will or not... that's the question, isn't it?"

*

"I was born here," Irrian said. He eased Sarul down on the rug, the hilt of the knife still sticking out of his chest. "Not far from the river Rielle. A long time ago I was working in the files and the Lady of the Hidden House came to see me, and we talked. I think," he added ruminatively, "that I've been a little in love with her ever since."

Sarul couldn't speak. He thought there might have been something on the blade in his heart, because from the moment it had gone in he hadn't been able to twitch a muscle. The Justified Highbinders used poisons that were said to achieve such a result. He struggled to thrash, to cry out for help, and only managed to drool from the corner of his mouth.

Irrian wiped it away absently. "It was me who sent the warning to Calesh Saissan, in the desert. You were sure it was a serving girl or a laundry boy, weren't you? But it was me, Sarul. Everything you planned, they knew about as soon as the words left your mouth.

"That bit didn't work out, of course. It was meant to give them enough advantage that they could hold out." Irrian sighed wearily. "Well, God makes fools of us all, doesn't he? Your God, my God, it's all the same, though you never saw it. I have to leave the knife in, by the way, because if it's there until you die there'll be hardly any blood. Amaury will be able to pass your death off as an accident, if he wishes. Then the Council will meet and elect a new Hierarch, and the Arch-

Prelates will bicker for years over which of them deserves the most credit for all the things you achieved. Won't that be nice?"

Sarul's breath was slow now, and pulling in air was becoming hard. Too hard. His vision was dim around the edges but he saw Irrian lean forward and put a hand on the knife again.

"I would never have let you become Hierarch," he said quietly. "*Never.* I have too much love for this world and its God to allow that. I will make restitution for my sins when the time comes. As you will."

He was about to, Sarul knew. He couldn't see Irrian's face at all now. And then his chest stopped moving, he couldn't suck in air anymore, and numbness began to spread out from the wound and throughout his body. He clung to the last vestiges of awareness as long as he could, but he could feel the darkness drawing him down long before it swallowed him.

*

It was announced to camp the following morning that Arch-Prelate Sarul, the Hierarch-Elect, had suffered a fatal seizure during the night and gone to his God in Heaven, as he surely so richly deserved.

It was usual for there to be twelve formal days of mourning, before the funeral took place. On this occasion things would have to be done differently, general Amaury said. The cleric had died high in the Raima Mountains, from where it would take twelve days just to get his body back to the burned ruins of Parrien, even if the weather held - never a certainty in the heights. By the time he reached his rightful burial place in Coristos his worldly flesh would have begun to decay, something the general found unacceptable in such a holy man.

But there was another way, happily. Sarul himself had declared that the pyre which had consumed the last of the heretics had been a punishment sent by God himself, to visit a last agony in the mortal world upon those of His children who had strayed so terribly from the fold. Well then, let the same fire burn his body, but this time in cleansing. Let it wither away the corruptible flesh and leave only bones, which could be placed within a reliquary and carried back to the Basilica in all honour, there no doubt to be treated with all the deference due to a man who would one day, surely, become a saint.

Sarul's mortal remains were burned that same day. General Amaury walked ahead of the casket the whole way down from the mountains, until the funeral party met a delegation from Coristos itself not far from what had once been Mayence. There priests took the reliquary and carried it away. A month later, at the same ceremony which saw the investiture of the new Hierarch, it was reburied in a temple adjacent to the Basilica, not very far from where the long line of Hierarchs themselves lay at their rest.

Not very far at all.

Nineteen

For Every Song

The boat was there, right where Gaudin said it would be.

On the west coast of Sarténe the ocean had cut deep bays into the hills, pirate coves tucked away so neatly it took an experienced eye to make out they were there. Most were useless though, blocked off by reefs or jutting rocks, and just as well: piracy added to the outlaws of the Raima crags might have been too potent a mix to be conquered. But some were safe, for captains who knew how to recognise the signs and had the nerve to guide their ships through narrow gaps between spume. Only a few did.

The ship put out a longboat, rowed by eight big men in shirtsleeves despite the cold ocean spray. Farajalla hardly watched it. Her attention was on Gaudin, as it had been for most of the trip. He stood with his hands clasped behind him, not far from Fara but not really near to her either, as though he couldn't quite bring himself to be as close to this new Lady as he'd been to the last.

"That," Calesh said, looking out across the rollers, "is old Seba's ship. The *Promise of Plenty.*"

Farajalla turned, startled. "Are you sure?"

"Dead sure," he answered. He hadn't spoken often enough during the three day journey from Adour, and even now he did his voice sounded dull. Farajalla thought he was struggling to summon interest in anything. No wonder, really, with what had happened behind them. All the hopes torn apart, and then the lives laid down at the end.

They would all be dead by now. It was hard for Farajalla, and she'd only known them for a few weeks. In that short time Luthien had become a friend, and Raigal had, and Ailiss something both more and less, like a mixture of aunt and sister. But they were dead, all of them. She knew it with the strange, inner certainty she was coming to recognise, since Ailiss had handed her the books of the Lore and told her it was time to learn.

One thing the books taught was this: there are few true coincidences. If Seba was here now, waiting to pick them up as he'd set them down back in the spring, that was because it was meant to be so. Farajalla half-turned to Gaudin and found him already looking at her, one eyebrow hoisted quizzically high.

"Ask," he said.

She hesitated. In the crook of her arms Segarn slept, hardly visible amid a huddle of blankets. "You don't know what I was thinking."

"Wager you a sester?" he asked. "I do know. Ask me."

Best not challenge him on that. Farajalla studied him for a long moment, which he bore with outward patience, and then she decided and said, "You're a Gondolier. Aren't you?"

"Yes," he said.

Calesh turned from his perusal of the sea, and by the chest Othaer gave a comical leap of surprise. Neither Farajalla nor Gaudin took the slightest notice. They watched each other, two cats waiting for the other to blink, until finally Gaudin broke the silence.

"When did you know?"

She shrugged. "When you said 'yes'. But I suspected days ago. In Adour Ailiss said to you, *You've been my touchstone and my conscience, these fifty years in the Hidden House'.* But you don't look more than fifty now. The ages don't match, and I began to wonder."

"The years don't add up for Gondoliers as they do for other people," Gaudin said. "We were a long-lived race from the start: fourscore years and ten, perhaps, instead of twenty fewer for your races. Our spans have grown longer since then. A Gondolier born today can fairly expect to live for a hundred and twenty years." He paused. "Though few babies are born now. Our years lengthen and our numbers dwindle. It may not be long, now, until there comes a day when there are no more Gondoliers in the world."

"You wrote the Lore."

He nodded. "Not me personally. But my ancestors did, yes."

"Then you've always known how this would end," she said, thinking it through. "You've seen the Hidden House rise and fall so many times. You must have seen disaster coming."

"Again, not me personally," Gaudin said. "But my people have seen it time and again. Think, though, Farajalla." She thought that might be the first time he'd ever used her name. "Should we give up hope, because we have failed before? I didn't think so. Neither did Ailiss. She had a will of oak. And she believed something else as well, something all humans are prone to believe, even in the face of all evidence and good sense."

"Believed what?"

"That things might be different this time," Gaudin said.

The sea breeze whipped their hair. The longboat was in the surf now, its crew heaving to keep her straight.

Things might be different this time. That was hope speaking, dressed in simple words. Farajalla remembered Harenc, the last time she'd been back, when the Crusaders were losing ground and the Madai warbands were roaming close to the town, and everyone expected an attack. It would succeed when it came: there were too few westerners to stop it. And the people of Harenc had said there might not be pillaging then, as there had been before. There might not be looting and rape, because the Madai were only taking back their own, and there was no sense in destroying what was yours.

Harenc had burned, of course. Because there was *always* pillage and loot, it was what fighting men did, almost all of them.

"What did you believe?" she asked.

Gaudin sighed. "Must we -"

"What?" she pressed him.

"I believed the chances were slim," he sighed. "But worth the risk, perhaps. The Dualism thriving… what a triumph that would have been, for every man and woman in the world. Freedom from the shackles of the All-Church, and all the other dead, stultifying religions that tell their worshippers what to say in prayer, and what to believe, and then demand payment for enslaving them." He stopped abruptly, just as the words had begun to tumble from him, and gave another sigh. "I hoped for too much, and now so many are dead."

"So did I," Calesh said, breaking in, and this time they both turned to look at him. "I knew how poor our chances were before I brought the Hand of the Lord home. I thought perhaps I could take a small possibility and make it a large one, all on my own. Or with my friends, anyway. And now so many are dead," he said, echoing Gaudin, "and that will weigh on me all the days of my life."

"As it will on me," Gaudin said.

They exchanged guarded looks, and then small smiles that made Farajalla's heart break to see them.

"Not everything that happens is the fault of men," Othaer said from beside the chest. He lifted his shrunken left arm, withered by disease in his childhood. "I know that for truth."

"He's right." Farajalla went to Gaudin and took his hand, then held out her other for Calesh to take. He did, with a wry twist of his lips. "You both did all you could. The mistakes were made by other men, and other women too, and sometimes just by Fate. Some of that happened years ago. Do you remember what Luthien always said? That there was no such thing as a new beginning?"

"I remember," Calesh said.

Gaudin was watching her with a peculiar smile playing around the corners of his mouth. "Your husband's armour was copper, but with a dash each of arsenic and bismuth, and a few other traces added besides. We Gondoliers made it, though the secret was lost long ago, thousands of years before any of us were born. That armour has seen wars in deserts and fields, been buried in a king's pyramid and then lost, only to surface again in a forgotten storeroom in a nowhere town in Tura d'Madai. And from there it found its way to Sarténe, and the latest flowering of the Lore, as though it was coming home."

"No new beginnings," Calesh said, having listened to the story with rapt attention. "Luthien would be pleased."

"I'm sure he *is* pleased," Farajalla said, "and is watching us now to be sure we get safely away. Shouldn't we board?"

The longboat was wallowing in the shadows, unable to come any closer to shore, and Calesh nodded. "We should."

He and Gaudin carried the chest out, the precious books tucked away inside it. Othaer splashed in behind them and Farajalla came last, feeling a pang of regret as he feet left Sarténi soil for the last time. She would never be back. She didn't need mystical powers to know that.

Seba was in the boat.

"Do you remember what I told you?" he asked as he helped her over the gunwale. "About a people who had sailed far from the world we know, and never been found?"

"I remember I said it sounded like foolishness," Farajalla said. "But you know where they are, don't you? That's where we're going."

He grinned and scratched his stubbled cheek. "She chose well in you, did the Lady. Yes, that's where we're going. The Lore needs to lie quiet for a while."

"You're a Gondolier as well," she said, realising it as she spoke.

"Born on the Far Isles themselves," he agreed. The boat rocked ominously as a swell caught it, and the sailors cursed as they fought to control the yaw. Segarn woke and looked around blearily, curled his hands into fists, and went right back to sleep. "That's how the Sea-Fish Guild knows all the sea lanes, Lady. We've been sailing them so long we've worn furrows in the sea."

"You must know so much."

"We've forgotten most of it," he said. "But what remains is yours to see. You are the Lady of the Hidden House, and among all the peoples of the world, there's no honour higher."

He gave an order, and the longboat began to back out of the surf.

*

Half an hour later the *Promise of Plenty* unfurled her sails, and Sarténe began to recede behind them.

Calesh leaned on the rail above the rudder to watch it fade away. He'd left it once before, heading for the desert and a lifetime of war: a short lifetime, for all he'd known then. Hundreds of new Armsmen always fell in the first year in Tura d'Madai, where the brutal realities of war made all the months of training all but meaningless. He'd never intended to go back. If it hadn't been for that mysterious letter from the Basilica, warning him of the attack to come, he never would have done.

This time it was for good, though. He would never see the orange groves again, or smell the rich soil and hear the woodland birds sing. Never walk Waggoner's Way, into Musicians' Square with its pipers and lute players, singers and poets, or past the fountain with its famous inscription: *For every song of joy, there must be a song of sorrow.* The Madai domes and Jaidi spires were gone, the Galleni porticoes, the Magani mathematicians and philosophers from Caileve. The ships in Parrien's harbour and the Academy in the woods behind. All lost.

"I meant what I said about Luthien," she says behind him.

He doesn't bother to turn. He knew she was there anyway, by the soft fall of her feet and the perfume of her skin. He thinks he will always know where she is, even from far away. "Oh?"

"There is no such thing as a new beginning," she says. "Creation is too complex for that. Origins always lie far back in time and shrouded in mystery, so what we think is a new start is actually only the next, necessary step in a long dance."

He smiles, hearing the words in Luthien's voice, though there is pain in the smile too. "So everything is preordained?"

"No," she answers. "There is always choice. What we choose to do marks us as the men and women we are. You chose to risk everything for a homeland you never wanted to see again. Your wife, the children you hoped to have, your life: you threw them all into danger for what you believed to be right."

That was true. It sounds like a ridiculously positive way to look at it to Calesh, given the disaster Sarténe had come to, because he has to accept some blame for that. But he knows he thinks so because his mood is so grim, at least in part. He feels so full of pain that it should be leaking out of him onto the deck, squeezing out through his pores like bile or fetid blood. He shakes his head, not really meaning a negation, thinking she'll take it as such.

"If there are no beginnings then there are no endings," she says. "Not truly. This is not the end of the Lore, my love, or the end of the dream. Dreams only die completely when hope does."

He turns to look at her, standing a few feet behind him on the deck, and thinks (for the hundredth time, at least) that she was beautiful the first time he saw her, in the courtyard at Harenc, and is more lovely yet every time his eyes find her. The wind has blown the braids of her hair half across her face, which somehow makes her even more desirable. He almost laughs, surprised he can find desire in himself now, then wondering why he should be.

"Dreams only die when hope does," he says, trying to smile. "That's very good. Did you make it up yourself?"

She shakes her head. "I learned it from a very clever man. The best friend my husband ever knew."

He masks the hurt of that, and says, "Not quite the best."

She comes to him in a rush then, and he understands belatedly that she has been afraid of him a little, in these past few days of choking grief. He never meant to do that to her, not for anything would be do that, and he finds himself weeping into her hair without knowing who the tears are for: himself, his love, the dead in their burned mounds. He weeps for a long time. She holds him throughout, saying nothing, a support and strength at his side.

"You stood by me when there were things I had to do," he says, when he can speak again. "Now it seems it's my turn. You're the Lady of the Hidden House, and I will go where you go."

"You'd better," she says, and he starts to laugh before she guides his hand down to her belly, and he understands what she means.

Dreams only die when hope does.

And for every song of sorrow, there must be a song of joy.

What to me is the multitude of your sacrifices? says the Lord; I have had enough of burnt offerings of rams and the fat of well-fed beasts; I do not delight in the blood of bulls, or of lambs, or of goats.

Isaiah 1:1

Made in the USA
Charleston, SC
06 July 2016